TULIP SEASON

A Mitra Basu Mystery

By

Bharti Kirchner

Booktrope Editions
Seattle, Washington
2012

Cover Design by Greg Simanson
Edited by Toddie Downs

This is a work of fiction. Names, characters, places, brands, media, and incidents are either the product of the author's imagination or are used fictitiously. Any resemblance to similarly named places or to persons living or deceased is unintentional.

ISBN 978-1-935961-47-5
HARDCOVER ISBN 978-1-62015-333-8

DISCOUNTS OR CUSTOMIZED EDITIONS MAY BE AVAILABLE FOR EDUCATIONAL AND OTHER GROUPS BASED ON BULK PURCHASE.

For further information please contact info@libertary.com

Library of Congress Control Number: 2012905630

For Didi, Rinku, Tinni, and Tom

For holding the light, as I take another step

And in loving memory of Kachi, Niveditamami, and Satyada

ACKNOWLEDGMENTS

I've been fortunate to have the help and encouragement of a number of friends in completing this project. Their names (in no particular order) are: Margaret Donsbach, Sarah Martinez, Holly Warah, and Christine Mason.

I would like to thank Mike Hawley, Mike McNeff, and Greg Mills for answering my questions about police procedures.

For their effort on the publishing side, I thank Toddie Downs, Katherine Sears, Heather Ludviksson, and Ken Shear.

I am indebted to my readers who have urged me to write another book.

And I am grateful to my husband Tom for his loving support. Without you, I couldn't have done it.

Nothing in the world is really precious until we know that it'll soon be gone. The lily, the starry daffodil, the regal irises are the lovelier for their imminent vanishing.

Donald Culross Peattie

ONE

"GUTEN MORGEN." Mitra rolled over on her side to face Ulrich, the sensual feel of his German name in her mouth. A sliver of sun winked through a crack in the window draperies.

Ulrich turned his golden blond head, nuzzled the pillow, and regarded her with his soft green eyes. "You look so ravishing," he whispered, "with your hair falling down over your face." Playfully, he reached out for her.

Mitra smiled at him, at the sculpted hardness visible beneath the sheets. Usually, she rose at dawn and slipped into her greenhouse, her heart swelling with new hope as she appraised the overnight progress of the seedlings. This morning was different. Swallowing a feeling of awkwardness, for he was still a stranger, she snuggled into the warmth of his chest and lay there curled up in the sheets, savoring the musky sweetness of his skin.

If her mother were to peek in at this instant, she would draw a corner of her sari over her mouth to stifle a scream. "Sin!" she'd say. "My unmarried daughter is sleeping with a man!"

Fortunately, Mother lived in Kolkata, whereas Mitra was half a world away in the bedroom of her bungalow in Wallingford, Seattle's garden district. And although she was unmarried, she was in fact twenty-nine, old enough to take a lover.

Ulrich glanced at the clock on the lamp stand, tossed the blanket aside, and bolted from the bed. "8:30? *Ach,* I was supposed to be at work by 8."

He scrambled toward the bathroom, mumbling to himself in his native tongue. Mitra could hear the sounds of water splashing in the sink and snatches of a German song. Although an engineer by training, Ulrich chose to do physical labor, to escape the tedium of days spent at a desk poring over equations and blueprints. It was a quirk that she had found intriguing last night. He happily hammered nails all day, fixing roofs, patios, kitchens, and basements. Siegfried, his German shepherd, always went along.

The silky, iris-patterned linen sheets were bunched up on his side. He slept more messily than she did but for some reason she liked the rumpled look.

The ringing of the telephone startled her. Not fair, this intrusion. If it was Kareena on the line, Mitra could whisper the truth to her: *I met a cool Deutscher last night. He's in the shower. Okay, so, it's not like the usual shy me, but . . . Look, I'll call you back later, okay?*

She had to answer; it could be a client. Tangles of long hair drowned her vision, as she reached for the receiver. "Mitra Basu speaking."

"Veen here." Her friend's voice lacked its usual bounce. "In the name of Ma Kali, have you heard? Kareena is missing."

"Missing?" Mitra felt shaken, the way a plant must feel when uprooted, the solid support of the firm earth stripped away. "What are you talking about?"

"I called Adi after I got stood up for tea this morning. He told me he hasn't heard from her in two days. I haven't seen her since girls' night out—over a week ago, was it? When's the last time you spoke with her?"

Mitra's heart thumped away. "She didn't show up at Toute La Soirée last night to meet with me."

She skipped the rest of the story. Last evening had not started out well. After waiting for about an hour and not getting even a beep on her cellphone, she'd driven to Kareena's house. Neither she nor her husband Adi answered the door. Mitra told herself that her friend had probably gotten caught up in another appointment. A little miffed, she'd opted for a distraction—something cold, sweet, and decadent—and made a beeline for an organic ice cream parlor, where an acquaintance introduced her to Ulrich. A long conversation, a second helping of parfait, and the evening had turned out delightfully.

"When did Adi find her missing?" Mitra asked.

"The night before last Adi apparently got home late. Her car was in the garage, but she wasn't home. There was no sign of a forced entry. Yesterday, he called 911. The police came over, asked a lot of questions about her—height, weight, eye color, tattoos, her habits, who's last seen her—things like that. They filled out a form and requested a photo. There aren't any leads." Veen paused. "I wonder if she had an argument with Adi and just left."

"She'd have told one of us, don't you think?" Mitra said. "You know I've been asking her to be extra cautious." Silently, Mitra repeated her warnings to Kareena: Don't use your last name with your clients, take a different route home every day, always let someone know where you are. She wondered which one Kareena had forgotten.

"Adi didn't have much more to say," Veen said. "He was leaving for the office. Speaking of the office, I'm late. Let's talk in about an hour."

Something wasn't right here. How could Adi go to work when his wife was missing?

Mitra searched for her clothes. Last night's coupling, with its wild tumbling, had put her into deep communion with her body, but she was also a bit out of her zone. The long-sleeved print dress she wore last evening, a tantrum of wildflowers, lay tangled on the floor, intermingled with her bra and panties and Ulrich's charcoal jeans. Hands trembling, she rummaged around in the closet, grabbed a pewter-gray bathrobe, and wrapped it around her body.

Adi says she's missing.

Adi? Who could trust what Adi said? At her cocktail party a few weeks ago, a paisley Kashmiri shawl had slid off Kareena's shoulders. Through the sheer sleeves of a tan silk top, Mitra glimpsed dark blue finger marks and a fresh swelling on her upper arm. She nearly shrieked. Had Kareena been mugged by a stranger, grabbed by a client's angry husband, or had Adi attacked her? Upon realizing that Mitra had noticed, Kareena glanced down and repositioned the shawl. Before Mitra could speak, a male friend approached, asked Kareena to dance, and they'd floated away. It'd be ironic and tragic, if Kareena, a domestic violence counselor, suffered abuse at home. *Was it possible?*

Ulrich stepped into the room. His well-scrubbed face shone, but the rest of his body looked unwashed. An awkward pause fell, which Mitra attributed to seeing each other for the first time in broad daylight.

"Everything okay?" Ulrich asked.

She registered the warm intimacy of his voice. "A friend has been reported missing."

"Missing? I'm sorry—I hope your friend turns up soon."

Standing close to her, so close that she could still smell the sweat of the night on his skin, he wiggled into his jeans. His large fingers fumbled with the buttons of his chambray shirt and a thin lower lip pouted as he struggled to insert a recalcitrant button in its hole. He threw on his herringbone jacket, wrapped her in an embrace, and with a candy-shop expression cupped her face in his hands.

"You look even prettier in the daytime," he said, "such luscious skin to go with those big dark eyes."

His eyes held a mirror in which she saw herself: a petite figure, not a beauty by either Indian or American standards; a careless dresser to boot, although Kareena had once praised the serenity on her face. At least that was something. Kareena—where was she?

Ulrich gave her a deep look, then a short warm kiss, which didn't soften her tense midsection. She managed a half-smile. Under a different circumstance, she'd have reveled in a morning romp, but her friend's absence was becoming more real to her with each passing second.

"You look so worried," he said. "Your friend is probably fine."

"Well, she has a dangerous job. She works as a counselor for abused women. Many husbands have it in for her."

"I would get her office involved." He gave her a soft kiss. "If I could, I'd stay here with you and I really want to, but . . ."

At another time, the word want or *vant*, as modulated by his accent, would have hinted at delicious possibilities, but not now.

"Shall we see each other again?" he asked.

She looked up at his pale-skinned face, and she really did have to look up, for he was a good nine inches taller, and nodded. "Call me this evening."

They walked to the doorway, his arm around her shoulder. As he skipped down the front steps, his face turned toward her budding tulip patch—soon to be an exuberant yellow salutation to the spring—and he held it in sight till the last second before turning away. Yellow was Kareena's color (and Mitra's, too). Tulips were a favorite of both of them. And Mitra had planted this double early variety in her yard just for Kareena. If only she were only here, she would surely shout in pleasure upon seeing how gorgeous even the buds were.

Mitra sighed, picturing Kareena's heart-shaped face, tailored pantsuits, dark sunglasses even in rain, and a stylish wristwatch. She just had to be okay. She must have snuck off somewhere for a breather. How like her to forget to tell anyone, even her husband. Mitra would find her dearest pal.

Ulrich gave her one last look and a wave, then loped toward a steel gray Saab parked across the street. Feeling a nip in the air, Mitra cinched the belt of her bathrobe. She walked back to the living room, opened the draperies, and hoped the fear signals inside her were wrong. A blue Volvo SUV cruised by, reminding her of Adi. He zipped around the city in a Volvo, too.

She dialed his number. The receiver to her ear, she paced frantically back and forth in front of the window, too keyed up to sit still. The plum tree in her north yard was a billowy cloud of delicate white blossoms. An upper branch had thrust itself dangerously close to a power line and she made a mental note to prune it back later.

Adi's recorded voice said, "Leave a message."

Mitra didn't. She studied the clock: still the commute hour.

Unable to wait another second, Mitra punched Veen's office number, only to be greeted by a voice-mail message. She kept trying every few minutes, then decided to go visit Veen in her office.

TWO

TEN MINUTES LATER, Mitra and Veen walked the extensive grounds of Good Shepherd Center, an Italianate-style building of late 1800's, now used for multiple business purposes. It was located only a few steps from Veen's office. They found an empty bench on the grassy yard, surrounded by tall oaks, and sat down. No one was about this early in the morning.

Mitra turned to Veen. A substantial woman, she had her hair pulled back in a ponytail, a gray wool jacket casting a shadow on her face. She wasn't a *shoi*, a friend of the heart like Kareena was, but still belonged to Mitra's inner circle of friends. Mitra thanked her for taking a break to meet with her.

"I damn near got in an accident coming to work." Veen's voice shook; she wasn't her usual assured businesswoman self. "Now I have a bitch of a headache."

Mitra felt for Veen, a go-getter, always dependable, always rushed, often blunt. She could use a break, this overworked architect who specialized in green design. Even when they hung out together, bumping out to a Sunday breakfast at Julia's, visiting the Flower and Garden show, or popping up at Seattle Arts and Lectures, Veen never seemed to be able to let go and enjoy the moment. Right now, she sipped a sickly brown tea from a carry-out cup, with the sorry teabag still inside.

"Why do you think Adi hasn't called either of us, if Kareena has been gone for two days?" Mitra asked.

"The bastard said he hadn't had time."

"You believe that?"

"No." Veen's voice rose. "And what do you make of this? I was passing by Umberto's restaurant last night and spotted him with a blonde, his assistant, I think. They were talking over wine. Do you think he's having an affair?"

"Affair? That doesn't sound right. He seems so much in love with Kareena." Mitra paused. "Actually, I don't know what to think. Other than calling the police, he seems to be taking this awfully casually."

"Shit." Veen winced. She'd just splashed hot tea on her lap. Mitra rummaged her purse, grabbed a tissue, and handed it to Veen, who got busy wiping the wet spots on her pants. Veen mumbled thanks and added, "Someone in my office said when a woman goes missing, nine times out of ten, it's the husband."

It's the husband. Mitra held back the rage inside her. For a moment she let her eyes roam the Pea-Patch just ahead, the serenity that rested over the plot, to get over the feelings she had against Adi. "Do we know who saw Kareena last?"

"I didn't ask Adi—I was so overwhelmed by the news. But you know I glimpsed her about two weeks ago at Toute La Soirée, with an Indian guy. He's straight out of GQ, if there were an Indian GQ. They were smiling, leaving the place. I happened to drive by. I don't think she saw me. I didn't wave. That'd not have been proper. At the time I'd assumed it was a friend or relative visiting her. Now I'm not so sure."

"Kareena and I met at the same place last week."

"So, did you two talk about anything that might throw some light on that guy?"

"Not really, but it was an interesting get-together." Mitra replayed the afternoon. She'd been waiting for Kareena at a corner table for about fifteen minutes, perusing the *Seattle Chronicle*, a cool breeze blowing though a half-open window. She looked out through the window and took in the sky-colored ship canal where a fishing vessel was working its way to the dry docks that lined the north shore of Lake Union. Sensing a rustle in the atmosphere, she raised her eyes and saw Kareena standing just inside the door. Kareena peered out over the crowd, spotted her, and flashed a smile. She looked chic, a get-up-and-go kind of a person in the maroon pantsuit (Mitra called it "maple," whereas Kareena referred to its shade as "Bordeaux"). Arms swaying loose and long, Kareena wove her way among the tables. A shining leather purse dangled from her shoulder.

As Kareena drew closer, a woman seated at a corner table called out to her. Kareena halted and, charming as always, exchanged pleasantries. The woman glanced in Mitra's direction. "Is that your sister?" she overheard the woman saying.

Kareena glanced over at Mitra and winked. They'd been subjected to the same question countless times. Did they really look alike or had they picked up each other's mannerisms from hanging out together? Aside from similar faces—sharp cheekbones and narrow foreheads— Mitra was three inches shorter and eight pounds lighter. She glanced down at her powder-blue workaday sweater, a practical watch, and sturdy walking flats. Her attire didn't follow current fashion dictates, but it was low-key and comfy, just right for an outdoors person. Fortunately, a place like Seattle accommodated both their styles.

"Sorry I'm late," Kareena said, pulling up a chair across Mitra. The corners of her mouth were lined, a sure sign of fatigue. "First, I had a gynecologist appointment, then a difficult DV case to wrap up."

Mitra pushed the newspaper to the far side of the table. DV— domestic violence—was an abbreviation that sounded like a fearsome disease. "A case from our community?"

"Unfortunately, yes. And you know how our uncles and aunties talk about these incidents?" Kareena mimicked a British accent. "'A bride got burned in fire? Oh, that's just a kitchen accident.'" She paused. The waitress was hovering by her shoulder. They placed their orders of Riesling.

"You're the only one I trust enough to talk about it," Kareena said to Mitra when the waitress departed. "My client is an H-4 dependent visa holder, worried about her personal safety and legal status. She was so scared that she couldn't even string a few coherent sentences together. I spoke a little Punjabi, which loosened her up. I explained that the law was on her side and will offer protection. She said her husband beats her up regularly. She'd be in worse trouble if he suspected she was out looking for help."

"Why doesn't she go hide in a women's crisis house?"

"It's called 'trauma bonding.' You develop what in DV counseling is known as a 'comfortable and sustained blind spot' for the one you love. You continue to stay in an abusive situation. You see yourself in him."

Might these definitions apply to Kareena as well? "Did you see bruises on her?" Mitra asked.

"Oh, yes, even though she hid her forehead with bangs."

Mitra hesitated, wondering if she should broach a delicate subject. "There's something I've been meaning to ask you. For some time. I just couldn't be sure." She paused. "You don't have similar problems at home, by any chance, do you?"

Kareena gazed off into the distance. A sense of wariness seeped into her voice. "What are you getting at?"

"Well, I happened to notice bruises on *your* arm at your last party. Who did that?"

Kareena's face turned mauve. "I don't want to talk about it."

"I can never forget what I saw." Mitra leaned toward her friend protectively. "I'm so worried, Kareena."

Her voice edged with embarrassment, Kareena said, "I said I didn't want to talk about it."

"Sorry. Forget it—I don't know what I was thinking."

"I accept your apology," Kareena said, a touch of resignation in her voice.

Mitra filed the matter away for a future conversation. Sooner or later, she'd nail down the truth behind those bruises. She took a sip from her wine, while Kareena drained hers with hurried gulps, not taking the time to appreciate the flavors fully. Mitra digressed from this aching topic to a pleasanter one—the upcoming tulip festival in Skagit Valley and the legend of the tulip.

"Every bulb holds a promise of something new to come?" Kareena exclaimed. "The Dutch actually believed that? I absolutely must go with you to that festival. You'll get the tickets?"

Mitra nodded. To lighten the mood further, she pointed out a cartoon clip from a magazine peeking out from under the glass cover of their table. A tiny boy craned his neck up and said to his glowering father, "Do I dare ask you what day of the week this is before you've had your double tall skinny?"

That had gotten a spontaneous laugh out of Kareena. Mitra had made a mental note to compliment the manager of Toute La Soirée, who appreciated humor and changed the jokes frequently.

Relaying the Soirée rendezvous to Veen, listening to the traffic rushing down the nearby 50th Street, Mitra wondered: had she been right to let Kareena off the hook so easily? She could still so easily visualize the nasty-looking bluish discoloration on Kareena's arm.

THREE

VEEN LISTENED TO MITRA'S RECOUNTING of that afternoon and at the end mumbled, "I keep going back to that stranger I saw Kareena with at Soirée. They seemed pretty tight. As I remember, he carried a jute shoulder bag. Remember *jhola*—how it used to be a fashion item?"

"Oh, yes." In India, *jholas*, or shoulder bags, were fashionable among male intellectuals—or rather pseudo-intellectuals. Mitra's scrawny next-door neighbor in Kolkata, who fancied himself a man of letters but was actually a film buff, toted books and papers in his *jhola*. He could often be seen running for the bus with the hefty jute bag dangling from one shoulder and bumping against his hip. Tagore novels? Chekov's story collection? Shelley's poems? The only thing Mitra ever saw him fishing out of the bag was a white box of colorful sweets from Jolojog when he thought no one was looking.

"I wonder if the man had recently arrived from India." Mitra took a moment to think. "So who is he and why was Kareena meeting with him?"

"Beats me."

"Aren't you surprised the police haven't contacted us yet?" Mitra asked.

"They have no reason to. There's no sign of foul play." Veen consulted her watch. "Shoot, I have to head into a meeting."

"I'll call the police as soon as I get home," Mitra said.

"Buzz me later, will you? We'll help each other through this."

Mitra hated to let go of Veen's supportive presence. As she drove home, elaborate scenarios occupied Mitra's mind. The *jhola* guy had blindfolded Kareena. She screamed. He clasped a hand over her mouth. She fought to free herself. He dragged her into a waiting car and drove off. She yelled for help, but no one heard her.

Then again Mitra could also see Kareena packing a small suitcase and checking into an unobtrusive pension, thereby fleeing from Adi's ill-treatment and finally calling a lawyer. Could the *jhola* guy be a lawyer?

But why would Kareena have done any of this covertly? As an abuse counselor, she knew how to protect herself. She'd have separated from Adi before the situation got sticky. She was way too sharp. Or did she try to maintain the same confidentiality for herself as she did for her clients by deciding not to say a word to anyone, even her best friend? Behind Kareena's bright public face, there lay a private person. Mitra was well aware of that.

Or maybe Kareena's eyes and judgment only worked for others, not herself.

She'd always seemed to have known when Mitra was heading down a bad path with a man. Two years ago, she'd warned Mitra against a date who would be later arrested for fondling a woman on a plane. A few months after that, Kareena had thrown a bash in honor of Subhas Jha, a visiting Indian film director, whose new offering, *Shadows*, had just opened to wide acclaim at the Seattle International Film Festival. For that occasion, Kareena had asked Mitra to provide the centerpiece. Mitra spent hours preparing an all-white lily arrangement. She didn't mind the expense. Clad in a beaded white ankle-length dress, holding a wine glass in her hand, Kareena fluttered among the guests. It pleased Mitra to see that Kareena frequently stopped to sniff the white lilies spilling out of an urn like a milky waterfall. She smiled at Mitra whenever their gazes met. Mitra had worn her best black pants and a white weskit blouse but, seized with shyness, stood alone in a corner, nursing a Crystal Geyser.

A member of the film crew, a 6'6" giant, approached her and asked if she'd like to go out with him for drinks. She said no. He kept insisting, pushing his bulky body closer and closer, until he shoved her against the wall. "I know what your problem is," he said. "You haven't had a man in awhile. But I'll fix that for you."

Mitra tried to angle away, but he grabbed her arm. Kareena, who must have been watching from across the room, rushed over and glared at the offender. "You have to get out right now," she commanded, pointing at the door and snatching a cellphone from her purse. "Or else I'll call the cops."

The man's shoulders bunched, his gaze darted to the door, and he scurried away. Mitra took a few choppy breaths.

Kareena poured her a drink. "Fight, Mitra, fight. Don't let a man ever harm you."

At her urging, the very next day, Mitra had signed up for a weekend workshop on personal safety and self-defense training for women. She was one of the first in her community to do so.

Letting go of that memory, Mitra prayed that Kareena hadn't been in a position where she needed to fight to keep a man from harming her.

Upon returning home from her visit with Veen, Mitra picked up her cellphone. She didn't know the protocol for calling the police. Nonetheless, she punched the number of the Seattle Police Department. Struggling to keep her voice calm, she asked for the officer assigned to Kareena's case.

Oh, God. She was a case, a number in the police computer system, her Kareena.

FOUR

MITRA ANSWERED A SERIES of routine questions from the investigating officer. Usually, she smiled whenever she thought of her closest confidante: now she felt as though a sharp knife were threatening her. The officer cleared his throat.

A peek through the draperies revealed a bruised, swollen April sky. "What happens from here?" Mitra asked.

"Call everybody who knew her. The more eyes that search, the quicker you'll get results." The officer informed her that Kareena was last seen at Soirée with an Indian man, as confirmed by a waitress there. He suggested starting out from Soirée, the primary search area, then radiating out in widening circles. "Also check the jails and hospitals."

The officer should offer help with a bloodhound, a search-and-rescue team, and state police helicopter. "Jails?" Mitra said. "She's never been in trouble. Aren't those your responsibilities? What kind of priority are you giving to this case?"

"Sorry, we don't go out looking for missing people, unless it's a minor. Your friend could simply have run away. It's not illegal for adults to go missing. In 99% of the cases, the person is found. They've just dropped out. Without evidence of abduction, violence, or even a threat, I can't requisition resources. We have only two detectives assigned to all missing persons' cases."

Mitra drew in a troubled breath. Even though she understood the reasons, she still couldn't accept them. "Kareena was named the top DV counselor in her office. She's an important person in our community. You're saying you can't do anything?"

"We haven't found a body."

Mitra's heart fell. She wouldn't disclose her suspicions to the authorities about Adi. It was only a gut level feeling that he'd given Kareena the bruise.

The officer encouraged her to call back if she ran into any new information. After hanging up, pumped by adrenaline, Mitra Googled "Missing Persons" and telephoned the National Center for Missing Adults.

"There are privacy issues," a representative said. "An adult who goes missing might wish to keep their locations anonymous. We ask people to wait thirty days. Missing adults often turn up in that length of time."

"Thirty days?" Were they crazy? This was Kareena they were talking about, her best friend, her comrade.

Mitra cut off the conversation, astounded to discover her tax dollars were not being used properly. She punched Kareena's cellphone number, only to find it had been switched off. Well, Mitra could try one more thing. She dialed Kareena's office and left a message for her supervisor.

Then Mitra worked the situation around in her mind, like breaking up packed soil to allow planting. But she couldn't get anything to line up. Even the cushioned chair didn't feel cozy.

She walked outside, over to her side yard. Blue bells were pushing up from the winter-hardened ground. An apple tree spread its skeletal arms studded with nascent buds. White clumps of mushrooms popped up here and there over the dark mulch. Mitra noticed a slug, picked it up, and deposited it on a safe spot.

Her career focus in art and botany—the study of the physiology of new growth, the awareness of color and light, and harmony of arrangements—hadn't prepared her to confront a situation like this. She looked up to the sky, out of a gardener's propensity to check the weather. The blue infinity helped her to see beyond the immediate, and provided her with an approach.

In her home office, she grabbed a notepad and a pen and began scribbling a list of friends and acquaintances she could call upon, not stopping until the page was filled. The Indian population in the Puget Sound area had recently been described as a "model community" in a feature article in the *Seattle Chronicle*. Its academic and professional accomplishments were "as lofty as Mount Rainier." Mitra was troubled by such laudatory phrases, being well aware that it had its fair share of warts and blemishes. According to Kareena, the rate of spouse abuse among the community's dignified doctors, elite engineers, and high-powered professors equaled, perhaps even exceeded the national average. Still in a crisis, this was a community that came together.

Mitra consulted her watch. It was pushing 10 o'clock, an hour when everyone was up and about. Adi would in his office, Adi who professed to be "furiously, stormily, achingly" in love with Kareena. "Every millisecond, wherever I might be, and whatever I am doing, I dream of you and you only," he had gushed in a birthday card Mitra had once seen pinned on the memo board in their kitchen. Still, the fact remained. They'd been married nine years, but didn't have any children.

Mitra relived a moment that had transpired a few months ago. She and Kareena were spending an afternoon at Soirée, when an enormously pregnant woman waddled past their table. Mitra shifted her chair to let her pass. Kareena put her fork down, wiped an invisible crumb from the corner of her mouth, and gazed with fascination at the woman.

In a teasing tone, Mitra asked, "Could that be you?"

"Adi doesn't want kids," Kareena said, her voice sad, low. "He says, 'I like it the way it is, just the two of us.'"

"I'm not married," Mitra said, "so couldn't offer you advice. But couldn't you discuss it with Adi? Maybe try to change his mind?"

"Adi's a good husband. He buys me everything I want. You have to understand the dynamics of a marriage, Mitra. There are personal limits you must respect. I try to be understanding of Adi. I don't push him about having kids."

"Why not, may I ask, if the issue is so important to you? Why make such a huge sacrifice? Wouldn't you some day regret—?"

Kareena butted in. "Hey, we came here to have a good time. I get gloomy issues from my clients all day long." She eyed her plum-almond tart, picked up her fork, and took a bite. "Just the right sweet-sour balance."

Her left wrist sported a pearl-studded bracelet-cum-watch, an expensive present from Adi, his way of "buying" her affection, or so Mitra conjectured. He stared at her, Mitra had noticed on numerous occasions, as though she was an *objet d'art* which had cost him no small sum.

And yet, on that day Mitra had seen the crack in their marriage, as clear as the broken branch on a young dogwood tree outside the café window. She couldn't quite put the puzzle pieces together.

It was time to visit Adi. Under normal circumstances, he loved to talk about himself in his Oxford-accented, popcorn-popping speech; this self-obsession might give Mitra a chance to tease information out of him, however distasteful the process might be, however dangerous.

As Mitra drove toward Adi's office, she almost saw Veen's words inscribed on a billboard: *When a woman goes missing, nine times out of ten it's the husband.*

FIVE

ON THE WAY TO ADI'S OFFICE, stalled in traffic on the I-90 Bridge, Mitra ruminated—she couldn't avoid it, her mind was on overdrive.

Three years ago, she'd met Adi for the first time at a dinner he and Kareena had hosted to celebrate Diwali. Mitra had known Kareena only about a week then. It had surprised and pleased Mitra to get an invitation.

A tanned man of medium height and broad chest, handsome with an Indian overtone, approached Mitra. "I am Adi." He shook her hand, his eyes straying elsewhere in the room. "Short for Aditta. Kareena's other half."

Kareena joined them and they began discussing their connections to India. Kareena had been raised in Mumbai and New Delhi; Adi hailed from the state of West Bengal in Eastern India, like Mitra. Even as she greeted him, *"Parichay korte bhalo laglo"* ("How nice to meet you," in their shared Bengali tongue), the name Aditta somehow brought to mind another word, *dhurta*: crook. The two words sort of rhymed in Bengali. Mitra never mentioned that to him or Kareena, but she couldn't help musing about the two words as she watched the indolent way Aditta flicked his gold cigarette lighter, the angle of the Marlboro between his lips, the shroud of smoke around him.

He informed Mitra that his company, Guha Software Services, was solidly in the black and that he'd recently purchased a deluxe beach cottage on the Olympic Peninsula.

Eventually, he finished bragging about himself and asked Mitra, "What do you do with your time?"

"I have a garden design business, Palette of Color."

"Are you a tree-hugger, too, mademoiselle?"

She laughed his question away, as well as the use of French. It might be the mocking tone of her laughter or her immediate turning away, but a chill had hung between them ever since.

"Two strong personalities," Kareena would maintain in the years to come. She also warned Mitra that Adi could be blunt. A nice way of saying "jerk," Mitra assumed. Or that his charm was in the budding stage.

Still thinking about that first meeting with Adi, Mitra parked her car a block from his office and crossed the street in a hurry, the light turning red.

A passing motorcyclist yelled at her: "Get out of my way, you fucking idiot!"

Surely this was an overreaction in her usually polite city. Still, it bugged Mitra. She arrived at Adi's office building with a sense of discomfort, marched through a large lobby, signed her name at the guard's desk, went past a row of workstations, and entered a lavish office, all leather and mahogany.

Thank God, Adi wasn't there. She needed a moment. She drew up a chair and studied the room. A number of award plaques lined one wall. The desk held a black-and-white photo of Kareena that Adi had snapped on vacation in the Greek Isles. Dolled up in a camisole and gypsy skirt, she leaned against a tree and smiled. *Kareena—where are you?*

Next to that photo rested their wedding picture from nine years ago in a gold-tone wood frame. The bride and the groom both wore their wedding gear; a red silk sari and gold jewelry for Kareena, and an off-white brocaded *sherwani* and contrasting black *churida*r for Adi.

Kareena had once told Mitra the story of Adi's family. Adi was an only son, heir to a fortune. Growing up in New Delhi, he had intelligence, if not good behavior, and bagged many academic honors. His mother spoiled him, the God Krishna incarnate, as Indian mothers of that generation were accustomed to do. Even on the day he'd punched a sickly classmate at school, she treated him to sweet rounds of besan laddoos.

In his late twenties, Adi had met Kareena. By then, a successful executive, he fell hard for her. Adi's wealthy family didn't approve of their relationship. "Her mother is low class," they'd said, "practically a whore. How can the daughter be any good? Just wait and see—she won't stick around."

"They were so petty," Kareena had told Mitra in a strained voice at the time. "How can they speak like that about my mother? She's a respectable woman. She has her own mind, so they don't like her."

Adi had decided to marry Kareena against their wishes and given up his huge inheritance for her sake. His family disowned him. Not only that, his uncle sabotaged his efforts to obtain a coveted position with an electronics firm by taking the job himself. Adi endured a year of that type of humiliation before giving up.

Eight years ago, Adi and his new bride had left India and flown to the opposite side of the world, as far away from his family as he could possibly go. He settled in the Pacific Northwest, where he found a plethora of opportunities. Before long, he formed his own software outfit. There was a price to be paid: long hours, constant travel, and worry about finances. In spite of this, he persisted and ultimately succeeded. He created "value" for his customers. He had "recurring revenues." Even though a success, he was still pariah to his family. Rumor had it that these days, although he often jetted to India on business and phoned his family from his hotel room in Mumbai, his mother would not take his call.

Mitra's memory faded as she noticed the emperor walking in through the door. Attired in an impeccable navy suit and black leather shoes, Adi wore no socks, which was part of his fashion statement. His eyes were red-rimmed with exasperation possibly at some luckless underling behind on a project.

He frowned when he saw Mitra, bumping awkwardly into the edge of the desk, and took his swivel chair on the other side. In light-challenged Seattle, his deep tan usually elicited envy, but today a grayish cast dominated his complexion. The eyes were sunken, as though his spirit had flown out of them.

"What brings you here to see me?" he asked in a business-friendly manner.

"Where is Kareena?" Too worked up, Mitra threw another question back at him. "Why haven't you called me?"

Easy, Mitra. Don't panic. Don't push. Don't hurl so many questions all at once. Adi was, after all, a Bengali. Their ancient culture had come of age—Mother's words echoed in Mitra—under the benevolent gaze of a blazing sun in an abundant land laced with magnificent rivers.

Crops were easy to grow and so people had copious leisure time, which led to dazzling rituals and a penchant for art and philosophy. To the Bengalis, rushing was not only alien, it was gauche. Even in this speedy era, Bengalis tried to prevail with soft gestures, moral reasoning, and delicate persuasion, rather than blunt confrontation. Mitra shouldn't be so tense. She should try to behave like a silkily polite Bengali lady.

Adi straightened, put his elbows on the desk. "Calm down, Mitra," he said in a voice rising slightly. "Your core competency is handling dirt. You play with weeds, worms, slugs, and horse poop. You grow lovely petunias. I'm not saying it's menial labor, but neither is it nuclear physics or private investigation. Go back to your weeds and leave this situation in more competent hands, like mine."

His remark stung her, but she observed him. The eyes were shifty, the hands were stiff, and the mouth was gloomy.

"I can't help but be involved, Adi. What about the stranger she was seen with at Soirée?"

He touched his wedding ring, a small gesture that distracted him for a moment. "I'm not worried about that. She's a big girl. She can take care of herself."

"Could I ask you why you filed a report with the police then?"

Avoiding her gaze, he studied his Day-at-a-Glance calendar.

She stared at him hard. Again, she was blowing it. Adi would not open up to a strong woman he viewed as a threat. She needed to be delicate, like the blush-white blossoms of baby's breath that lit up the corner of her yard.

"Do you think Kareena needed a break and decided to sneak away for a few days?" Mitra asked in a gentle tone. "There have been times, like at your birthday party a few weeks ago, when she looked like she could use a break."

Adi glared at her with a deep frown that was somehow tragic, somehow frightening. "Everything is fine between us, Mitra, just fine."

Mitra heard the staccato rumbling of a dump truck cruising by. Adi had some nerve telling her everything was fine with Kareena when he hadn't heard from her in more than forty-eight hours. Get real.

"Have you checked her closet?" Mitra asked. "What about her purse, cellphone, and credit cards? Is her toothbrush gone?"

He jerked at the question. "Her clothes are all there, but her purse and cellphone are missing."

Would he even recognize her alligator handbag, jeweled mules, the flowing shawls she favored over the structured feel of a coat, or a newly acquired camellia scarf? Would he be able to detect her perfume? Mitra believed he only remembered the totality of Kareena's being.

"Have you checked her recently visited websites? And all the e-mails she'd sent and received lately."

He shook his head, but stayed silent.

"Have you opened her safety deposit box? Has she taken her passport out?"

"I don't know where the key is." He paused. "Do you know how stressful this is for me? First thing this morning I got a call. They asked me to ID a body at the morgue."

A scalp-prickling moment. "What?"

Adi fiddled with his elaborate watch. "They found a woman's body in an alley in Pioneer Square. It wasn't her."

"Omygod!" Mitra shook her head. "I don't know what I'd do if—"

"Look, Mitra, I have a busy day. I have to chair a six-hour offsite. Technology stocks have run into speed bumps. We need to get our cash-burn rate under control. It may be necessary to de-hire some people."

She almost choked at the expression he used for firing an employee. De-hire. Was that how he thought about the body pulled from the alleyway—de-lifted?

"This is a life-or-death situation, Adi, not business as usual. Time is not on our side. We need to put our heads together and mobilize our community."

He looked her in the eye, as though loosing an arrow. "Hold on now, Mitra. I don't even want my *friends* to get wind of this, never mind the whole community. Don't you know how things get blown out of proportion when the rumor mill cranks up?"

She folded her arms. "Losing face is more important to you than asking for help to find your wife?"

His silence conveyed a latent hostility. In a way, she got it. Their community was small. It had at most two degrees of separation between people. Word spread quickly and rumor insinuated itself in every chit-chat. Still, in this dark situation, how silly, how counter-productive, Adi's pride seemed.

Maybe he suspected she didn't fully trust him, or perhaps there were things he'd rather conceal from her. He might be wondering what she knew that he didn't.

His cellphone beeped. Adi dug it out of his pants pocket, switched it off, shoved it back in its place, and made a motion to rise.

Strange. What if it were a call from Kareena or the authorities? What was he hiding? She needed to talk more with him. "Shall we meet again this evening?"

Adi stood up, pushed a few papers across his desk. His silence indicated a no answer. Why wasn't he doing his best to locate his czarina, the woman on whose behalf he sacrificed the love of his family?

Mitra stayed seated and stared at him until he nodded and said, "At Soirée around 8."

Why Soirée, unless he wanted to look for her there? How empty the place would seem to Mitra if she went back there without Kareena. But she didn't want to risk a change of location. It would give Adi an excuse to weasel out of their meeting.

She got up. He bid her farewell, not with his usual supercilious "Ta ta" but rather a low and serious, "I expect you to keep quiet."

SIX

BACK TO HER HOUSE, disregarding Adi's warning, Mitra began calling friends and community members from her list. Everyone seemed spooked by someone missing in their midst, but in the end she managed to persuade eleven people to form a task force. Although she was the youngest in the group, she agreed to lead the effort.

She invited Mrs. Barman, a prominent community member, to this evening's "Missing K" committee meeting. The buxom, retired history professor with thinning hair said, "Why are you meddling in their marriage? It's a private family matter. Let the family take care of it."

"I'm like family to her," Mitra said before terminating the conversation. "I want to bring her back safely."

Hoping to clear her head, Mitra wandered into her yard, to the row of flower patches. Petunias were pushing up and out toward the light. They'd soon explode into a storm of burgundy. The daffodils, white with frilly orange cups, had began to wither, their fleeting season almost over. No matter. Soon it'd be time to usher in the tulips.

She turned toward the tulip patch. To her dismay, some of the shoots were stunted. Others looked withered. The buds were still closed and a trifle wan. She shook her head. Not only could she not find Kareena, but she was also losing touch with her beloved bulbs.

She wandered back indoors, over to her bedroom. Herr Ulrich floated into her mind, a man who had turned out to be tender and pliant on those silky sheets. She wished she could confide in Kareena about him. She would exclaim: *A shy thing like you?*

Right now, somewhere in the brown-gray jumble of a construction site, Ulrich's taut body pushed, lifted, and stooped, the angles of his face accentuated by the strain. Did he pause for a split second, stare out into the distance, and re-experience Mitra's lips, her skin, her way of curling up with him?

Too soon to get moony about a man, Kareena would surely advise her.

Just picturing Ulrich, however, warmed her body. Not just the electric tingling of sex, but going beyond to a kind of communion. Sitting and talking, eyes only for each other, holding hands, knowing each other's innermost secrets, the occasional silence between them full. She never would have thought a single night could bring two people so close together.

Piano music soared from the Tudor across the street and encouraged her. Mitra reached for the receiver, her gaze falling on the blank Post-It pad next to the phone. Ulrich hadn't jotted down his phone number or even his last name.

He'd promised he would, but he hadn't.

Her dreamy interlude broke.

She noticed a pill lying on the floor, small, round, and yellow. It must have fallen from Ulrich's pocket. What was this med for? Did she even want to know? She stood still for a moment, then picked up the pill, and threw it into the wastebasket.

Late that afternoon, the search party huddled at her house, gloomy-faced, eleven of them. Mitra looked around the room. Veen swirled the fennel tea in her cup absent-mindedly. Sue, short for Suparna, kept her eyes lowered. Usually she had plenty of gossip to spare. Jean's dark hair skimmed her gold hoops. A loquacious woman, she simply asked, "Do you suppose Kareena is voluntarily missing?"

"Yes, she could have run away," Mitra said. "But suppose she didn't. We must look for her."

"What if she doesn't want to be found?" Jean said.

"Can we make assumptions and regret later?" Sue said.

Mitra talked up the urgency of the situation and assigned each person a task: preparing and handing out leaflets, combing the parks and neighborhoods, and urging the India Association of Western Washington to step in. Veen, such a helping soul, took on more than her share of responsibilities. When Pradeep, a Microsoftie and a newcomer to the community, volunteered to build a website, www.Looking ForKareena.Com, everyone cheered him.

Around 7 P.M., the meeting was adjourned. The task force members filed out the door, promising to carry on their respective tasks and reporting the results to Mitra. Their goodbyes rang with sadness.

Mitra walked out the back door and slipped into her greenhouse: a spacious room with barn-style roof and glass-paneled walls and strewn with plants in containers of various sizes. A pine-like fragrance filled the air. Plants were her refuge, her salvation and, fortuitously, her vocation, but today she'd neglected them, which she now regretted.

She picked up a hand-sprayer and misted the trays, dispensing growth-producing moisture to the germinating seeds and fragile sprouts tentatively poking up through the soil. For a moment, she pondered the miraculous ability of even the tiniest seeds of pansies, snapdragon, violas, and marigolds to execute the complex chemical instructions that aided their development. A honey bee hummed over a seed flat, performing its mundane but integral part in the symphony of creation. All around her, the life force was triumphant: surely that'd happen with Kareena, too. Whatever the cause, her disappearance would be temporary, explainable, reversible.

As Mitra rearranged the trays, her thoughts stretched to the weeks ahead. When the flower starts were sturdier and could tolerate the rigors of outdoor life, she'd transfer them into the backyard of her adopted grandmother Glow. It would be one more step in the process of designing a garden for Grandmother, a place for repose and emotional restoration.

Mitra heard the house phone ring. In her haste to set the hand-sprayer aside, she misjudged. The plastic bottle toppled and landed on top of an eight-pack, smashing the lobelia sprouts and spilling crumbly dark soil on the floor. She stifled a sigh. Then she sprinted to the phone, grabbing a towel and wiping her hands as she went, her insides throbbing in the hope of hearing Kareena's hello.

SEVEN

HOW COULD ADI DO THIS? He canceled their 8 P.M. meeting at the last minute, apologizing that he had a "product roll-out" the next day and needed the rest.

"Do you suppose Kareena has wandered off?" Mitra asked and listened for his reaction.

"Yeah, I think she's flown somewhere for an impromptu vacation," he said in a voice that held no humor. "She's punishing me for not taking her to Fiji last February. Don't worry. She'll get a big scolding from me when she gets back. And a trip to Fiji. That'll be my deliverable."

Another business-speak, possibly another lie. Mitra analyzed Adi's speech and voice pattern: he swallowed words; his voice often faded; he projected fake cheer. He was hiding something.

"Just to be sure, why don't you hire a private investigator?" she asked.

Silence. Had he murdered his wife and hidden her body? It gave Mitra the shakes to even contemplate such a possibility.

"Are you telling me everything, Adi?"

He said nothing. She heard a click from the other end.

Her stomach grumbled. She'd subsisted the whole day on nothing more than a few crackers. She decided to make an investigative trip to Soirée. A glass of wine might just be the treat she needed.

She pulled into a parking place only a block away, next to a rock garden lit up with the rosy buds of a heather bush, and checked her watch. Despite the catchy name, Toute La Soirée—all evening— closed at 9 P.M., less than an hour from now.

Inside, the busy café pulsed with after-work chumminess. She threaded her way through, concentrating on finding an empty seat, as well as looking for clues.

The table she and Kareena usually wanted was taken by a couple; how could it be otherwise, at this prime hour? Mitra was half-hoping for a minor miracle, but finding that parking spot must have filled her evening quota of luck. She gave a close look at the couple. They were each having a slice of strawberry shortcake. Mitra found even the thought of such sugary excess revolting.

Oh, no, it was Adi, dressed in a worn polo shirt, and looking slightly upset. He wasn't resting at home, after all. Accompanying him was a blonde who wore rather festive, crystal-accented chandelier earrings.

Should Mitra approach Adi, point out his lying?

It might have to do with the bleeding strawberries on their plates, but she felt sick in her stomach, nausea and a rumbling. She had no choice but to dash out.

On the way to the door, she knocked over a chair, which she put back in its place, so embarrassed to make a racket that her hands shook. Then she almost collided head-on with an Indian man who had just entered the shop. Young, dark, and devastatingly handsome, he had all the bones stacked just right, as Mitra's mother would put it. Clad smartly in a silver woolen vest, this prince headed straight for the take-out counter. His impressive carriage and smoldering eyes caused a stir among women patrons seated nearby. A college student-type tried to catch his glance. He touched the jute bag, an Indian-style *jhola*, dangling from his shoulder, in a practiced gesture.

Mitra slipped out the door, too drained to absorb anything further. After taking a deep breath, she hopped into her car, and peeled out onto the road. *Please, Goddess Durga, get me home in one piece.*

It drizzled but mercifully traffic was light. Within minutes, she pulled into her garage. As she stepped out of her Honda, her mind flashed on the enchanting prince from the café.

Hadn't Veen mentioned that Kareena was last sighted with a handsome *jhola*-carrier at that very spot?

Adrenaline shot through Mitra's body. Why couldn't she have been more alert? Stuck around longer to scrutinize Kareena's mysterious companion?

Should she drive back? Her watch said 9 P.M. Soirée had just closed.

Filled with nervous excitement, she entered her house. Neither the hot shower she took, nor the mug of holy basil tea she drank, tempered the anxious thoughts racing through her head. What really had happened to Kareena?

*   *   *

The next morning, Mitra stepped outside to get the newspaper. It hadn't arrived yet. The morning light shone on her front flower bed. An errant branch of camellia needed to be pruned. Its shadow stole sunlight from her plants. A stray buttercup had established itself at the base of a velvety coleus. She pulled the buttercup and threw it onto an impromptu compost heap, she'd just started. Next, she noticed the prolific clovers, threatening to overtake part of the space occupied by the tulips. Suddenly angry, she bent over and grasped a handful of the clover blossoms by their throats. Her muscles tensing, the blossoms practically bleeding on her fingers from the tight grip, she pulled and pulled them and tossed them into the compost pile. How dare they invade Kareena's tulips? Mitra wouldn't allow it. She refused to let them win.

With the weeds gone and blank spots in the soil staring up at her, she inspected her beloved tulips closer, an ache in her belly. All their buds were shriveled and brown, as though singed by blight, the dried stalks drooping over to return to brown earth.

Why were they dying on her so soon?

She fell to her knees and caressed the plants, lifting a wilted leaf to examine it, and squeezing its brittle stalk. She rolled each wizened bud between her fingers, but failed to find a single one with any hope.

With a pebble in her throat, she brooded about the broken promise of these tulips and reflected on Kareena, so vibrant, so full of life.

EIGHT

THE NEXT MORNING, Mitra sat down to a breakfast of steaming whole grain cereal, soy milk, and maple syrup. The kernels were soft and puffy, promising a satisfying fullness in her belly. Ulrich's dense face and wary green gaze floated in her mind. She finished only half of the bowl, losing her hunger thinking about him, and dumped the rest into the kitchen compost bucket.

On the evening she'd first met him at a fancy modern ice cream parlor, the place was packed, so packed that she had decided to head for the exit. She heard someone at a table calling her name. Carrie, a former neighbor, sat at a crammed communal table for eight. "Come sit with us. There's an extra chair."

She introduced Mitra to her friend, Ulrich, first names only. Mitra got her parfait and joined them.

On her own, she might not have noticed this brooding man, with a round face and a neat haircut. His eyes were a tame tortured green. He seemed quiet and content, aloof from the clamor of the scene and blending into the bone-white walls. Fit enough to suggest narrow hips, he was dressed in a wool-knit sports jacket. Speaking above the cello music that poured from the sound system, he informed her in his slightly accented English that he'd only recently moved here from Hamburg.

Mitra liked the foreignness about him, a closed window she'd like to open. "I've visited only one town in Germany for any length—Heidelberg," she said. "I went there for a week when I was on summer vacation from college." She recounted for him how she got caught up in the drama of the sky and mountains and loveliness of the university campus, the thrills experienced when trains pulled into the station on time—the way you wish your prayers were responded to, as one fellow American traveler put it. "My grammar wasn't perfect—I'd often forget to put the verb at the end of the sentence—I had had only one semester of German. But no one laughed and most of the time they understood me."

He leaned closer. "Why did you study German?"

"To satisfy the foreign language requirement, but mostly because I loved the long syllables. To call a grocery store *Lebensmittelgeschäft* is to give it heft."

Silence for a moment. She listened to the cello. "Do you like the music?" he asked, eyes sparkling.

She was glad he asked. Quite likely, they had a common taste. "Is that David Geringer? I seem to recognize the fingering."

"Yes." He lowered his gaze to her hands. "Are you a musician?"

"No, I'm a landscape designer."

"I appreciate the earth sciences. Tell me more about what you do."

Thank God Shiva, she didn't disappoint him. Sitting up straight, she described her typical day—visualizing, sketching, digging, transplanting, and appreciating the nature. But then did she really have to talk about the sheer delight of composting? She knew she was talking too much, but he stared at her with fascination, affecting her the way early spring lighting did. She shed her usual bashfulness, handed him her business card, and asked him how he liked the rainy city.

"I've found a good barber," he said, "as well as a European deli and German beer at Trader Joe's, and I don't mind the rain, but I can't find my way around here. Yesterday, it took me an hour to locate the house of an older German couple. I didn't think I'd be making friends with retired Germans here, but that's the way it has turned out to be."

She almost liked it that he didn't have many friends yet. She heard him saying, "But you have a circle of friends here, correct? From the way you carry yourself, you seem like what we call *gemütlich*, cozy."

"Well, my first three months in Seattle weren't *gemütlich*. I'd just moved from Alaska." She related to him the joy of strolling through one landscaped Seattle neighborhood after another in a state of touristy euphoria. Premature calendula blossoms lent a yellow-orange cast to the atmosphere—in February, no less. Compare that with Alaskan roads, as solidly frozen as a reign on death. But, as she'd soon discover, Seattle had a wintry side. If the weather was easy here, forging a network wasn't. In cafés she connected with bright, interesting minds. They discussed monorail as mass transit, the Koolhaas-original library, and the farmers' markets. But it wouldn't go further than that; she'd go home and curl up on her couch with a blanket and a book. She concluded by saying, "I did volunteer work at the Arboretum and met people on a casual basis, but didn't become intimate with anyone."

"You had—what do they call it here—trust issues?"

She nodded slightly. He fixed her with a gaze that said she was the only woman in the universe, at least in that room. She didn't know why but a slight discomfort rose in her, a feeling she pushed down.

He moved to other topics. Between chilled sweet bites, she disagreed with him in a pleasant manner when he suggested that the universe could be reduced to a giant computer program. She argued in a happy voice that billions of lines of codes wouldn't be enough to explain the life-force that transformed a tiny seed into a colossal pine tree, the determination in the heart that inspired a human of average strength to conquer Mount Rainier, or even what made each person's iris individually unique. If a computer program could decipher the mysteries of life, then they ought to destroy those lines of code. Some things were best left unexplained.

He didn't offer a differing opinion, just smiled. There was enough in that smile to distract her. She didn't even notice when Carrie and the others left.

By the time they had gotten up to leave, Mitra's head spun with abstract ideas, whereas her insides quivered with a delicious anticipation. She didn't head home alone that night.

Closing the compost bucket and heading toward the sink to wash the breakfast bowl, Mitra thought of the Deutscher, the green of his eyes, his caress. She couldn't wait to hear his sleepy sexy mumble. Why hadn't he called? They had so much in common: both came from far-away places; both spoke a foreign tongue; both were cello aficionados. In the past few days, she'd imagined seeing Ulrich everywhere; as she fidgeted in the grocery store check-out line, mended a garden hose, waited her turn at the ATM machine, or fed the parking meter.

Walking over to the kitchen window, she replayed his voice in her head. She practiced pronouncing *gut* for good, bobbed her head up and down, said *ja, doch,* the way he conveyed agreement. She injected a musical "z" for "th" in certain words, as if she, too, were a German struggling with English pronunciation.

Was that one night with him no more than a casual dalliance? She felt a blush of embarrassment creep into her cheeks.

Still, she couldn't help picking up the cellphone and calling her friend Carrie, who had introduced her to Ulrich, and dropping his name in the conversation. It was spring, after all, with waves of green growth just outside the window, and what else could Mitra think of?

Carrie caught on. "Oh, he's probably still around. He's finished putting new cabinets in my cousin's kitchen. I don't know what he's doing next. I'll call you back with his work number. You two seemed so cozy that night."

Within a couple of hours, Carrie called back. "Ulrich doesn't work for that outfit anymore. But my cousin says she's seen him painting a house at the northwest corner of 42nd and Latona. You know the rambler with a holly tree shading the front? Good luck."

Following an impulse, Mitra picked up the car keys, fired up her car, hurried to the said intersection, and parked on the curb, then looked through the car window. Sure enough, Ulrich was standing on the grass, scraping the exterior paint of a house across the street, his body snug in a gray sweatshirt, his back turned toward her. He seemed so much into the task at hand. His movements were smooth, with no wasted motion. She watched his hands going up and down, how the breeze ruffled his hair. His tall frame was a solace. She'd like to confide in him.

If only he would turn around so she could see the depth of his eyes, the determined jaw. If only he'd notice her and dash out in her direction, saying, "*Mitra!*"

He picked up a bucket and moved to another corner, no longer visible to her. Should she exit the car and approach him?

No. Mitra put her hands on the steering wheel, lurched away from the parking spot, and started toward her house. She'd seen him at least, which was satisfaction of some sort.

That afternoon, Mitra went to a private reception for Professor Devi Laal, a visiting social studies lecturer from Jawaharlal Nehru University in New Delhi on domestic abuse. Even though she didn't feel festive, Mitra had a twofold purpose in attending the reception. She wanted to meet Professor Laal—Kareena had more than once mentioned her name with respect—and she wanted to exploit this opportunity to mingle with the Indian community. Kareena remained her highest priority and the community could be of help.

In the reception hall, Mitra joined a small web of guests. Professor Laal, a stout woman in a simple white sari, spouted the creepy worldwide statistics of one in three women suffering physical abuse at home. Mitra recognized one of the people listening to Professor Laal from another community function; it was Dr. Sardar, a biotech engineer in his forties.

Dr. Sardar lifted his shoulders under his pricey sport jacket. His huge dark eyes made him appear perpetually curious or cross. "Of course, family violence happens," he countered, "but it doesn't happen with *us*. I'm sure the police get loads of calls from Rainier Valley and Central District."

A hush fell over the group. Mitra wanted to laugh at Dr. Sardar's denial. Blame it all on the working class and their neighborhoods.

Before Professor Laal had a chance to respond, Mitra stared Dr. Sardar in the eye and said, "Excuse me. I'm friends with a woman who's a DV counselor. Do you know where Kareena Sinha's clients come from?" She surprised herself by asserting that violence occurred as often in million dollar lakefront mansions as in apartment houses with chipped paint, shattered windows, and streaming cockroaches. Several women spoke up in agreement.

Mitra went one step farther and suggested, as Kareena would have, that it was time to educate the men. Such teaching should start at diaper age. Boys mustn't witness violence at home, or they'll carry germs of that behavior in their psyche forever.

Dr. Sardar blinked, seemingly in annoyance. "Excuse me," he said and headed for the samosa table.

Mitra wouldn't let him off. Minutes later, she cornered him as he dug into a flaky vegetable pastry, and talked to him about her effort in finding Kareena. When she finished, she noticed his eyes softening. "If you need any help," he said. "Call my office."

It gave Mitra momentary pleasure that she'd overcome her shyness, stood up for what she considered was right, and taken Kareena's message forward.

Although the evening had been a success, alone in bed that night, Mitra found herself puzzling over Ulrich's absence. She pictured him lying next to her, the warm comfort of his skin. Her breasts craved his touch. Her mouth pined for his clinging kisses. She stayed awake a long time.

NINE

MITRA'S GAZE FELL ON the vase of dried eucalyptus on the accent table in her living room. Kareena had always admired the fragrant arrangement—she adored all objects of beauty. Now she, a beautiful soul, was reported missing. On the morning of day five, Mitra considered it good fortune to finally be able to get an appointment with Kareena's supervisor.

Twenty minutes later, Mitra made her way through the corridors of the Domestic Violence Prevention Office to a cubicle, expecting to meet with a friendly face. Sandra Williamson hung up the phone. A sturdy woman with bitterness around her eyes, dressed in a well-fitted black twin-set, she appeared to be approaching fifty.

She shot Mitra a nasty look. "What can I do for you, Ms. Basu?"

"I'm trying to find Kareena. As you know, she's been missing for several days. Could you share with me what you're doing to find her?"

Williamson crossed her arms. "I've spoken with the police. They plan to form a multi-disciplinary missing person task force. They haven't gotten back to me with any new information."

Mitra settled deeper into her chair. "Multi-disciplinary missing person task force? That's long term stuff."

"There doesn't seem to be any immediate course of action to pursue."

"Do you believe that? Are you going to sit around and watch the police do little?" She paused. "Let me ask you this. Did you notice anything unusual during Kareena's last few days? Neighborhoods she might have ventured to? People she might have met?"

"We don't watch our counselors. They operate on their own."

"Couldn't you Mapquest the searches she's made on her computer? That might give you an indication about her whereabouts."

The look on Williamson's face said she'd just as soon Mitra got lost.

Mitra leaned forward. "You won't do anything at all for her?"

"Relax, Ms. Basu. This is way above my pay grade. We only deal with family issues. We don't give out information about our employees or their whereabouts. We deal with partner violence. Period. Maintaining privacy is of the utmost importance to our organization. This is for the safety of our clients and, I might add, a legal requirement."

Mitra stared at the oak tree outside the window. She mustn't raise her voice or Williamson would show her the door.

"You're confusing the issues. Kareena was a counselor, not an abuse victim. Or are you saying she was being battered at home?"

"I think your time is up. And this is no place for gossip. I wouldn't have made an appointment to meet with you, except you're so persistent. You must have left, what, ten messages?"

"No, twelve. Look, I'm not here to waste your precious time or mine. My friend is a top employee of yours. There must be some clues here."

"She *was* a top employee."

"Are you saying her work had been slipping? And, if so, what do you attribute that to?"

Williamson lowered her gaze to the ground. Her deeply lined forehead was capped with a lock of gray hair.

"Please, Ms. Williamson. You may be able to help our search for her. She's your best employee."

"Best employee? Ha! She'd been talking about quitting."

"Quitting? I find that hard to believe. She's totally dedicated. How can you be sure?"

Williamson laughed derisively. "Counselors resign all the time. Often because they can't take it any more or they have other plans. Kareena is no different. She'd been struggling with that decision. She thought it'd be her life's work, but then . . ."

"What other plans did she have?"

Williamson stayed mute. Mitra heard argumentative voices from a nearby workstation.

"Could somebody have abducted her? The husband of one of her clients, for instance?"

Williamson laughed. "She was not in any obvious danger. Only once in my quarter-century career, have I seen a case where a husband kidnapped a counselor, and then only for an hour. You just don't understand, Ms. Basu."

"You're right. I don't understand why you're not taking this seriously."

"You're young, Ms. Basu. You'll learn not to get excited over everything. We all do eventually."

Mitra stood up. "But I'll always get excited when it concerns someone I love dearly. Good day, Ms. Williamson."

Mitra strode out of the office building, legs stiff and mouth dry, and climbed into her car. She'd learned something new about Kareena—she was considering quitting her job. How did that fact fit in with her disappearance? She couldn't tell for sure.

Under the bright sun, Mitra made a resolve: no one was going to stop her, not Ms. Williamson, not the police. Once she made up her mind about doing something, she stuck to it. She didn't normally use the cellphone while driving, but this time she gave in. She reached the investigative officer in the SPD office.

"The longer the wait, the colder the trail," the officer said. "But you seem to be doing all the right things. You have a pretty cool head. And we're in touch with Adi Guha. We'll give him status information. He's our primary contact."

The officer was probably rifling through papers on his desk with one hand and cradling his cellphone with the other. To him, Kareena was no more than a computer profile of another lost soul to be summarized in a paragraph, another poster to be printed, whereas to Mitra and their mutual friends Kareena was a person of importance.

She said goodbye to the officer, frustration percolating in her. On second thought, he didn't really owe her anything. She wasn't family to Kareena.

TEN

HOW MITRA WISHED she had raised a little more money. $7,000 wouldn't do it. Yesterday, on day six, wanting to raise enough money to offer a reward for information on Kareena's return, she and the task force had held a benefit auction. Mrs. Talukdar, a community elder, contributed her wedding silk sari worked with gold threads. Another community member gave away a pricey rosewood throne. Mitra donated five gardening consultations and her entire sari collection, many gifted by relatives back home, thus parting with many sweet childhood memories.

She had to dip into her savings to come up with the amount needed to announce a reward for Kareena's safe return: $10,000.

She continued her search this morning. One other place to try: Aunt Saroja, a cousin of her late father. Mitra would never have met Kareena if not for this aunt. All the more amazing when you consider that she'd maneuvered such a feat from New Delhi, thousands of miles away. She knew a few of Kareena's relatives and might be able to provide Mitra with information she wouldn't otherwise get.

As a child, Mitra had a special affection for Aunt Saroja, a wise woman, willowy and well groomed. She called her Masimoni, Jewel of an Aunt.

When Mitra went to college in Alaska, Masimoni, wrote often, speaking her mind on pale lavender pages, her script firm. After graduation, Mitra was trying to decide on where to settle when Masimoni suggested in her usual direct style, "Why don't you give Seattle a try? I hear it rains constantly there, but that should be ideal for growing plants."

Much as Mitra adored her aunt, she stayed in Alaska for nearly four years, taking a job on an organic farm in the Matanuska Valley. Eventually, the winters got to her. She pulled up stakes, moved to

Seattle, and got hired by the Seattle Parks Department. At that point Aunt Saroja wrote again: "My friend's cousin's daughter lives in Seattle and likes it. Her name is Kareena. You two are alike in so many ways. I think you'll really hit it off. She'll help you get situated."

A month later, Mitra picked up the phone, called Kareena, and introduced herself. She did this more for Aunt Saroja's sake than out of any personal desire. Kareena sounded lively and approachable and suggested having coffee the next day. During their long coffee session, they shared everything about themselves and also their memories of home. Kareena said she was undergoing a periodic episode of homesickness for India, the country she'd left behind, but not entirely. Mitra, too, experienced the same longing from time to time. Her country was always there, soft-edged like breathing, hard-edged like crunching ice between your teeth. She didn't usually talk about it, but in Kareena's company she did. It was as though her voice had freed up.

Three weeks later, Mitra moved from her apartment into this house she'd just bought. On that day, it was snowing heavily and she lived on a hilly street. She'd have stayed put but her lease was up and someone else was moving in. Friends who promised to help didn't show up and she didn't blame them. Then the doorbell rang. Kareena stood there, perky in her corduroy slacks, wool hat, and boots, all in matching black. What a relief. Kareena immediately took control, called Adi and a friend. The roads were slick and stalled cars blocked traffic. It took them the whole day to get the move done, but Kareena was just as cool at the end of the day as when she came in.

"You've introduced me to an angel," Mitra said to Aunt Saroja on the phone later that evening.

A month later, in another conversation, she further told Aunt Saroja that Kareena was who she wanted to be. Kareena dressed well, entertained fabulously, had a wide circle of friends, and was always ready to lend a hand when a friend needed it.

"We have a splendid time whenever we get together, you know," Mitra told Aunt Saroja. "I'm really comfortable with her. It's like we've known each other forever. There's nothing I couldn't discuss with her."

"I am just so pleased," Aunt Saroja said.

In the months to come, with Kareena's encouragement, Mitra opened a landscaping business of her own, and that shifted her life for the better. What a joy to be your own boss, even though the hours were longer. She'd been thankful to Kareena ever since. Kareena, who had an extravagant taste, often asked Mitra to provide flower arrangements for her parties. Mitra did so free of charge. The gigantic bouquets she supplied often cost her several hundred dollars each, but she didn't mind.

They got together on most Fridays. Day would turn into twilight as they relaxed over drinks, gabbing, laughing, and trading opinions, oblivious to the time. As the years passed, all through the days and nights and springs and summers of their friendship, Mitra thanked Aunt Saroja silently and in her letters. She, suffering ill health, answered only sporadically.

"You're always there for me," Kareena once said to Mitra, "more than any other friend. If I were ever in trouble, you'd be the first person I'd call."

But she hadn't.

On this day, the seventh day after the vanishing of her friend, sitting in her living room, Mitra punched Aunt Saroja's number.

She came on the line. "So nice to hear from you, Mitoo," she said, calling Mitra by a nickname only she used.

Mitra gave her an account of Kareena's disappearance and the shadowy events surrounding it.

"A lovely person disappeared into thin air like that? How terrible. There's a cause. I smell something." Aunt Saroja paused. "I know how much she means to you. I still remember one of your letters. You talked about your time with her so poetically that I memorized it. 'We don't parse our friendship. It just is. We scatter the gems of our hours freely, then retrieve them richer in value.'"

"You knew Kareena through her relatives long before I met her. What can you tell me about her?" Mitra asked.

The line went silent for a moment. "There's something I can tell you, my dear Mitoo. In fact, it's been on my mind a long while, also something of value."

"What is it, Masimoni?"

"Will you promise to keep it to yourself and not say a word about this to your mother? The poor woman has a weak constitution and I wouldn't wish to disturb whatever peace she has in life."

"I promise."

"Well, dear, Kareena is your half-sister, your father's child from his first marriage."

Mitra jumped up from her chair. "Half sister? How can that be?"

"Well, it might shock you, but here it is."

Mitra's stunned ears absorbed the disclosure: Her father Nalin had taken a job after college as a technician with a film studio in Mumbai. At the studio, he fell in love with a sexy struggling young actress and married her. In the fifteen months the marriage lasted, they had a child, Kareena. After their divorce, Nalin, shattered and disillusioned, packed his bags and took the train back to Kolkata, where he met Mitra's mother. They were married within a year. Nalin's ex-wife never allowed him any contact with his daughter.

Kareena was Mitra's half-sister. She was family. That felt so right. Mitra's cheeks burned in joy.

"Are you happy that I've told you?" Aunt Saroja asked.

"Oh, yes," Mitra said. "What a surprise that'd be for Kareena. I don't believe she knows. I've never mentioned father's first name to her. And Basu is such a common surname in India. Do you know what puzzles me? My mother has never mentioned father's first marriage to me."

"Your mother had a hard time accepting that marriage. Remember, it was over thirty years ago. Divorces were considered a matter of shame and acting wasn't a respected profession, not to mention the low reputation that an actress had. Relatives who had the knowledge didn't consider it proper to talk."

"So Mother wasn't told about father's first child?"

"Never."

"Why didn't anyone tell me sooner?"

"There's much in my long life I regret," Aunt Saroja said. "This is one of them. Ultimately, your secrets drag you down. The longer you wait, the more monstrous they get. They eat at you, they make you frail." Her voice broke.

"Are you okay?" Mitra asked.

Aunt Saroja assured Mitra that her health was sound and that she'd check with her large circle of friends to see if anyone had heard from Kareena. "God, who knows what's behind it? We won't waste a minute."

After cradling the phone, Mitra stayed seated for awhile pondering the irony. A distant cousin did once whisper to her something about her father's first wife. She didn't believe it then.

She would have to track Kareena down even more urgently and confide in her what she'd learned. They shared a father. God Vishnu be praised, they had blood connection—their lives were forever joined. The sisterly closeness they felt was just as it should be. Kareena would stare at her in wide-eyed silence, then embrace her with a cry of joy.

ELEVEN

STILL THINKING ABOUT THE SECRET spilled by Aunt Saroja, Mitra plunked down at her home office desk. The phone jangled. Robert Anderson-Haas, Gardening Editor at the *Seattle Chronicle*, reminded her she'd missed the deadline for her twice-monthly gardening column.

"Could you give me a little more time?" Mitra said. "My best friend has gone missing and I've been involved in the effort to locate her."

"Get back to me by the end of the day." Robert paused. "You said somebody disappeared? You know I started out as a crime reporter. I also know a detective with the SPD, if you care to speak with him."

"Yes, please."

"His name is Nobuo Yoshihama. He used to live in my apartment building, then bought a house and moved out. I gave him a hand when he moved. He owes me."

Mitra jotted down the particulars. "How do I work with him? I know so little about police protocol."

"Just be open with him. Nobuo is a little hard to figure out at first. A little on the shy side, but he's a good guy. He might be interested in talking with you about gardening, too. He often complains about having to manage a yard all by himself. He works long hours at his job."

So the detective was single. Mitra laughed to herself. *No, Robert, I don't need a date right now. I want to find Kareena.*

"Since you have connection to crime reporting," Mitra said, "might you be able to give me any suggestions about this case? If it doesn't take up too much of your time, that is."

"Is there any proof she's been kidnapped? Or is there a chance she's run off?"

"Wish I could tell you." Mitra related her fears and concerns, but couldn't answer Robert's questions.

"Actually, since she's your friend, I'd like to dig into the case. Nobuo can update me. Believe me, it's not extra work on my part. I like to read true crime reports in my spare time. Methods and motives fascinate me. I have a tough stomach, you might say."

How interesting, Mitra thought, a garden editor who read bloody crime stories to amuse himself. She saw a glimmer of hope, however. After hanging up, she left a voice message on the detective's cellphone and waited in vain for a few minutes, pacing up and down the living room, for his call back.

Then, sitting in front of the computer, she positioned her fingers on the keyboard. Facing up to writing the gardening column was exactly what she needed. It'd transport her back to her familiar world where plants ruled, events made sense, the day ran according to an order, and confusion didn't hang like a cloud cover. She stared at the opalescent screen, which stared back with glee, as if delighted with its own resistance. She glanced out the window and saw a few buttercups—weeds. The topic she opted for was weeding.

WEEDING: A Somewhat Holistic Approach
A weed is no more than a flower in disguise.
James Russell Lowell

She heard the tiptoeing of a noun, the whisper of an adjective, the aggressiveness of an adverb, and eventually the whistle of a sentence. She pecked away at the keyboard, trying and failing and trying again to hold together a proto-idea. Finally, a paragraph became whole.

A start, but Kareena wouldn't leave her thoughts.

About this time last year, on a balmy weekend day, Kareena had stopped by to visit. She watched from a nearby wicker chair as Mitra crawled around on her hands and knees, pulling out grass and dandelion from a flowerbed.

Mitra showed Kareena a patch with grass tendrils shooting every which way. "See these creepers? The season has just begun and they are already so aggressive."

"Weeding looks like a lot of dirty work to me."

"But it's therapeutic. And you do get joy out of it in the long run when you see your flowers blooming sooner."

Kareena stirred her glass of green ice tea. "You know, on second thought, I envy your healthy life-style. Wish I could be spending hours and hours outdoors, surrounded by beauty, color, and fresh air. That's not possible with Adi. He wants me to look perfect, not with dirt under my nails."

Was she trying to tell Mitra something? She'd long suspected Kareena had marital challenges. Pulling and digging might give her an outlet.

"Why don't you try weeding with me, despite what Adi says?" Mitra asked. "See how you like it?"

"Yeah, I'll give it a shot."

And so Kareena had her first try at yanking out dandelions. After half-an-hour, she complained that her back got sore. An obnoxious yellow jacket harassed her. And she chipped a French-manicured nail trying to swat it with the shovel.

"I'll leave you with it, Mitra," she said with obvious relief. "I have a charity luncheon to go to."

Mitra's gaze returned to the computer screen, to her column-in-progress. A thought emerged. Suppose Kareena had shown more interest in chasing weeds. Then perhaps she'd have grasped the underlying principle: one must let go of that which no longer served a purpose in one's life, or that which threatened one's existence. As a result, she'd have weeded Adi out. She'd given up her life in India, given up all she'd ever known, to be married to him. That marriage didn't turn out the way she'd have expected. Adi had been choking the bloom of her happiness, or so it seemed to Mitra.

TWELVE

THE NEXT MORNING Mitra decided to pay a visit to Glow Martinelli, her adopted grandmother and a septuagenarian sprite. Mitra had turned to her in the last week, even though she was one of the few people ambivalent about Kareena. They'd met once at Mitra's house, exchanged niceties, then gravitated to opposite ends of the room. Mitra could feel an icy chill between them. Just chemistry, she'd assumed.

She had another reason for this visit. Grandmother's ex son-in-law, Henry, worked for the Snohomish County Sheriff's office and she'd promised Mitra on the phone to speak with him about the Kareena situation.

As she snatched her purse and keys and headed for the garage, Mitra recalled how she'd met Glow. About six months earlier, Glow had trekked to Zoka in Wallingford for an afternoon cup of espresso and stepped on Mitra's business card. It'd probably fallen from someone's pocket. Mitra's "Palette of Color" business name described the way Glow pictured her garden, so she phoned Mitra, even though she had already gotten bids from two landscapers.

The next day, Glow showed her a messy weedy yard in need of attention and "healing." Though the task appeared to be challenging, Glow's open face and inclusive manner heartened Mitra. She offered some initial ideas for design such as, closely planted annuals anchored by longer blooming perennials and islands of ornamental glass. She suggested cleaning the debris and doing much of the site preparation before the rains started, but holding off on planting until early spring.

Without commenting on her suggestions, Glow invited her to a glass of fresh pear cider. They grabbed canvas chairs under an Asian pear tree and chatted over the sweet cider, the conversation soon gravitating to the topic of India.

"From what I've seen in movies and read about India," Glow mimicked the affected British manner, pronouncing it as "Inja," and adding, "Women seem so companionable with each other over there." She described a scene from a Bollywood film depicting women in their inner courtyards. Flowers blossomed, children and grandchildren played, relatives dropped by, and servants plied everyone with trays full of tempting sweets, all happy, hectic, and connected.

A breeze had whispered over their heads. Mitra gave Glow a synopsis of what her childhood had been like. She and her mother hadn't had a courtyard. Their relatives, most of them barely getting by, were notoriously unsociable. When a classmate complained during the autumnal Durga Puja celebration that her parents had to buy presents for ten cousins, Mitra wished her mother had the same problem.

"And my mother never seemed happy," Mitra put in.

"Even if Indian women aren't completely fulfilled," Glow replied, "and indeed how many of us can hope to be, they don't seem to mind the limits and responsibilities placed on them. And they don't need champagne to cheer themselves up." Then she added that she'd go with Mitra's bid, even though it was higher than the other two, because she liked her suggestions.

Mitra had barely finished expressing her gratitude when Glow said, "Perhaps it's destiny that has brought us together. Each of us has scores of destinies preplanned and stored away like pretty boxes lined on a shelf, or so I believe. You are free to lift the box that catches your fancy and carry it home. You, the enchanted buyer," she cautioned, her eyes twinkling, "beware."

Trained to respect her elders, Mitra didn't argue. Nor did she mention that she'd left the oppressiveness of destiny back in India along with her saris, bangles, and elaborate earrings. Clearly, something had clicked between her and Glow, even though they belonged to different generations and her dependence on destiny rubbed Mitra the wrong way.

The next day they went to Mollbak's nursery to purchase new gardening tools. There they selected a round-point shovel, turning fork, garden spade, pruning shears, and a utility cart. In the checkout line, a snooty woman gave Mitra a look and Glow introduced her as her granddaughter.

That evening, Mitra's phone trilled. "This is your Grandmother." Glow gave out a laugh—a happy, natural one. "Am I disturbing you?"

Grandmother? The strain of the day vanished for Mitra, replaced by an unexpected flush of happy sentiments. She attributed it to her Indian upbringing. She had always appreciated the older generation who provided support, steadiness, continuity, and humor. Both her grandmothers had passed on before Mitra was born, but here was Glow, just the right age, slipping easily into a corner in her life.

"You're not disturbing anything, Grandmother," she said.

She questioned whether Glow could really fill her need for a grandmother, but as it would turn out over the next several months, she did. They had fun hanging out together, generation gap be damned. And Mitra loved her explanation of why she'd changed her name from Gloria to Glow. She was no longer the "caged-bird wife," "Sichuan carry-out mom," "buttoned-down nonprofit administrator," or "silly greetings card saleswoman." She was free to glow.

Thinking warmly about Glow, Mitra now drove to her house in Fremont and reached it in a few minutes. She buzzed the bell and instantly the door opened. There stood Grandmother, her plump, self-described "Cabbage-Patch doll" body dressed in a color-splashed caftan. Her cat Tampopo, with her glossy fur and large alert eyes, stood next to her, purring.

Grandmother hugged Mitra and asked her to follow her to the kitchen. She poured a glass of mango lemonade for Mitra and a Scotch from a tall sturdy bottle for herself. She swirled the pale yellow liquor in her glass, backed into the counter. *What's with the drink?* Mitra wondered. Grandmother's doctor had advised her to avoid alcohol.

"Has Henry called back?" Mitra asked, a quaver in her throat.

"Yes, just before you came," Grandmother said.

"And?"

"I don't want you to panic. He said that the body of a 32-year-old woman was found in Lake Stevens at about 5 P.M. yesterday. She might have fallen off a boat. Henry wants you to call the Medical Examiner's office."

Mitra's cheeks went cold. She set the juice glass on the counter and, with a numb hand, dug her cellphone out of the pocket of her jumper. She got hold of the Medical Examiner's office. The person who would have the answer was out to lunch. Mitra's shoulders sagged.

At Grandmother's suggestion, they carried their beverages to the living room and sat on the couches. Tampopo stalked in and jumped on Mitra's lap.

Perhaps to lighten the moment, Grandmother touched the top of her hair. It was tinted red, but the result looked nearly natural, save for the extra sheen. "I need a new hairstyle," she said. "It's the same modified Mitzi Gaynor cut I've been wearing for decades. She was a movie star eons ago."

Mitra nodded, her mind occupied with the telephone call. Tampopo leaped out toward an invisible insect. The conversation went back to Kareena.

"She's always there when someone needs her," Mitra said, her voice thickened. "I remember when Veen's sister had emergency surgery in Dallas and she couldn't get there on time because she had pneumonia, Kareena offered to go in her place. Her boss wouldn't give her the time off, but she flew there anyway and risked the consequences because there was no one else to go. That's just the way she is."

"Who's Veen?"

"Veen Ganguly is a mutual friend of ours. Anyway, Kareena had no place to stay in Dallas. I guess she camped out in the hospital's waiting room. That selfless act ended up costing her greatly. Adi gave her a hard time for going against his wishes, her supervisor docked her pay, and she had to cancel plans for a holiday weekend getaway."

"You spend way too much time with her. I know you both like to go out to restaurants and enjoy yourselves, but I get the impression she uses you. Didn't you say you do the flower arrangements for her parties? I bet you do it for free."

From a neighboring house, there rose the metronomic clanging of a hammer. *You're right about the flower part, but wrong about Kareena,* Mitra was about to say when her cellphone beeped.

Her pulse racing, she held the phone to her ears. It was the Medical Examiner's office. The dead woman had turned out to be a tourist, not Kareena. Mitra breathed a sigh of relief. Despite the scare, Mitra felt glad that Grandmother was keeping an eye on things for her.

Grandmother glanced down at the empty glass on her hand and shook her head. "It's been quite a day. I got a letter in the mail from my fourth husband. He signed it 'Sincerely, Georgio.' Can you believe it?" Grandmother laughed, perhaps to massage away the day's wear-and-tear and callousness of those once close to her. "I didn't mean to get your spirits down by talking against Kareena. On my way home, I had a clear view of the Cascades, so tall, so glorious, so other-worldly, no matter how many times I've seen it. I parked my car to have a better view. No matter what, we have these high peaks to look up to."

Mitra rose. Grandmother stood up, gave her a hug, and they clung to each other for a moment.

Mitra stepped to the porch and turned to wave. Glow stood on the doorway, fingering her bangs. How like Mitra, her adopted grandmother from another era, who had another sensibility and another hairstyle, but who navigated similar losses. She felt for her in a way she hadn't before.

THIRTEEN

THE FOLLOWING MORNING, Mitra was working in her home office when the doorbell chimed. She scrambled to her feet and flung open the door in a sudden motion, startling a tall man in his mid-thirties poised on the porch.

"Ms. Basu?" Their gazes locked. "Nobuo Yoshihama. I'm the detective assigned to the Ms. Sinha's case. I thought I'd stop by to see you. You left a message on my cellphone. You work with Robert?"

He even knew where she lived. Before she could size him up, he'd flipped open his wallet to flash his police badge and identification card. She barely glanced at them.

"May I come in?"

The air was thick, the sky the color of soot, and the silent trees bristled with an uneasy stillness. "Yes, please," she said.

He took a seat in a leather armchair in the living room, declined her offer of a cup of tea. His beige windbreaker seemed pale against the green glaze of her north wall.

"The last few days must have been difficult for you." He asked a few questions about where she'd first met Kareena, took notes in a slim notepad, and seemed satisfied with her answers. "Any information you provide is confidential. Do you have any idea where Ms. Sinha could have gone?"

"No. Every year she travels to India for a month. She plans for it and tells me long before the trip."

"Did she seem depressed recently? Do you know if she has had any psychological problems in the past?"

Was he going to psycho-analyze Kareena? "Oh, no, she's a friendly, outgoing, centered person."

"Any indication of trouble? Any financial concerns?"

"No to both. She makes a decent salary. Her husband has an excellent income. They both come from money."

"I'm told you're someone Ms. Sinha was close to. When you last saw her, how did she seem?"

"Yes, we were close. We were alike in so many ways. We last met at Toute La Soirée. Aside from being fatigued after a long day, she seemed happy."

"Toute La Soirée." Yoshihama lifted his head from the notebook and inquired about its location, décor, clientele, and even what one ordered there.

Mitra responded with minutiae that under more pleasant circumstances would have been fun to share. Kareena, who had no special loyalty to any one place, somehow had taken a fancy to rendezvousing there with her. Mitra concluded with: "I'm told that's where she was last seen. A young, well-dressed Indian man was with her."

"Do you have any idea who he might be?" Yoshihama asked.

"No."

"Did Ms. Sinha ever tell you why she chose to be a DV advocate?"

"She likes to help abused women who have no money or family support, women who don't understand the legal system."

"Do you know what her typical day is like?"

Mitra peered through the window at a Fed-Ex truck speeding down the street. "No, Kareena doesn't talk a lot about her job." Another fact percolated at the back of her mind. Kareena had a bumper sticker with the DV helpline number on it. She asked Yoshihama if someone could have traced her from that.

Yoshihama expressed his doubt, paused, and said, "Tell me about Ms. Sinha's marriage. Does she have any marital problems that you know of?"

To assume that Kareena had marital difficulties was mere speculation on Mitra's part. Still, recalling the telltale brown swelling on Kareena's upper arm, Mitra decided to be open. "I can't help but be suspicious of Adi. I've seen bruises on Kareena's arm that looked like someone grabbed her. And Adi isn't cooperating in this matter."

Yoshihama asked her to elaborate, leaned back, and listened as she laid out the details. He seemed cool, professional, thorough, and somewhat Zen. His quietness and deliberate manner, even after she'd spilled out her worst fears, began to get on her nerves. How did he plan to find Kareena?

"I saw your greenhouse," Yoshihama said. "Did Ms. Sinha have any interest in gardening?"

"None at all, although I've tried to get her interested."

"You work with plants?"

She nodded her assent and briefly described her small business.

"I admire people who can get beauty out of the ground. What's your favorite flower?"

How unusual for any man to ask such a question, especially a cop. "Tulips. Yellow tulips, for that matter. I grow them, although this year they're not doing so well."

Yoshihama's brown eyes roamed the room. He nodded. Maybe he viewed Mitra's décor the same way she did, as Asian-style austerity. Her rooms were minimally furnished. She considered blank space to be restful and harmonious, and it freed your mind to create beauty, not to mention that it was easier to keep tidy. Kareena had once said just the opposite. She'd suggested that Mitra needed heavier furniture "to graft personality, to inject *chi*, and achieve a fuller, more built-out appearance" that she believed this Craftsman bungalow called for. Of course she'd think that. She and Adi had a large bank account, which Mitra didn't. And yet she didn't resent her friend for spending freely or giving her a tip or two on interior decorating.

"I like this room," Yoshihama said. "It's peaceful." He gazed down at his notebook.

"What's being done to find Kareena?"

"We have questioned six or so persons—none has panned out. We're auditing Ms. Sinha's credit card usage and waiting for the cellphone company to release her records. As I promised Mr. Guha, I'll do my best to help him. But I let him know we field more than two thousand disappearance cases every year." Yoshihama shut his notebook, rose, drew a business card from his breast pocket, and offered it to Mitra, brushing against her hand. "Please call me right away if Ms. Sinha gets in touch with you."

He gave her a warm handshake. At the door, with a strong motion of his wrist, he twisted the slightly loose knob. Before she could help him, he yanked the door open, again caressing her hand. Usually, her visitors had problems with this door. Not him.

Their gazes, two appraising pairs, met. With a nod of assurance, he turned and descended the front steps, pausing a moment to examine the pink flowering cherry tree on her parking strip. He touched a branch—leafy, dark brown and reaching up to meet the sunlight—and his expression turned tender. Did he have a cherry tree of his own? He walked a few steps, glanced back at her, waved, ducked into his black SUV, and drove off.

Mitra sighed. Although she could see that the police were doing what they could, in her heart she felt as though their attitude was rather casual. She didn't, however, write Yoshihama off completely. They'd made a connection of sorts and that might help speed things up.

She wandered into the kitchen, opened and closed the cupboard, rearranged items in the refrigerator, and filled the tea kettle with water. With a cup of black tea and a slice of toast, she sat at the table. Bananas protruded from a sunny ceramic bowl within arm's reach. She fiddled with her iPod.

As she grappled with various possibilities in her mind, the tea tempered to lukewarm, toast became dense, and bananas remained untouched. She stared at the large "Trees are not trivial" poster on the sea blue wall. Mitra's mother had sent that poster from Kolkata on her last birthday. In it, a sari-clad Indian woman lowered her head in respect before a gigantic leafy tree.

And that made her recall an incident involving Kareena's mother. Mitra and Kareena had been hanging out on her back deck one weekend, when Kareena's cellphone sang out. It was impolite to eavesdrop and so Mitra walked over to the evergreen kalmia shrub and pretended to ignore the conversation.

"Stop yelling," she heard Kareena imploring. "Stop it, Ma."

Kareena hung up, visibly shaken, her mouth slack and the sparkle in her eyes reduced to a dull sheen. Mitra walked back to join her.

In a small raspy voice, Kareena said, "That was my mother."

"Is everything okay?" Mitra asked.

"Oh, she's being the usual drama queen. She still thinks her life is like one of those Bollywood movies she acted in a zillion years ago."

Taking a sip of her lukewarm tea, Mitra wondered if that long-ago afternoon could shed new light about her sister and whether she should have remembered to mention it to Yoshihama.

Mitra had seen how a catchy song from a movie, a dance scene, a dream sequence, but most of all a dashing actor would keep Kareena's heart and mind soaring. Had she gotten that passion for Bollywood films from her mother? Mitra remembered a particular incident that took place about two-and-a-half years ago. On that day, she'd come down with a cold and stayed in bed.

As the evening fell, Kareena turned up at Mitra's doorstep, a soup tureen on her hand. They slurped the rasam, what Kareena called, "the Mumbai version of mother's chicken soup," and munched on boat-shaped chamcham sweets, which she'd toted back from a recent trip to India. Afterwards, they'd pored over the garishly colored pages of an issue of *FilmDunya*, a fantasy rag from Mumbai.

"Look at this *lehenga*," Kareena said, pointing to a woman's red-and-purple bare-midriff costume.

"I wouldn't wear it myself, but—"

"Look at him. Isn't he gorgeous?"

Different tastes for different folks. Despite the closeness she felt for Kareena, Mitra realized their tastes were galaxies apart.

Finally, Kareena popped in a DVD in the player, a "cop romp," as she described it. For the next three hours, they watched a shadowy gangster story, a blend of gun play, car chase, rapes, dance sequences, and sappy romantic interludes. Kareena laughed, hooted, and applauded often, whereas Mitra had a hard time coping with the fights, blood, high decibel, and fake tears.

As the credits rolled, Kareena said in a cozy voice, "That was great. Could we watch it again? Oh, just that part where they dance on a glacier. Such a terrific background score. You don't mind, do you?"

Mitra really didn't want to, but seeing her friend so happy and rosy, she went along with it. This was a yet another Kareena. Mitra wondered if, in her mind, Kareena tamed the beast of aggression she saw daily as an abuse counselor by making it an object of fantasy.

"If I took your temperature now," Mitra teased her friend at the end of the repeat viewing, "It'd break the thermometer. The diagnosis? Bollywood fever."

Kareena threw her head back and laughed. "It gets me going, the melodrama, the craziness, even the tacky songs. If it's fever, I want no cure for it."

Mitra had accepted her friend's school-girlish enthusiasm. In her gardening pursuit, she had long ago learned to love and nurture a wide assortment of plants, even those exhibiting peculiar characteristics. As with plants, so it was with people.

* * *

After another sleepless night thinking about Kareena and missing the warmth of their friendship, Mitra sat at her desk, pulled a sheet of featherweight lilac stationery, and held her pen poised over it. She would write a letter to her sister; otherwise, her insides would burst.

> Dearest Kareena,
>
> I've always loved you and cherished you as a friend, and now that Aunt Saroja has spilled a huge secret, I feel even closer to you. I can't wait for you to come back. It's still hard for me to believe it, this secret, so tender and so sacred. It keeps me up all night.
>
> We're half-sisters.
>
> Yes, the warm way we feel toward each other is just what it should be.
>
> This is the biggest thrill of my life. You see, I never had a sibling and always wanted one to play with, to mess around with. To have you as a sister is the best thing in the world. I wish you'd come back soon, so I could tell you this in person and welcome you to my family.

Mitra filled the page and spilled over to another sheet, recounting her memories of their father, Nalin. Once finished, she sealed the letter and slid it inside a matching lilac envelope.

She had no mailing address.

She stowed the envelope in a dresser drawer. Well, she'd hold on to this letter, until such time as they met again. She'd love to watch her sister's reactions as she read it.

She knew what to do next. Adi hadn't kept his word about staying in touch. She'd have to visit him. She wanted answers.

FOURTEEN

MITRA ARRIVED AT Adi's corner office unannounced at lunchtime, knowing his watchdog assistant wouldn't be there. Standing by the window, Adi checked his iPhone. He had on a pricey well-fitted blue shirt (which Kareena had gifted him on his last birthday), casual khaki trousers, and no tie. Mitra paused at the open doorway and waited for Adi to notice her. He raised his eyes, frowned as usual, and waved for her to sit in the chair across from him.

He wore a bewildered expression, as though someone had just awakened him from a deep sleep without telling him why. The face was fleshier, the complexion mottled, the eyes puffy as new pillows. Here perhaps was a more human Adi, more fallible, and even vulnerable.

Putting the iPhone down on the desk, Adi clenched his hand into a fist, then asked Mitra to sit tight for two seconds so he could handle an "action item," and walked out of the room.

A black metal file cabinet situated next to a wall was partially open. Mitra glanced at the door and saw no one nearby. Should she open it? What might be in there? After a moment, she sidled over to the cabinet, pulled it open, and thumbed through the hanging files, reading their labels. One titled, "Kolkata Investigation," drew her attention. Why Kolkata? She extracted the folder. It held newspaper clippings and several business letters. Voilà. She might find a clue here. She picked up a letter.

Hearing footsteps, she put the letter back, without having read a single word, and returned the folder to the cabinet drawer. She shut the drawer and rushed back to her seat, heart thudding. The file cabinet didn't close completely. Adi entered, skirted the desk, and moved toward his swivel chair, shutting the file cabinet with one hand and turning to face her at the same time. Thank God, he hadn't noticed anything unusual.

"I don't suppose you have an update for me?" Mitra said, trying to sound interested, but not too aggressive.

"I do as a matter of fact," Adi whispered, his eyes clouding over. "I got a ransom note in yesterday's mail. Yes, it's payment time."

The breath Mitra took fluttered in her throat. She sat unmoving with horror. Ransom—the stuff of violent movies or the bloody plotlines in the mystery novels Mother liked to dip into. "Ransom?" she echoed.

Face stricken, his left eye twitching, Adi described receiving an unsigned typed letter the previous day. He read it once, twice, three times, four times, digested the implications, stared at the outrageous demand again, and quivered. He even entertained the possibility he'd lost his mind. But the note was real.

"Who sent it? Where are they holding her? For what amount?"

"They're demanding a million dollars."

"What did the cops say?"

He squirmed in his seat. "I'm keeping them out of the loop."

She leaned forward in frustration, her elbows on his desk. "But why? Aren't there instructions in the note that can be traced? What about fingerprints?"

He shook his head, glanced down at his fingers. "Now, take it easy, Mitra."

"Do you have the note with you?"

He scooted his chair back and again shook his head. "Look, you're overstepping your boundaries. You're putting yourself in the path of the criminals. Go back to your garden."

"Why are *you* dealing with the criminals?"

"The note says I should keep the police out of it, if I want—"

Would the criminals harm Kareena? Put a gun on her throat? No!

"How can you expect to handle all this on your own?" An icy shiver down her body nearly choked Mitra's words. "How will you live with yourself if things go wrong?"

He lurched to his feet. "I'm handling this as delicately as I can."

"Delicately? When Kareena is in danger? Have you paid?"

"I'm getting ready to pay half."

"Why only half?"

"I'm not cash-flow positive right now. I have to liquidate some properties. That'll take weeks. Whoever sent this will just have to wait. I don't have a choice."

Mitra stared at him. "What'll happen to Kareena in the meantime? How did you exchange the money?" Seeing him stay silent, she mentioned the fund she'd raised in an auction as a reward for Kareena's safe return. "It won't be much, but I'd be happy to offer it to you. Don't you think we should get our community involved to raise more money?"

As though in denial, as though unwilling to witness the anxiety on her face, he closed his eyes.

"Damn," she said.

He opened his eyes; there was desperation in them. "Not your usual language, Mitra. Listen, if you blow the whistle on me, I'm ruined and you . . . you won't know what happened to you."

She got it. He'd make sure that she lost all her gardening clients. And worse. She waved a hand. "Go ahead, intimidate me, Chairman Guha."

"Look, I know you two are very close. Kareena trusts you like she trusts very few people. She calls you a bestie. You deserve a positive performance review for your dedication, but stay out of it. This is not a situation for you to butt into. It's dangerous. *Bujhley*? Do you read me?"

"*Bujhina*. I don't follow why you're all of a sudden worried about me. I don't follow why you're not doing what's necessary to bring Kareena back safely."

Adi's red-ringed eyes sparked with anger, confusion, despair, and possibly even hatred. Kareena's wellbeing didn't seem uppermost in his mind. Could it be that Kareena wasn't missing at all? Mitra felt as though she'd stepped into a ghost town. She didn't know where to go, what to do next, or what to believe.

Adi picked up his iPhone. End of conversation. Mitra scrambled to her feet. He didn't raise his eyes.

As she stormed out of Adi's office, his blonde assistant gave her a dirty look from a nearby cubicle, as though Mitra had come to harass her boss. She strode back to the sidewalk.

Standing there, Mitra debated whether she should call Detective Yoshihama. That little piece of ransom note had shaken things up and the detective should be informed of it. And yet the warning from Adi hung over her head, a rock about to slip down a hillside. Eventually, she retrieved the cellphone from her purse and called the detective.

"How are you, Ms. Basu?" Yoshihama asked when he recognized her voice. He sounded pleasant, as though glad to hear from her.

"Not too good." Mitra shared with him the highlights of Adi's extortion story. "There's more to it. I don't think Adi's telling me everything he knows."

"Neither has he contacted us. Kidnapping is a federal crime. Let me speak with Mr. Guha. Stand by—I'll get back to you. Thanks for the heads-up."

After returning home and consulting her calendar, Mitra belatedly realized it was Veen's birthday. Of course, she wanted to celebrate. Everyone in the task force needed a break, especially Veen, who regularly worked ten-hour days. How much closer she and Veen had become since Kareena's disappearance. Veen was always there when Mitra needed her. They talked on the phone nearly every day. They'd become each other's sounding board.

Mitra buzzed Veen and announced her intention. She could almost see Veen's eyes lighting up. She decided to withhold the ransom information for now.

Mitra selected Tuscany, a trendy Eastlake trattoria, and arranged a birthday dinner for Veen there. With a galaxy of women friends circling her at a large table that evening, Veen smiled, her cheeks blushing, a cloud of perfume about her. She was attired in a metallic satin top, unusually dressy for her. Add to that a sinister red lipstick. This was a different Veen. Their middle-aged waiter, an earthy man of indeterminate Mediterranean origin, stole glances at her all evening and inhaled the scent of her perfume while refilling her wine glass. Later, waving his hand like a symphony conductor, he led the whole room in a serenade of *Hebby Bearthday* in his charming, heavily accented English. Mitra only wished Kareena was there.

After dinner, Mitra decided to drop Veen at her place. On the way, Veen talked about having had a lunch date with a coworker that weekend. "I like him," she said, with obvious enthusiasm. "He's a nice man, an interesting man."

Mitra lost her reticence and confided in Veen about Ulrich and how much she wanted to get back together with him.

Veen's face darkened. "Get over it," replied the ever-outspoken woman. "He wasn't interested in anything serious or he'd have called." After a pause, she added, "My cute brother will take you out. He's the youngest and cutest of my three brothers. You met him when you came over to my apartment last February. Remember?"

Oh, yes. Mitra recalled the intense information technology specialist with curly hair, piercing dark gaze, and a morbid air about him. He had stared at her from across the room. Ulrich's face came to her mind and wiped out that memory. Mitra casually suggested to Veen the names of a few unattached women acquaintances who might be interested in a "cute" guy.

"What's happening with the investigation?" Veen asked, changing the topic.

Mitra gave her the details about the ransom note and Adi's attempt to keep her out of the picture. She disclosed her fears about Kareena's safety.

"Ransom? For real?" Veen said in a panicky voice. "Are they going to kill her?"

They consoled each other until they reached Veen's house in Capitol Hill. After expressing appreciation for the dinner, Veen added, "I'll stop by Adi's house tomorrow. See what shitty explanation he gives *me* about that damn ransom note."

FIFTEEN

MITRA HAD DROPPED BY Soirée most nights on the off-chance that she might glimpse Kareena, with no success. She had also contacted Kareena's acquaintances, visited Kareena's acupuncturist, the gas station she frequented, the blind Thai masseuse she patronized, and her Korean hair dresser. But there was no sign as yet of what might have happened to her.

This evening, exhausted from all the running around, Mitra stopped at Sascha's Scoop, an organic ice cream parlor in Belltown. This place, with its carved lettering in terra cotta above the entrance, had caught her attention last year; a fashionable ice cream parlor meant for young moderns. It had charmed Mitra doubly when along with her order came an ivory napkin emblazoned with the owner's motto printed in black: "Straight from our very own cows." Like most Indians, Mitra had an abiding affection for cows. Back home, they referred to them as *go-mata*, cow-mother.

Scoop was also where she'd first met Ulrich. She nurtured a tender hope of running into him here again.

An aromatic haze of milk, sugar, berries, and nuts welcomed her. She scanned the parlor, her heart palpitating. The owner had changed the décor since her last visit. The once-white walls were now painted a smart black and they sported a collection of hand fans, made of lace and bamboo and exquisitely pleated. (Were hand fans making a come back?) She saw a few patrons scattered among the tables. No Ulrich.

Taking her gaze away from the empty chairs, Mitra approached the counter. In a monotone, the young cashier at the register asked what she wanted. The black chalkboard on the wall bore bold artful inscriptions, seducing her with superlatives such as "moon-glow" this, "passion-struck" that, or even a "blissful-sinful" combination of items. The owner was reported to be a bearded expatriate Russian poet, who lived for vodka and verses.

Mitra's lips were rounding to pronounce "Moon-Glow Almond Parfait," the same concoction she'd indulged in last time, when she felt a breath on her neck. She pivoted.

Ulrich stood there, handsome in a white sweater and a new haircut, smiling slightly. Her pulse picked up. The right words didn't form in her mouth. She'd wanted to see him, obsessively even, this past week. So why did she suddenly want to edge away, without saying a word?

"I just called you," Ulrich said.

And I bet you booked a trip to Paris for us. Her cheeks tingling, she glanced at him. She had the discomfiting feeling that he was peering into her soul, seeking out any stirring of a negative reaction. "Did you leave a message?"

A twinkle stole into his eyes. "No, I thought I might see you here."

"Seriously?" She didn't want him to get away lying to her, even if his German accent worked its charm on her. "You don't know where usually I hang out, do you?"

"But it worked."

She looked away, focusing on nothing in particular, aware of his fibbing. So what if he did fib? Maybe she'd invested too much sentiment into one intense shared night. "Small planet, similar palette, I guess."

Towel in hand, the cashier leaned over the counter and wiped the milk stains from stainless steel cylinders marked "Cream," "Low fat milk," and "An extra ten years of life."

"May I help you?" the cashier repeated.

If only he understood the torment Mitra was going through. She'd forgotten what she intended to order, but was aware that another customer, a young mother, had just entered the parlor. The mother fidgeted, a baby squirming in her arms. The baby's blueberry eyes peeked out from under a navy cap. Mitra looked away from Ulrich and the new arrival and refocused on the chalkboard, her body and mind inhabiting different realms.

"A Moon-Glow Almond Parfait," Ulrich spoke from behind her. "A Haughty-Naughty Cherry Cone, a Rosebacher Mineral Water, and a Perrier."

Well done—that was a mouthful. He pulled out his billfold and deposited a twenty-dollar bill in the server's outstretched hand, despite her murmur of protest. He smiled, and she reconciled herself to accepting his peace offering. Together they walked to a table that allowed a view of the starry night sky, with Ulrich carrying the tray.

"I must apologize to you for not calling sooner," he said. "I've been very—how do you say it—preoccupied. *Ja,* preoccupied. Siegfried, my dog, died. I had back spasms from the grief and the doctor said I must stay in bed. Then I must buy a new mattress. But the store's website, In Bed We Trust, was out of stock for what in Germany we call *federdecke*—a down comforter. But *naja,* no complaining. My back is better now. And I've been coming here for the last two days looking for you, and here you are. Have you been well?"

She hadn't been exactly well, worrying about Kareena and frustrated by her desire for him. "We're still looking for my friend, but there are days when I feel stuck and helpless. The police haven't come up with any real lead so far."

"She isn't back? I'm very sorry to hear that. It doesn't surprise me about the police, though. They're useless."

Mitra caught him up on recent events, including the fact that Kareena was last sighted at Soirée.

"Soirée falls on the way home from the house I'm remodeling. I stop by there often. I might have seen her. Do you have a picture?"

Mitra delved through her purse and held out a 3x5 snapshot of Kareena standing, her black hair in a sleek bob. She was dressed in a clinging white blouse and matching white pants.

He studied the photo. "She looks a bit like you."

"You don't really see it in here, but anyone who knows her will tell you how cool she is. She's a kindred spirit. She was last seen with an Indian man."

He lifted his eyebrow, as though to share in the admiration. Examining the shot more closely, he stirred. "I recognize her. I have seen her."

"How recently?"

He stayed quiet.

"Think. How long ago? Where? Was anyone with her?"

A flicker of annoyance passed over Ulrich's face. "I can't remember."

She must not press him so hard. She repositioned herself on the chair.

He returned the photo to her. "An Indian man, you said? He'd be noticeable. We have many Indian doctors, scientists, and engineers in Germany. Fine-featured, gentle, respectful, distinctive clipped speech, either painfully reserved or chatterboxes. Am I stereotyping?"

Teasingly, Mitra said, "Unbearably so." She paused and added, "You'll keep an eye out for my friend?"

"*Ja*. Julie, our friendly barista at Soirée, can do that for me. She always notices a good-looking guy, even if she's served him only once. I'll ask her. I *vant* to help you." He sounded firm and sincere.

"Okay, but we have to keep it quiet. Her husband doesn't want us to look for her."

He squeezed her hand, a stroke of playfulness as well as masculine assertion. "It's really good to see you."

She shifted back in her chair, hard against her back. Something bothered her, the intimate atmosphere he'd created, just like the last time. What assurance did she have that he wouldn't disappear again?

"But it distresses me to see you so concerned," he said, eyes fully on her. "I know what it means to lose a kindred spirit."

She poked at the remains of her parfait and didn't reply, hoping that he'd say more. She wanted to understand his thought processes. Otherwise, she wouldn't rest easy.

"I didn't have friends when I was young," he said. "There was one boy, Klaus, a bully. He was bigger than me, and mean. He would practice all the curse words he'd learned on me. I'd say *schlecht*, and run away. Later in high school, when we were older, he began to like me and gradually we became the best of buddies. Then one day, he broke down while studying with me. His mother had run off with another man, leaving him and his father. He said he was flawed. He said he was good for nothing. I tried to talk to him. That only made him mad. He sweated. All of a sudden, he yelled at me, slapped me, and walked out of the room. Then he also dropped out of school. I thought I'd never see him again, but a year later, he called. He'd gotten a job fixing elevators. A month later, he lost that job. He came to see me and cried on my shoulders. Again, he lost his temper because I couldn't loan him money. His emotions seemed to climb up and down—he couldn't control them. Still, we stayed in touch. I became closer to him than my parents. Then we lost touch again."

She put the spoon down, wondering why he'd told her this story when he could have talked about his family. And yet she had to admit to herself she was enjoying listening to him. Wanting to stay a little longer, she asked, "Now that you're here, do you miss Klaus?"

His foot brushed against her leg, although he made it seem casual. "Yes, very much. But a teacher of mine once said that in the broad scheme of things, everyone is disposable."

She felt tingling all over the leg, a kind of pleasant warning. "I disagree. I like to think that each of us counts. Our thoughts, words, actions, our very presence make a ripple somewhere, at least in people closest to us. If not, why do we bother to shop, cook, sprinkle the lawn, or even open the curtains in the morning?"

His hand found hers and held it for a moment. "So you're saying that whatever we do, we do for the sake of love, either getting it or giving it?"

"I'd rather not dissect love." And yet she uttered the word love silently, wrapping her tongue around its sweet roundedness. Love: *pyar, prem, muhabbat* in her native country.

He lavished her with a long warm inclusive gaze. "I had plenty of time to read this past week," he said. "It seemed like every magazine I picked up, even the German ones, had a piece on India. Do you miss your country?"

Mitra had been asked that question quite frequently. Sometimes happily, at other times painfully, it had reminded her of her other existence. How do you convey there was no 'missing your country?' Your country was always there, as integral to your existence as the pillow that cradled your head at night.

"My friend Kareena puts it so well," Mitra replied. "When she last visited India, she wrote me a letter. How everything washes over her all at once. How she surrenders herself unconditionally to the experience, how she's shocked and charmed and crushed by its huge weight. There she remembers her dreams, every single one in all its colors, but never in Seattle. Isn't that amazing?"

He looked down at the table, contemplating. "What do you miss the most about your country?" Mitra asked.

"The bread." He laughed, as though trying hard to make a joke. "Our bread is dark, heavy, dense, and filling. Where I lived, you could find a baker's shop at every corner. In the morning, the whole neighborhood smelled of yeast. I still have trouble starting the day well without that smell." He stayed silent for a moment. "I like this parlor. It reminds me of a café back home. This is the first time I've lived outside Europe. It takes a lot to really feel at home—how do you say it?—to sink new roots."

Mitra commented on how she daily observed the phenomenon of a plant slowly putting down its primary and adventitious roots. "My friend, Kareena, is good at putting roots down, making new friends. I wish she was back."

His foot danced over hers. "Anytime you need help in finding her, you can call me. Let me give you my number."

She jotted it down, then peeked at her watch. It was 9 P.M, time for her to break this slightly strange, somewhat cozy encounter and go home.

With an eye to her, he stuck a hand in his breast pocket and pulled out a tiny book with an elegant gesture. Opening the book to a dog-eared page, he recited from a poem by Heinrich Heine about palm trees and burning sand. The words roused feelings in her. She visualized the two of them lying on a warm beach, bodies touching, an ecstatic feeling pervading, palm fronds nearby being ruffled by the wind.

He shut the book. Something shook inside her. "That was lovely," she said.

He must have picked up on her feelings, for he placed a hand on the table and leaned toward her, a sensuous flicker in his eyes. "Why don't I take you out to dinner tomorrow night and read more poems?" He might have been inwardly rehearsing this invitation for the last fifteen minutes, but acted as though it had just now clicked inside him.

What did she hear inside her? An alarm bell?

"I have a meeting." She lied and didn't like it that she did, but had no choice. She just couldn't possibly deal with another disappearance of his.

"How about Friday?"

"Sorry. Meeting with a girl friend." Lied again, feeling worse.

"Saturday?"

Her heart fluttered in a way it shouldn't. He hadn't been around lately and tonight had been just a chance meeting. Had another date stood him up? Despite these misgivings and against her best judgment, she nodded, then wondered what was it about him that she gave in so easily.

She rose to leave. Tall as he was, he leaned forward, as though sniffing a flower, and met her lips. He captured her, just for that instant. They left the table together, her mouth slackened, her stroll to the door a bit unsteady.

A sixty-something woman sitting at an aisle table glared at her from over her half-moon spectacles. *These shameless youngsters,* she was probably muttering to herself. Or it might be that a kiss bestowed on another pair of lips had taken her to a long-ago missed opportunity. Yet something in the disapproving glance from that stern matriarch made Mitra snap out of her dream. Why did Ulrich have to confide in her so much about Klaus, the crazy guy? As she drove home, that story stayed fishbone-stuck in her mind.

SIXTEEN

THE NEXT DAY, Mitra rang Detective Yoshihama. She had reasons to call him, didn't she?

His voice brimmed with hidden cheer. "I was just thinking about you, Ms. Basu. What's on your mind?"

"Have you spoken with Adi?"

"Yes, the money demand is not a hoax. Mr. Guha said he wanted to handle the matter himself—he doesn't want us in the picture. But I advised him against secrecy, told him of the potential danger he faced. We've got to do our job. We want to bring Ms. Sinha back alive. We're getting more people involved."

"Why do you think is Adi so bent on keeping it under wraps? Does the note contain a threat to his life if he divulged any information?"

"That could very well be the case. He's also conscious of his community's reaction and has asked us to respect that." The detective paused briefly, then asked, "How're your flowers doing?"

"Oh, I'm not spending as much time with them this season as I usually do. My tulips didn't bloom. This is the first year that has happened to me."

Yoshihama seemed to have covered the phone to speak with the dispatcher. "I wish I could talk with you longer," he said, "but I've just gotten a call. I need to rush to a school shooting in Rainier Valley."

Mitra said goodbye and hung up. Obviously, Yoshihama had a more urgent matter to deal with. She understood that. But Adi—he made her feel as though she didn't deserve to be let on in this matter.

In the evening, still feeling deflated, Mitra busied herself making a marigold garland, threading a needle into the stem and out through the heart of a blossom, then on to the next. This side gig, contracted by an Indian couple for their daughter's wedding, would bring her some much-needed cash. And it steeled her mind. As she tied the ends of the last garland, her eyes darted to the clock: 8 P.M. This would be the perfect time to telephone Mother; it was morning in Kolkata. Mother adored marigolds, so much so that she'd put its lemon-scented, filigreed foliage in a small bowl and place it on her lamp table. She'd be tickled to hear of the lush marigold specimens Mitra grew—tiger eye, yellow fire, and tangerine gem.

Mother came on the line, talked about the novel she'd finished last night, ignored Mitra's question about her health, and asked, "Did you go shopping with your girl-friend?"

How should Mitra reply? Wouldn't Mother be enraged if Mitra revealed her blood connection with Kareena? She couldn't risk it. Then, in a moment of either weakness or rationalization, in her need to express grief, she confided that Kareena had vanished. The kidnappers were trying to extort money from her husband.

"Kidnapping and extortion is a growth industry in India," Mother said. "Easy money, I guess, but it's a crime. The Section 364 of Indian Penal Code can be used to punish the criminals. Careful now. Big country, all kinds of *bapper,* and you're alone."

Mother's favorite word *bapper* implied happenings with an unsavory connotation. "Don't call it a *bapper,* Ma. I live in a safe neighborhood."

"Speaking of neighborhoods, I just opened this morning's *Hindustan Standard.* The headline talks about gang activity in Kolkata, not far from my place." She paused. "This is not the city you grew up in. Gang wars from Mumbai are spilling over here. Five hooligans broke into the office of my neighbor's cousin. They fired several rounds at him. He died instantly. They believe it's a case of extortion. Another time, the same thugs threw chili powder on a guy they were angry with at Howra Station. The poor fellow got serious injuries to his eyes. Those gangsters are ruthless, brutal. They're still at large." Mother paused and added, "But eve-teasing incidents in public busses are down."

Eve-teasing—sexual harassment of women; a term Mitra considered rather cute. "Should I be worried about those gangsters, Ma? Are you safe in your apartment?"

Mother laughed. "I'm quite safe. I keep myself up-to-date on what's going on and avoid certain streets. The other day, I was coming home in the evening. An evil-looking guy approached me. 'What's your name?' I yelled at him. 'What's your game? What do you want?' The guy looked confused and turned away." She paused. "But I should be helping you find your friend."

"You mean that?"

Mother gave such an emphatic yes that Mitra stood up in surprise. "You'll fly all the way here to play armchair detective?"

"I don't want to armchair anything. I want to act. I'll follow directions to the right place and meet whomever I need to speak with. No one is threatened by a gray-haired lady who wears wrong colors, doesn't talk sports, and is not snooty. When you're invisible, you don't rouse suspicion."

Mitra smiled to herself. Then, picturing her mother scurrying through Seattle's speeding cars, bicycles, trucks, and impatient pedestrians, she trembled. Suppose Mother, a frail woman, collapsed in the middle of traffic? At the same time, Mitra couldn't spoil the intimacy of this moment. Her clever, resourceful mother could certainly be of help. But then, what'd happen when she found out Kareena's parentage? Wouldn't she feel betrayed?

"I don't want to take you away from your books," Mitra said.

"How often does one face a challenge like the 'Kareena Affair'? Pardon me. An affair is what a novelist would call it. I live a hermit's life. It's time I got back into the grind, became a useful member of the society, contributed to the collective good, cracked a real-life mystery, wouldn't you say?"

"You'll have to fly for more than twenty hours to get here, Ma. Wouldn't that be strenuous?"

"You think I'm a weakling, don't you? How I wish you'd seen me in my college days. All I had to do was breeze through the door wearing a pretty sari, my mother's locket, and a smile, and doors would swing open for me. I'd leave with treasures—satisfactory results—in my handbag. In those days, happy endings didn't seem corny, delusional, or fictionalized, just a natural outcome of events. Maybe I could have a taste of those days again."

In Mother's mind, in her memory, she must have always been a dashing heroine who could take on any task she wanted and finish it with aplomb.

Mitra was about to blurt out a yes when Mother said, "Wait just a second. I have to take my medicine."

When she returned to the line, Mitra asked, "Are you sick?" Mother cleared her throat, which took a few tries, then mumbled what could be either a yes or a no. "Ma, don't you feel well?"

Mother said she was fine, which Mitra didn't buy. It was the quiver in her voice, the thinness of her protest, the brevity of her remark.

"Why don't you hire help to do your chores?" Mitra asked. "I'll send a money draft right away."

"I need a head bath," Mother said. Hair-washing time, a stalling technique. She simply didn't wish to speak about her illness. She said goodbye.

Click, her last command, indicating that Mitra should get back to her work.

Though she'd put the receiver back, Mitra knew the conversation wasn't finished in Mother's mind. Her arm curved on the table, she'd rehash the exchange for half the night, refilling the brass tumbler with water many times. She had a tendency to discard the present moment as valueless and dwell on what had happened in the past.

Mitra rose from the sofa. She loved her mother to a degree that went beyond the rational. How desperately she wanted to close the distance between them and establish a deeper intimacy that allowed no secrets to lurk.

SEVENTEEN

A DAY LATER, on a balmy afternoon, the doorbell shrilled and Mitra saw Veen standing there. She flung one arm around Mitra in an embrace. On the other arm, she toted a plastic bag containing several cartons of food. In a camel-colored pantsuit, Veen appeared professional, as well as approachable, but Mitra couldn't ignore the look of concern on her face.

"I decided to bring you dinner," Veen said. "You probably won't even eat otherwise."

They settled on a bench in Mitra's backyard and served themselves pullao rice, vegetable kebob, samosa, mint chutney, and lustrous chai, all carried out from Bombay Grill on Roosevelt Street.

A stray black curl straggled down Veen's forehead. "I wanted to see you before I left," she said. "I'm taking off for Bangalore tomorrow to attend my niece's wedding. It happened quite suddenly. She's younger than me and getting married. That's not fair. You know how in India they think you're an old maid if a younger sister or cousin gets hitched before you do. Anyway, I'll be gone for a week."

Oh, no. Veen, her biggest supporter, would be gone.

Veen then shifted the conversation over to Kareena. "Something peculiar about Adi's routine. He's been telecommuting a lot these days. My neighbor sees him coming in and out of his home in the daytime a lot. Last night, I knocked at his door just to check up on him. He pissed me off. He's found out about our task force and fucking demanded that we disband it to 'reduce redundancies.' He's also extremely irritated that you've been talking to Detective Yoshihama."

"Adi's extremely irritated with me? What else is new?"

"Goddamn it, he's hired a private eye."

"Well, isn't that a bit late? After he's gotten a ransom demand? By the way, I'm the one who'd suggested that he hire a P.I."

Veen caught a breath. "Listen, we've gone through so much together. I must warn you. For my sake, be extra careful. The P.I. is not to find Kareena. Adi didn't mention her in that part of our conversation, but he sure mentioned you. How you've rushed into 'uncharted territories.' How he'd like to keep an eye on you no matter where you go. I got the impression that he'll have you watched."

*   *   *

The next evening, despite that threat from Adi hanging over her, Mitra took time to dress up. Her cool Deutscher was taking her to Ponti Seafood Grill. She coiled up her collarbone-length hair for added height. The white sequined top draped gently over her shoulders. The black pencil-thin skirt gave her more shape than she believed she had. A gold necklace and high-heels completed her look. Kareena would approve of this outfit, this hairdo, and the restaurant.

Ulrich parked two blocks away from the place, a pleasant walk, except that the night had smoothed out the sharp edges of the street. Happily careless, Mitra tripped when one of her heels caught on a crack on the sidewalk. Her quick and observant date grabbed her arm. She stood up straight and laughed. He hung on to her until they reached the restaurant door.

They talked over a leisurely five-course meal made richer by soft light, unobtrusive staff, and the most terrific marinated asparagus she'd ever tasted. He told her his last name is Schultheiss. She liked the consonants or rather the way his lips curled and plumped as he pronounced them.

Halfway through the meal, he looked in the direction of a departing family of four—father, mother, and two quarreling teenage princesses.

"I'm of the opinion," Ulrich said, "the family as a nuclear unit is dead." He blamed mechanization and human greed, and expressed fear that the demise of the nuclear family signaled the demise of civilization.

"I disagree," Mitra replied, taking a sip of the jaunty mint tea. "We'll revert to larger units of living and sharing like our ancestors did. That's my hope."

"Hope makes you look beautiful," he said. "And I like your new hair-do."

They returned to her house and watched the full moon from her back yard as their "nightcap," surrounded by greenery tinged with a silver sheen. Together, they speculated on the makeup of the moon's core.

"Molten rock," Ulrich said, "nothing more."

"But there's more." Mitra spoke of an age-old Indian belief that the moon's benevolent shine, the life force inside it, nourished the plants.

Clouds obscured the moon and soon the first drops of rain anointed Mitra's skin. They went inside and danced first to Bhangra-pop, then cello music, laughing like teenagers, working up sleepy muscles. After a few songs, he begged off and grimaced, one arm going across the opposite shoulder and rubbing.

"I love to dance, but my back hurts," he said.

"Would you like a back rub?"

He nodded. She stood behind him, as he perched on a chair. She started at the spine, her fingers gliding outward and making deep circles to loose the tension knots. Her fingers adjusted the pressure as needed; no thinking required. Nothing else existed for her but the warm touch of his skin, the strong resistance of the bones, the rise and fall of his chest as he took a breath. She melted, and watched him yielding to the workings of her hand, as though similarly giving in to the moment.

He smiled at her when she finished. "You make me feel so much at home. This will get me through the night. I should have had the pain medication with me, but I forgot."

Mitra did a rewind and went back to that morning to that yellow pill lying on the bedroom floor, the first time he was here. Casually, she mentioned it to him and asked what the med was meant for.

He startled and looked away. Then, after a brief pause, "Oh, it's for a sinus condition I have."

She didn't believe him. What might he be avoiding to discuss? Her thought pattern was interrupted when he rose, turned, drew her to his arms, and kissed her deeply. He put himself so much into the kiss that her concerns faded. Later, they made love, which happened naturally and rhythmically, going slower, longer, and deeper than before. Mitra sank, floated, and soared in the comfort that was Uli. He was fully present. He was there only for her. Any reservation she had about him about holding a matter of importance back dissolved into nothingness.

Climbing out of bed the next morning, Mitra put on her favorite navy wool slippers that covered her feet like a blanket. Kareena had given her these slippers on her last birthday. They'd come encased in a gift box wrapped in gold paper and tied with green ribbon. Stylized letters on top of the box had proclaimed: Sabnam's Sandals.

"It's a nice little shop," Kareena had said. "I know the owner—she was a client of mine. We still have coffee every now and then. I'd buy out her whole inventory if I could. Oh, by the way, Sabnam will take these back if they don't fit or you don't like the color."

Sabnam—Mitra liked the music of that name.

At the kitchen table, Ulrich poured Swiss muesli into his bowl. Mitra slid a coffee mug toward him, then ran down the steps of her investigation so far into Kareena's disappearance.

"I've talked to just about everybody who knew Kareena, but not the store clerks of shops where she bought her clothes and shoes," she said. "I want to get started on that. I'll show them a picture of her, ask if they recall her, and when was the last time they'd seen her. She was a big shopper." She looked down at her slippers. "I'll start with a shoe store owner."

"Plan your questions," he replied.

"Here is one of my planned questions to you. Could you tell me when and where you met Kareena?"

Ulrich frowned at the milk carton. "You don't have whole milk? I can't stand this skim stuff."

"Sorry, I don't. I'll put it on the shopping list." She dropped into the other chair. "When you said you recognized Kareena, how did you recognize her? Did you know her?"

Ulrich reached out and gently traced the scar under her left eye caused by a childhood brush with a low-hanging tree branch. "Let's drop the topic, shall we? She isn't important to me. You are, sweetheart. You're more beautiful than her." He paused. "Let's enjoy the breakfast together."

Mitra grabbed the muesli box, thoughts fluttering around her mind. They'd had a terrific night together, but his reactions about Kareena gave her unease, as did his line: *You're more beautiful than her.* She didn't trust those words. Nor did she like the comparison. Mainly because he seemed to be avoiding a discussion about Kareena.

EIGHTEEN

IT HAD BEEN eleven days. Kareena—her desertion had the flawless perfection of a blank sheet of paper. Every evening, Mitra curled up with the Police Beat and neighborhood tabloids, searching for any snippet of evidence. The papers had a discount-store smell. Their greasy print stained her fingers. They made for an altogether depressing read and provided no answers. And yet, Mitra never considered giving up.

Haunted by her thoughts of Kareena, on this afternoon, Mitra went to work in her adopted grandmother's yard. She hoped that turning the soil for the flowerbed and tidying a lot choked with weeds, grass, and rocks would diminish her nightmarish concerns. The air was redolent with the faint fragrance of newly opened pear blossoms. A robin chirped from a treetop. In this perfect ambience, the long oak handle of the spade felt like an extension of her arms.

She heard the click of the back door. Glow, dressed in relaxed-fit aquamarine sweats, her rouged cheeks shining peachy-bright in the sun, approached her. "You're moving all those rocks by yourself?"

Mitra wiped the sweat from her forehead. "I'm used to it. Mother Nature willing, this garden will be ready in time for your birthday."

Grandmother broke into a smile. Her small eyes closed, as though she were receiving a blessing. She settled into a deck chair beneath a forsythia bush. If the arthritis in her knees hadn't been acting up, she'd be on her feet, meandering around and plucking a vagrant root here, stick or pebble there, Mitra was well aware. Grandmother asked about Kareena.

Mitra's spade struck a walnut-sized pebble, making a grating metallic sound. She leaned down, picked up the pebble, and tossed it aside. "There are times when I wonder if Kareena's not contacting me intentionally."

"That wouldn't surprise me. I've never told you about my daughter Alice. She ran away from home when she was seventeen." Grandmother's voice trailed off; the contours of her face hardened. "We had no contact between us for a whole year. Then Alice called to say she'd been living with a man in Bellingham. She was pregnant and had decided to keep the baby. Boom. She hung up. That was twenty years ago. We didn't speak again till last May when I met my granddaughter Isabel for the first time."

Might Kareena be pregnant? Mitra tried to picture her with a baby. Kareena—lovingly glancing at the warm bundle in her arms. The picture formed so easily that it astounded Mitra.

She took a few steps back, skirting a heap of stones. "Kareena would love to start a family, but Adi doesn't. Hard as I try to connect that information with her disappearance, I don't come up with an answer."

"Well, you've done all you could. She's lucky to have a friend like you." Grandmother nodded, radiating sympathy Mitra could feel from several feet away. "But is it necessary to spend so much time on it? It's like holding two fulltime jobs."

"I couldn't bear any harm coming to her. I won't rest until I've unraveled the mystery."

"Drat!" Grandmother said. "My intuition isn't worth a dime today. Or I'd be able to tell you where she is, what her scheme is."

"She's not cold and scheming. She's a generous soul. Last winter, she even organized a huge fund-raising dinner for abused women. I helped her out on that."

Grandmother twisted a dandelion bud between her coral-tipped fingers. "Could that have earned her a few points at work? Did she take that on because she could count on your help? Listen, I used to be a saleswoman for a greeting card company, which had a friendly working atmosphere. I was still new when one of my colleagues organized a Tupperware-style party and asked for my assistance. I spent hours of my spare time on it. She never returned the favor. She was just taking advantage of me. I must tell you I've been disappointed by women more often than men, in spite of my four failed marriages."

Mitra watched a blue jay strutting along the ridge line of a neighbor's roof. Once again, she and Grandmother weren't in sync. In the past, she and Kareena had leaned toward each other in support, like plants naturally bending in the sun's direction. She'd never thought of Kareena using her.

"My experience has been different," Mitra said. "My women friends are like family to me."

"You're still such a romantic, my dear."

It became clear to Mitra, vivid as the sun flaring on her forehead, where Grandmother stood. The woman lived alone. She'd once alluded, with a catch in her throat, that her daughter Alice didn't send her a Christmas card. No wonder she felt clingy toward Mitra. She'd rather not have Kareena's shadow falling between them.

"As you grow older," Grandmother continued, "you stop treasure-hunting. You start worrying about what you might lose, rather than what you might gain. You keep an eye out for the quicksand."

Mitra spread organic matter—a mixture of steer manure, compost, and peat moss, each component asserting its own smell—into the dense clay soil. The flowerbed was ready.

"It's best to let the bed rest for a day," she said. "Then we'll plant."

"Righto, Mitra, my garden nymph. Mitra—what a pretty name. Does it have a meaning?"

Mitra brushed dirt off her dark workpants. "Yes. Mitra means friend. My parents wanted to give me a more poetic name, like Anamika, Sukanya, or Neelanjana. But they chose Mitra. It's short and brisk. And isn't a loyal friend the best thing you can be? That's what my mother said."

"You're way too loyal, Mitra-friend. Loyalty never pays much, just gives you a stomach-ache." She scrutinized Mitra's face and figure in a motherly vein. "You're stressed. You're ruining your health over something you can do nothing about. Let her go. Goodness knows what she's up to. Besides, I worry about the risk you're taking, the danger." She paused. "You've exposed Kareena's vanishing act as well as Adi's lack of effort to the community. If he has something to hide and, more than likely he does, he's not going to like that. He's already warned you, hasn't he? Or it could be some other criminal altogether. In any and all cases, you're interfering."

Mitra didn't have an answer. She only bristled with Grandmother's negative attitude toward Kareena. Then again, she told herself, the other side of having a grandparent was being a grandchild, which involved a certain amount of deference to their opinion or at least maintaining the appearance of it.

Tampopo meowed at the back door, a sure sign she wanted to be fed. She grazed at just about anything edible. Grandmother trudged back inside, saying she'd be back in a minute.

The setting sun cast its last rays over the yard. Once again, an inner voice confirmed the conviction that Kareena was hibernating somewhere. Mitra would see her again.

And yet the muscles in her shoulders tightened.

NINETEEN

IN THE FAINT LIGHT of late afternoon, Mitra scrutinized the chic hand-painted sign at the entrance to Sabnam's Sandals in an upscale strip mall in Bellevue. She'd called the proprietor earlier in the day and made an appointment to speak with her. Now she inspected the window display, a cheerful jumble of women's clogs, thongs, sandals, and flip-flops in earth and sun tones, all style, flutter, and whimsy, and all obviously imported from India. In contrast, Mitra's feet were encased in a pair of constricting loafers.

Had this been a happier time, she'd have been tempted to march inside and scoop up the red-and-blue thongs so attractively arranged on the bottom of a shoe tree, or the white two-strap slides on top. Suddenly, Mitra was transported back to India where her open-air footwear kept her lower extremities cool, gave her freedom to stride, and lent her a sense of playfulness even when seated.

Through the glass panes of the store, a petite forty-something woman waved and motioned her to come in.

"Mitra Basu. We have an appointment."

"I'm Sabnam Garg, the proprietor. May I be of service?" When she spoke, it was as though temple bells were chiming a melody. Underneath an ankle-length tangerine-print dress, her feet were bare, save for an emerald toe ring. Her cheeks exuded a glow that showed through her dark complexion.

"One of your customers, Kareena Sinha, is a friend of mine. She's missing, if you haven't heard. I'm desperately trying to put all the puzzle pieces together. Any information will help. As it stands now, I'm stymied."

"Why do you think I might know something?" Her tone of voice turned cold and brittle. "Are you from the police?"

Mitra shook her head, a strong shake. Sabnam, apparently mollified, waved toward a comfy couch pushed up against a wall.

Mitra took one corner of the couch. Sabnam swerved around her, hurried to a tea table situated just beyond the cash register and pressed the button on top of a tall black thermos. Amber liquid accompanied by a gurgling sound streamed from the spout into two ruby tea glasses. Sabnam offered Mitra a glass, without asking first, and edged in beside her. She held her glass beneath her nose and inhaled, a dreamy expression stealing over her face.

Searching for a way to begin that would set Sabnam at ease, Mitra zeroed in on the windowsills painted the color of young turmeric. "You've chosen your colors well."

"Kareena thought it was an encouraging sign that I broke out of my brown funk and went instead for reds, oranges, and yellows. She's not only a customer, you see. I'm a survivor. I owe my life to her."

"Maybe now you can help save her life," Mitra said. "Did she ever confide in you about any marital problems, or about being abused herself?"

"No, Adi would never hurt her. He can be gruff and he's complicated, but he loves her. He's not like the *dushman* I was married to." Evil man.

Mitra took a swallow of her glass and found the strong taste to her liking. "What's in this tea?"

"You like it? It's Kareena's favorite, too. It's my own formula. I doctor up Darjeeling tea leaves with honey, cardamom, black pepper, hazelnut flavoring, and a few ingredients I prefer to keep a secret. I sell only a limited quantity of this tea. An Indian gentleman was just here to buy a pound, a stylish man." She paused. "Do you know how to forget the pain of nightly beatings by your husband? Drown your senses in excess." Her body sagged into the couch under the huge weight of memories that she must have wanted to erase. "I loved my husband—I still do. He was my temple, my *mandir*. You can never make yourself believe that you'll get severe, severe injuries in the temple. I required four operations."

The scalding glass Mitra held caused a burning sensation on her palm. She had never before met a survivor of such terrible physical abuse. From Kareena's brief descriptions of the violence suffered by her clients, Mitra could piece together a scene at the "temple" — closed doors, sounds of slaps and crashes of furniture, shrieks of pain followed by trickles of blood and years of painful memory.

A ghost-like pall hung over the room, but Mitra cut through it. "How many years?"

A shadow of regret passed across Sabnam's face. "Twelve."

Kareena and Adi had been married eight years. "Twelve? Did you think that—?"

"Yes, every morning I'd wake up and say to myself he'll be different today, and he would be from time to time. He'd be waiting there with a tea tray in hand when I woke up. He'd smile and kiss me before going to work, as if the night before hadn't happened. Once he came home with a dozen yellow roses and knelt before me. It was like seeing Taj Mahal on a moonlit night. And like a love-struck teenager, I stupidly forgave him."

"How did you meet Kareena?"

Sabnam looked around the room, then began giving the details. She'd found a calling card of a women's advocacy agency by the washbasin of a restaurant in Bellevue and shoved it in her shoe. She'd gone straight to a pay phone, called the advocacy number, and spoken to an counselor with a kind voice.

Mitra leaned forward. "Aren't you glad Kareena was there for you?"

"An angel is what she is. She showed up at precisely the right time, just as I was giving up hope. The first time we sat down together, she held my hand and I felt reassured enough to talk. It was plain to her I wasn't 'crazy making,' as my relatives would put it. 'Clear out as soon as you can,' she advised me. 'Make a new movie with your life.' She could tell what I'd been going through all these years, like a dear sister would." Sabnam gazed at a wall, as though haunted by heartache, shame, and secrecy. "She asked me to temporarily hide in a women's shelter.

"Once I found a place of my own, I went through the legal process. It was then that Kareena suggested that I open a shoe shop. In those days, I looked like a mess, but still always had the smartest shoes on. Kareena saw me as a born entrepreneur, a retailer, trendsetter, and nurturer of women. When I applied for a bank loan, Kareena came with me. Oh, how she flirted with the bank officer. I was jealous. I didn't have the confidence to laugh and joke with a man. But I got the loan." Sabnam paused, apparently noting Mitra's raised eyebrows. "Why do you look so surprised? Kareena was a sharp woman who knew how to use her looks. Of course, she also had a weakness for handsome, well-dressed types—didn't you know?"

Mitra hadn't known. What else about her sister didn't she know? "Could you tell me which bank it was and the name of that loan officer?"

"I don't remember. I'm sorry, but now business is picking up and I have a wonderful rapport with my customers. It's like having a second family. They give me flowers, truffles, show tickets. Someone even gave me a puppy. I owe it all to Kareena. She helped me make my own movie." Sabnam paused. "You said you needed help finding her? Did you watch the old Nixon movie on television last night?"

Mitra set the empty tea glass down, fighting the frustration in her throat. "*All the President's Men*? I've seen it."

"Remember what Deep Throat said? 'Follow the money.'" Sabnam laughed sarcastically. "I say follow the love. Love takes you to more troubled spots."

Mitra had the sensation of being knee-deep in mud and fighting to take the next step. Yet hope hovered over the air. She had just gotten the first hint about a new possibility as to why Kareena vanished: she had a lover.

"So are you saying Kareena had an extra-marital affair?" she asked.

Outside, a man laughed, laughter with a bite, likely some drunk from the tavern next door.

"You ask too many questions," Sabnam said. "Slow down, Mitra girl. Tell me more about yourself. I want to know you better. You remind me of Kareena, same vibes. Are you privileged like her?"

Privileged? Mitra recounted to Sabnam how her mother couldn't afford tuition money for her college education. When she turned eighteen, Mother had shipped her off to an uncle and aunt in Anchorage, relatives she'd never met. She had never been outside her hometown of Kolkata either, but Mother gave her no choice. "Go west, young woman," she told Mitra. Mother had picked up that phrase from a Western novel. Mitra's uncle and aunt weren't overjoyed to receive her, nor was she ecstatic at the prospect of staying with them for four years. They didn't let her go out of the house, except to her classes and the corner store for six miserable months, those backward folks. Finally, Mitra moved out, rented a studio apartment, and picked up a full-time job of cashiering in a tattoo parlor while carrying a full load at the university.

"I was brought up differently from Kareena," Mitra said. "And we *are* different. Only now I'm finding out how much she didn't share with me."

Sabnam's gaze fell on Mitra's shoes. "Why don't you have a look at my new-season sandals? I just got a shipment from Sultan, Kareena's favorite brand. You won't find that brand in any department store. We women live on our feet. When we stop indulging in shoes, you know the economy has gone south, households have turned more dysfunctional, and our society is in danger of collapsing." She paused. "Do you have a boyfriend?"

Mitra felt herself smiling. "I'm seeing someone."

Sabnam stood and turned toward a shoe display. "Then try a new style. I'll give you an excellent price." She held a pair of three-inch heel, iridescent sling-backs before Mitra. "Go ahead! Be outrageous! Make your own movie."

Buying a pair of shoes just might help Mitra get through the afternoon. And if Kareena liked the brand, so would she. She shook the loafers off her feet and slid inside the straps. Suddenly she was on her way to a carnival, feeling foolish, impractical, and reckless, responding to the insistent throbbing of drums in the distance. She couldn't wait to tell Ulrich about this encounter, or to go out with him wearing this impractical footwear.

"Your new man will go wild when he sees you in these sandals," Sabnam said. "He'll kneel down and kiss your toes."

Mitra followed Sabnam to the cash register. Through the window she noticed a handsome, well-dressed man ambling toward a motorcycle at the far end of the parking lot. Whether it was his posture, his agility, or the cocksure quality he projected, he stood out somehow and piqued her interest. She noticed the *jhola* on his shoulder and her heart thumped faster. She gave him another look. Yes, it was the same man she'd encountered at Soirée.

"Excuse me," she said to Sabnam. "I'll be back in a few minutes."

She rushed through the door and sprinted toward the *jhola* man, waving and shouting, "Wait, please, I want to speak with you."

He whipped around, narrowed his eyes when he noticed her, donned a helmet, and jumped onto a parked motorcycle, a Suzuki maxi-scooter. Before she could get the license number, he'd exited the lot, the noise deafening her ears.

You jerk, she said silently.

He tore up the street and soon faded from view. No trace of him remained, only the wind howling.

A missed opportunity. A sour feeling on the stomach weighed on Mitra, but on second thought, she'd sighted him. The *jhola* man. He was still around.

TWENTY

AFTER HER VISIT with Sabnam and that sighting of the jhola man, Mitra returned home. Her thoughts turned to dinner. She went to the kitchen, heated up a pot of leftover potato-cauliflower curry, and placed slices of fresh focaccia bread from Essential Bakery in the oven. She put together a relish plate of cucumber, tomatoes, sweet onion, green chili, and cilantro and allowed it to rest on the counter to develop flavor.

Hearing the crunching note of leaves, someone stepping on the porch, she bustled to the door and looked through the peephole. Ulrich stood there, looking casual in a polo shirt and khaki shorts, his hair disheveled. Her insides went through a foolish, twisted motion on seeing his smooth bare skin. Today's temperature, scrambling to an unseasonable 70 degrees, could be considered an April bonus.

The neighbor's dog set to yammering, as he always did when Ulrich showed up.

"Hi, Uli, come on in," Mitra said in a bright voice.

Ulrich glided in, a six-pack of Pilsner cradled in one hand and a cluster of white wisteria in the other. Bundles of tiny blossoms—shy, delicate, and fragrant—drooped like snowy grapes from thin stems. He handed her the flowers and spoke of the luxuriant vine that covered the fence of the apartment complex where he lived, the blossoms that maddened him with its sweet fragrance.

He nibbled her lips. "They reminded me of you."

She skipped into the pantry, grabbed a slim-neck crystal vase, filled it with water at the kitchen sink, and crisscrossed the stems for a cascading effect. He watched her finish the arrangement, then drew near and kissed her fingers. "Your fingers are as pretty as your lips."

Mitra tried but failed to suppress a spontaneous laugh. Her hands—calloused, chapped, and specimen of labor—weren't her proudest feature. Even her nails, naturally pink, were cut in utilitarian half-moon shapes and polish-free.

They ambled into the kitchen and stood against the counter. She brought him up to speed on her visit to Sabnam's shoe store and her accidental encounter with the mysterious *jhola* man.

"Strange coincidence." He opened the upper cabinet and began poking around the glasses, pushing them into each other, with no apparent care of protecting them. Pink-faced, he mumbled some German expletives, adding, "Where's my beer mug? It's supposed to be here."

"Did you check the dishwasher?" she asked. Why was he pissed off about such a small matter? The lover who brought her flowers only minutes earlier had turned a stranger. If every person has a beastly side . . . But Mitra refused to look in that direction.

Ulrich shook his head. Pressing a big arm upward, he reached for a tall glass on the back of the cabinet, grabbed it with unnecessary force, and poured his beer. Golden liquid cascaded into the glass and a fizzy effervescent sound charged the air. He mixed in a splash of energy cola which he stocked in her refrigerator. As he looked over his shoulder and caught her shocked expression, he made a point of grinning mischievously. His grin bridged the opening in their communication, but a seed of doubt took root in her mind.

He joined her at the table. "I had a chance to speak with the barista at Soirée," he said. "She's the one who'd seen that *jhola* man with your friend. Ah, yes, Julie says the guy is a charmer."

"A charmer?"

"The guy lives in India, but he didn't say what he did there or what brought him here. She asked him if he was an actor, and he said he was."

"What made her think he was an actor?"

"She's studying at The Ron Bear School of Acting. She can spot her own kind."

"He's graceful, vain, even shouldered, et cetera?"

"*Ja.* She said he spoke each word like it was the first sip of a fine hot chocolate drink. She thought he was a bit slimy."

"Kareena never mentioned having an actor acquaintance, much less a slimy one, even though she's obsessed with Bollywood. Maybe that guy has bad intentions toward her. Does Julie have any idea of when exactly she saw him, how long before Kareena went missing?"

"Early afternoon. Not sure of the day of the week or which month." Ulrich took a long pull of his beer. "The *jhola* guy came alone most of the time. He always ordered hot chocolate with a splash of amaretto. Your friend met him there once. Julie said there was chemistry between them. They looked into each other's eyes, and whispered. They didn't stay long. Julie saw them going outside, walking arm-in-arm toward a car parked across the street from the café. That was the last and only time she saw them together. He's been back since then. Julie was about to tell me more when she got interrupted."

Mitra itched in her chair as she imagined Kareena, a married woman, her arm intertwined with that of a slimy character. Kareena, throbbing like a teenager, and he, in turn, mesmerized by her. Still, the picture didn't fit—Mitra didn't want it to, not when the adulterous woman was her best friend.

"Why would she hide this liaison from me?" she asked Ulrich.

"Do we ever know another person completely?" He shrugged. "Since I'm five years older, I've probably gone through a few more disappointments than you. Sometimes the best course of action is to move on. How do you say it? Cut your losses?"

"I can't move on," Mitra said. "Once I'm onto something, I can't quit. Even if Kareena didn't tell me everything, she's still missing, and there's a ransom note. She might be in danger. What if we drive to Soirée now and continue the conversation with Julie?"

"It's rather odd, but this afternoon I didn't see her at the counter. I asked another barista and was told Julie no longer worked there."

Mitra slumped in her chair. The longer Kareena's absence stretched on, the more she felt she'd been set loose in a maze.

"It now makes perfect sense for me to go through with what I'd been beginning to plan," she said.

"I'm listening."

"I need to look through Kareena's things. I'll have to get into her house in Adi's absence. I can zip through her closet, dresser drawers, file folders, anything that might tell me something. She must have left some trace in her house, some detail that others have passed right by without a second look. I know her tastes and quirks, almost as well as my own. I'm likely to spot what has eluded others. And if there's any information to be found about this man, even if she hid it, I should be able to find it."

Urichi tightened his hand into a fist. "And what if that damn detective is keeping his eyes on their house? Checking to see who is coming and who is going? You're not a suspect by any means, but this might put wrong ideas in his head. No, Mit."

His uneasiness could be attributed to an innate Germanic respect for rules and the law. Not that Mitra was the kind of person to break the law, but given the circumstances what choice did she have?

"I have to take the risk. Sabnam told me to follow the love."

"This is unbelievable. How will you get in?"

She told him how Kareena had once given her the key code of her garage door over the phone to let in the guests and the caterer to a surprise birthday party for Adi. Mitra had written it down on her Day Planner. It should still be there.

Ulrich lifted a hand, as though trying to stop her from rushing out. "Are you sure this is a good idea? Think it through. That shoe store owner—can you really trust her?"

"I believe her. She didn't spill the beans, just hinted at a few things. She probably had more to say, but was afraid to speak. What little she told me was real. When the words 'Follow the love' slipped out of her, she looked like she'd let something out she wanted to take back. I've always been able to judge who's telling the truth and who isn't. You should have seen me in Kolkata. I grew up street-smart or, should I say alley-smart?"

He looks into her eyes. "I could see you as a little girl. What were you like?"

Mitra began describing the kitchen window of her ground-floor flat in Kolkata that faced an alleyway. She spent hours watching the neighbors and figuring out what they were up to. What she saw: a crow stealing a gold bangle from an old woman's window and being cursed; a six-year-old smoking a joint; a shadow of an unmarried pregnant woman being maneuvered out of the house by relatives after dark. The relatives would later lie to Mitra and her mother, insisting that the woman had gone to Dubai to visit a cousin and that she'd be back. *You're lying*, Mitra wanted to say to them. The woman never returned.

"You can judge truth from lies, I'm sure of that." Ulrich reached out and gripped her hand. "But I don't want anything to happen to you."

"I'm not going to back out now. It seems like Kareena could have run off with this man, but then where does the ransom note come from?"

Ulrich rose to get another beer. "Let me come with you. *Bitte.* " His voice turned cautious, heavy. "I'll go crazy worrying. What if Adi comes back while you're in his house? What excuse will you give him?"

"Oh, I'll tell him I left a casserole dish there that I really need."

"If that creep catches you," Ulrich said, "he could do anything he wants to you."

Mitra winced. "He may have beaten up Kareena, but he wouldn't dare do anything to me."

Ulrich's face reddened. In an ominous tone, he said, "If he does, he won't see the daylight again."

However much she appreciated the safety net Ulrich had proposed for her, she winced again, inwardly this time, at this hint of physical violence. Briefly, she mentioned the weekend-long session on self-defense for women that she'd attended. Looking down her nimble gardening fingers and strong knees, she reminded herself of the teacher's advice: *Go for the attacker's eyes or kick him in the groin. He'll go down.*

Ulrich smiled; a caring smile. "I approve of women learning to defend themselves. But what would a one-day session do? Let me at least drive you there and wait for you."

Mitra agreed. They fixed a tentative Sunday date. She'd still have to check with Veen, who lived only a few blocks from Adi, about the feasibility of Adi being gone on that particular Sunday.

She lit a jar candle with sage fragrance, and placed it between them. The notion of entering someone's house *sans* permission made Mitra edgy. Never had she believed she'd go to that length. Planning such a gambit with her *Mann*, however, gave it solidity. Outside, a hummingbird made a peep sound. Ulrich said he loved to hear the hummers.

As she served dinner, Ulrich bent over the vegetable platter, his face flooding with pleasure. "What's in this curry? I hope you don't mind my asking."

"Let me think—cumin and turmeric, a splash of broth, potatoes, cauliflower, onion, garlic, and a dash of olive oil, that's about all. I'll leave the analysis part to you— and the food critics."

He took a forkful. "What a wonderful spicy mellow taste. As they say—hot weather and spices go together like a honeymooning couple."

As though in a dream, she saw herself as a bride. Ulrich would wear a suit and she would dress in ivory. The springtime ceremony would take place in Woodland Park's Rose Garden under the shade of a cherry tree blushing with blossoms. They'd have kids, at least two. Their house would be filled with rambunctious little hellions.

The candle flame shivered, then died.

"I have to admit I like meat," Ulrich was saying. "Back home, I'd order curry sausage, curry ketchup, and French fries only as a—how do you put it?—afterthought. This dish proves how good vegetables can taste. Maybe I should change my diet. Did you grow any of these vegetables yourself?"

"Yes, the cauliflower. I planted it last fall. It over-wintered. That's what happens when you take good care of your crop even in the off-season. It keeps on producing, one floret at a time, and soon there's enough to harvest."

"You not only take good care of your garden, you take good care of your friends."

He insisted on rinsing the dishes and stacking them on the dish washer. She stood there, keeping him company, and reveling in his particular scent. As he shoved the last dish into the dishwasher, their eyes met. He cozied up, his toes sliding next to her. Lost in the warmth of each other and clinging together, they headed for the bedroom, slipped off their clothes, and flung them over chairs, the dresser, and the floor. She watched her charmer, the broad expanse of his back, his smooth pale skin accentuated by three moles, and just enough body hair to be attractive. He murmured that her skin had a lovely natural smell. She sensed that there was an awakening in him, and in her.

Much later, Ulrich, now fully clothed, walked with her to the door. After an affectionate kiss, he proposed that should she care to try a new cuisine, they could head out to the new Sicilian hangout in his neighborhood the next evening.

"I can't. Jean wants to meet with me after work."

"What if we have a late supper?" It appeared as though Ulrich wouldn't take no for an answer. He praised the local restaurant scene. And oh, he could pick up her dry-cleaning; it was on his way. He'd be happy to do what he could to make it easier for her. "I don't like to see sadness in my favorite eyes."

How could she ignore such generous offers? She gazed at her good fortune, how he was filling the gaps in her life, and she could go on gazing forever. "*Vielen Dank.*"

"Sounds sweet, coming from you. Let's practice more Deutsch the next time. Someday, I'll take you to my country."

Just as Ulrich stepped onto the porch, with Mitra behind him, a car pulled in the driveway. Grandmother climbed out, ascended the front steps, and joined Mitra and Ulrich on the porch. She had a cloth hat in her hand.

"You left this on the garden bench," she said to Mitra, extending her hand.

Mitra thanked her adopted grandmother, but before she could make the introductions, Ulrich ducked away, mumbling a goodbye.

Grandmother arched an eyebrow, as she watched him leave. She'd assessed Ulrich as a loser, Mitra could see that. She chatted with Mitra for a minute, said she had an errand to run, descended the steps, and walked back to her car. She hopped into the driver's seat, and was gone. A twinge of gloom settled in Mitra.

They hadn't clicked. They hadn't exchanged even one word. Two people who meant so much to her.

TWENTY-ONE

EARLY SATURDAY MORNING, Mitra was dusting off furniture and listening to the radio news when the phone rang. Mother's hello from the other end sounded a little off.

"I'm beside myself." Her tone dark, Mother spoke as though she were having difficulty focusing her thoughts. "Why did God take her away? Why her?"

When overwhelmed, Mother had a tendency to flip out. "What is it, Ma?"

"My heart has been ripped off. I couldn't get up from my chair. Then when I finally did, I slipped on the floor, although don't worry I didn't hurt myself. I tried to dial your number and dialed wrong several times, because my fingers don't work."

"What actually happened?"

"Saroja's granddaughter called me early this morning," Mother said. "Poor girl. She's having a difficult time, to say the least. Saroja, kind soul, died in her sleep last night."

"Aunt Saroja?" Mitra stammered. The news hit her with such a blow that her mind went blank.

"I'm so wiped out," Mother said. "I can't talk anymore. Call me back a little later."

Mitra felt drained as she replaced the receiver in its cradle. In the bleakness, she picked up her aunt's photo from a side table. Aunt Saroja had given her so much. She and Kareena would not have met, if not for her aunt's generosity. Mitra had dreamt of one day thanking her in person. She wouldn't be there, hard as it was for Mitra to accept, save as a portrait in a frame.

A welcome spring shower cascaded down outside the window, the sky's attempt to cleanse and set things right.

Nothing could set her aunt's death right.

A few hours later, Mitra pulled herself together. She spoke with Mother again and they reminisced about Aunt Saroja's letters, how they kept her going during her college years in Alaska.

"She was the best correspondent in the family," Mother said. "Everyone said so, although she rarely wrote to me or called me. I was never her favorite."

"Why didn't you two get along?"

"She didn't think I *deserved* to marry her cousin brother. May she rest in peace, but her disapproval colored our marriage. She didn't believe I could make him happy."

"Ma, did her disapproval have anything to do with father's first marriage? Did you wish she liked you better?"

"Yes, especially since I loved Nalin so much. We were a mismatch, but every time I looked at him, I melted inside. How can you not fall for someone so well-mannered, so cultured, so gentle, and handsome to boot? But he gave most of his heart to his first wife."

"Why did you keep his first marriage a secret from me?"

"I feared you wouldn't respect him, or his memory. You see, he'd been married to none other than Dimple Sinha, the dragon lady of Bollywood films. She'd spread the rumor that he'd punched her on the face and she'd thrown him out because of that. All lies. I can't believe I'm telling you this after all these years." She paused. "Have you heard of Dimple Sinha?"

Mitra couldn't answer for a moment, as she wrestled with slipping out of the memory of her favorite aunt. "No. Who's she?"

"She was an actress before your time," Mother said. "She couldn't act, sing, or dance, yet was always featured in *FilmDunya* for the gossip around her. She married and divorced at the drop of a handkerchief, had affairs galore, always treated the press reporters shabbily. God bless Nalin's soul, but how did he get mixed up with that shrew? It's beyond belief. She ruined his life and mine, too."

Mother spilled out the rest of the tale. After the actress had divorced Mitra's father, she'd married three more times. Finally, she bowed out of films. She had her hands full with the offspring of her failed marriages—one girl and four boys. The children took her maiden name, Sinha.

"I got all this from movie magazines," Mother said. "Your father wouldn't tell me much. He held it all inside. Part of the reason he neglected us was he could never let go of his memory of his first love. That bitch. She's my *shatru*." Enemy.

Mitra kept quiet so Mother would say more.

"You came into this world a sweet innocent child, content with what little came your way. We ruined your perfection. Your big eyes searched for love. You didn't get it. Your father couldn't afford toys, clothes, or vacation. Feeling like a failure, he turned to gambling and spent his time and money on betting on horses. He failed in that, too. Yes, my dear, your father cheated you out of a happy childhood. If you ask me, it doesn't take only ability to raise a child, it takes sacrifice, and he just wouldn't make the necessary sacrifices. And, I didn't do much better."

"Ma, you tried."

"You never demanded much from me. You went your own way. After your father died, I was no better than a walking skeleton. I had no life in me, no appetite for food or living. I was of no use to myself. But I stayed alive for you."

Listening to the melody seeping through her walls from a neighbor's house, Mitra accepted what she believed was an apology from Mother. She rose from the sofa. Aunt Saroja's death had uncovered a truth: why Mother had neglected her so much. She was scarred in her marriage, scarred again as a widow. Mitra reminded her too much of a difficult past.

"No apology is necessary," Mitra said. "I love you and appreciate having you as my mother."

"Saroja loved you very much. She also said, 'Celebrate the people in your life who are still alive.' A wise woman. She'd have wanted us to enjoy this day."

They said goodbye. Putting the phone back, Mitra felt as though she'd traveled through a turbulent weather zone and been ravaged by it. Her aunt's death coupled with Mother's grief about the past weighed on her. Worse yet, Kareena now appeared in their family album, Mitra's chief ally, half-sister, and the daughter of Mother's worst *shatru*.

TWENTY-TWO

WITH AUNT SAROJA'S DEATH, bereavement had settled into Mitra's chest. The next morning, she turned the soil in a corner of her south yard, removed weeds, rocks, and twigs, and planted an already blooming lavender bush. This sweet smelling plant, with its silvery gray leaves and purple blossoms, would be just the right memorial for Aunt Saroja. Mitra took time to mulch the bush. Branches of a neighbor's apple tree formed an irregular lattice above her head. In the months to come, the plant would grow full, dense, and tall. Aunt Saroja would have swooned over its whirl of color.

A few drops of rain fell. Mitra went back inside and booted up her computer, then sat staring at her screen. The Auto Reminder feature flashed the image of a huge green thumb and a warning that her gardening column was due tomorrow. She checked her year-at a-glance calendar on the wall. Although it wasn't quite May yet, she was reminded of a most ceremonious event—Mother's Day. Not a topic she embraced, now that she feared Mother's reaction about Kareena.

Her gaze wandered to the window. She craned her neck to peer at the newly planted lavender and flashed on Aunt Saroja's face. Next her eyes traveled to a delphinium patch that hugged the side of the house. And now Glow glided through her mind. Grandmother appreciated it when Mitra opened the car door for her or poured her tangerine juice, but she smiled the brightest when Mitra walked in with a spray of flowers on her arms.

The delphiniums, already blooming, oscillated in the wind, raising a question for Mitra: shouldn't there be a day to celebrate grandmothers?

This must be the right topic, for suddenly she could type again.

My Grandmother's Garden
"The flower is an example of the eternal seductiveness of life."
Jean Giradoux

Mitra kept herself occupied for the next few hours, each tap on the keyboard a sweet affirmation of her regard for both Aunt Saroja and Grandmother. Once finished, she squinted out the window. The patter of rain had abated. The sun had cracked the sky open.

The last time she'd watered her plants, Ulrich was there with her. She hadn't seen him in the last two days. It was quite unusual for him not to call or come by. Mitra felt that familiar ache for him. She grabbed the cellphone and left him a message.

Less than a minute later, a call came in from Detective Yoshihama. He must be responding to a message she'd left earlier asking how the investigation was proceeding.

"We're working as many avenues as we can," Yoshihama said, "checking phone transcripts and the contacts and the like."

"And the ransom note?"

"Did Mr. Guha tell you he's received a second ransom letter? He's negotiating with them."

"Couldn't you override Adi's opposition, given that it's a matter of life-or-death for Kareena? Do they have a release strategy worked out for her?"

"Release strategy? I don't believe so." Silence for a moment. "Actually, I called you about another matter. It's a bit personal and I hope you don't mind my asking. Do you have a boyfriend?"

Mitra startled. Did the detective want to ask her out? He cheered up when he spoke with her. Then again, she couldn't be sure. He was rather formal and still called her Ms. Basu. "I'm seeing someone, although we're not serious."

"I'm concerned about you." He paused. Mitra held her breath. The pause seemed too long. "Do you know Ulrich Schultheiss?" he asked. "Are you seeing him?"

The mention of the name hit Mitra like a closed door in the dark. "Yes, why?"

"This is only for your safety. And please keep this information to yourself. Recently, Ulrich Schultheiss was picked up on charges of assaulting a colleague, released from jail after 72 hours. You might want to consider staying away from him."

Mitra's pulse raced. "Might it be a case of mistaken identity? I can't imagine him being involved in a crime. And how did you know we were connected?"

"An officer found your card in his wallet."

"I gave it to him when we first met. He's not in any trouble, is he?"

"No. I'd still watch my back, Ms. Basu, if I were you."

For several moments after disconnecting the call, Mitra couldn't shake the icy grip at her throat.

TWENTY-THREE

ON THURSDAY, Mitra removed the *Seattle Chronicle* from its plastic casing. The day's paper should contain her column "Come Smell the Daisies." She opened the newspaper to Page D3, looking past the results of the U.S. Lawn Mower Association's race toward the top right. There, under her byline, was her tribute to all grandmothers. Glow didn't wake up till nine, so Mitra folded the daily away and planned to make a call later. It was childish to seek approval of your elders, but Mitra couldn't help it. Especially now. Her own investigations with Kareena had stalled due to the lack of any new leads. And Ulrich—she hadn't seen him in the last few days. The reason for his absence, as revealed by Detective Yoshiihama, scoured her internally.

The phone sang. She ran for it. It was Robert on the line.

"I've already got some enthusiastic e-mail responses to your column. I'll forward them so you could add them to your fan-mail collection." Then he said that he was cleaning out his "cube." He wanted to get rid of review copies of gardening books littering his office floor. "Want to come over and have a look?"

How could Mitra let this opportunity slip through her fingers? Robert's office also happened to be on the way to a client's home in West Seattle. "That's the best offer I've had in a week," she said. "I'll be there in twenty minutes."

On the way to the newspaper office, Mitra took side streets due to a traffic jam on Interstate 5, and that afforded her time to ruminate about her side career as a columnist.

For the better part of a year, it had frustrated Mitra that the *Seattle Chronicle*, the town's daily with the second-highest circulation, should have such a mediocre gardening page. "The Garden Path" was cold, impersonal, and dull, filled with articles on arcane subjects such as bee keeping and bonsai pruning, nothing that typical subscribers—sixty-hour-a-week urban dwellers—could apply in their modest plots.

"Why don't you do something about it?" Kareena suggested one day, no doubt fed up with Mitra's constant griping. She'd heard from someone that *Chronicle* was looking for a gardening columnist. "You should apply."

And so, six months ago, Mitra had made an appointment with Robert Anderson-Haas, *Chronicle's* Gardening Editor. Getting a face-to-face interview with an editor was no easy task and she took it as a good omen. Dressed in a lightweight wool gabardine suit, and carrying a leather-frame purse, the sort of outfit she imagined columnists wore, she made her way through the newspaper office. She reached a dead-end cubicle which faced tall steel shelves, expecting to meet someone who, if not young, at least was genial. Gardeners, Mitra believed, were a happy gregarious bunch; they loved to compare notes.

Robert hauled himself from his chair, nary a single muscle twitch disturbing his bland facade. He seemed as huge and imposing as Queen Anne Hill, located not too far away. The banks of harsh fluorescent light accentuated his sallow skin and the white specks of dandruff on his scalp. His desk held not a speck of green, nothing alive. Only a color photo of a pit bull was affixed on the cubicle's otherwise-virgin wall. Mitra thrust a firm hand forward, smiling and projecting enthusiasm.

He addressed Mitra coolly and looked sufficiently peeved, as though she'd spilled coffee on his desk and spoiled his morning. Even though Mitra hadn't knocked anything over or done much of anything except display a too-cheerful smile, he didn't appear to be in a mood to entertain her proposal. She pulled up a chair, took out a folder containing three sample columns and photos of gardens she'd designed, and handed it to Robert. He flipped through the pages with fleshy fingers, a man who seemed depressed, not much interested in anything.

Piped-in music bristled. Mitra kept her feet from jiggling by conjuring up a shining future in which she'd churn out a column every other week. So it crushed her when Robert set the folder down on the desk and looked up with a frown, as though her essays and the photographs were giving him indigestion.

"Do you have any questions about my qualifications?" Mitra asked.

He shook his head, a tiny shake that didn't reveal what he might be thinking.

"What's your garden like?" Mitra asked, expecting him to open up.

He mentioned living in an apartment with no gardening facilities. He had resorted to renting a P-Patch in a community garden. "I'm coasting this year."

"I know what you mean," Mitra replied. "I give my beds a rest every so often, too."

"I'm just being lazy. My 'complicata' rose needs to be controlled. It's gotten up to eight feet. Arugula and parsley are all over the patch—they're worse than weeds." He heaved himself up from his chair, glancing toward the entranceway. "Come see me Monday, ten o'clock."

On Monday at the appointed hour, after some preliminary throat-clearing, Robert announced he'd try her on an "experimental basis" for a few months, the same dark shadow clouding his face. See how "they" responded to her column. "We're sensitive to our subscribers, you know," he added, as though she'd implied he had been ignoring them.

"Thank you, Robert." Mentally, she thrust her fist toward the ceiling in a gesture of victory. She would have given Robert a hug, but that probably would have offended him. "I'm sure we'll work together well."

And she meant that. True to her old country roots, she always tried to turn every acquaintance into a friend or relative. Robert proceeded to go over the rules for freelancers—the word count, the salary, and to whom she should e-mail the invoice. He emphasized how strict the deadlines were. Without explaining the reason, he suggested she took a pseudonym.

Thus Mitra began her career as a columnist for a major metropolitan daily under the assumed name of Ms. Em Bloom.

That was five months ago. Every other Thursday, her column appeared on the garden page of the Arts & Living Section. The assignment had turned out harder than she expected, much like digging into the area's glaciated soil and having to cart away wheelbarrows of stones and boulders. She had to rack her brain to squeeze the material into the paltry few inches allocated to her. The pay was crummy. Robert had reacted to her piece on wild flowers with the phrase "soporifically mundane." He'd deemed the column before that, a cheery essay on the delights of browsing through seed catalogs on a gloomy winter evening, as bordering on "fantasy."

It bothered Mitra that she and Robert didn't seem to breathe the same air. He seemed so detached and depressed at times. He viewed her as a migraine-inducing freelancer, a thistle in his rose patch, when in fact Mitra was ready to be a friend. So it pleased her, on her way to having a face-to-face with Robert, that he'd offered her some of his gardening books. What if she asked him to lunch and they spent a little time talking shop over a plate of something delicious? Then he might view her in a gentler light and devising a column wouldn't be such a mutual ordeal.

Robert did have a caring side and he'd begun showing it. When she needed to interview an expert on fertilizers, he got her in touch with a woman from Urban Horticulture.

The review date for Mitra's columnist status was fast approaching. Wouldn't it be grand if Robert kept her column beyond the test period? If he went back to his garden? If they became friends? Mitra still hadn't managed to make Robert laugh, though she vowed to get a chuckle out of the old curmudgeon before she was through.

TWENTY-FOUR

STILL ON HER WAY to the *Seattle Chronicle's* offices, taking a detour due to an accident and waiting for the light to change at the intersection of 50th and Roosevelt Way, Mitra noticed a pedestrian who looked familiar. Absent-mindedly, as he crossed the street, with quick intense steps, she examined him closer. It was Adi.

A flash-chill coursed through her arms. She was still processing the dread of a partially paid ransom and its potential consequences. Clothed in an old blue sweatshirt and jeans, Adi entered Cinema Books, located at the southwest corner of the intersection.

Wait a minute. Why wasn't he at work? Why wasn't he dressed in his usual business attire? She'd never known him to be a movie buff.

She made a quick decision, took a right turn, parked in an alley only a block away, and jumped out of her car. After walking up to Roosevelt Way, she hid herself behind a chestnut tree located two doors down from Cinema Books, feeling foolish. Even though she wasn't sure what she'd find, she had to do this silly bit of sleuthing.

In a few minutes, Adi exited the store, holding a plastic bag loaded with books, and took several quick steps in her direction. She edged her way around the thick trunk of the chestnut tree, trying to avoid his line of sight.

He looked straight at her. Her breath quickened. She stood immobilized, weighing her options of either running or confronting him. She chose the latter.

He planted himself boldly in front of her, holding a contemptuous expression on his face. "Hey, Mitra. Isn't it a little early in the year for chestnuts?"

She caught the irony in his voice. Veen had warned her about Adi. And he might be wondering if she was following him. If he did, that might not go well for her. Regardless, she decided to stay and act casual. In broad daylight, on this major thoroughfare, with pedestrians buzzing about, what could he do to her?

She smiled. "But apparently not too early for film books."

"Why don't you ever give up looking for Kareena?"

"I simply want to find out what films I should watch," she said lightly.

"You have time to watch films? Don't you write that gardening column in the newspaper? Doesn't that occupy you? I read your essay on weeding."

She tensed. "Why are you asking me about my column when there are so many more important things? Let me ask you this—did you pay the rest of the ransom?"

"Mitra, can't you just leave the fuck alone? I mean—"

He stopped speaking, turning his attention toward a bespectacled clerk who had rushed out of Cinema Books and was rapidly approaching him. "A mistake in your credit card transaction, sir," the clerk said. "If you'd be kind enough to step in—I'd like to run your card through one more time, if you don't mind."

Adi looked bewildered, but followed the clerk, turning back once to glare at Mitra.

She hurried to her car and drove away.

*   *   *

Robert—portly and middle-aged, with a bland façade—stooped over an open cardboard box on the floor and slid a stack of ten or so books across the large metal desk toward her.

Her mind still agitated from that encounter with Adi, Mitra sorted through the books, sitting cross-legged on the floor. The subjects were varied: Northwest mushrooms, now-fashionable ornamental grass, and boutique dahlias. Perusing these, sifting through fresh ideas and putting them to use, would give her overworked mental faculties a rest.

She collected a set of four under her arm and stood up. "Thanks, Robert. I'll enjoy reading them and also build muscles carrying them."

Robert didn't smile. "Have a chair, Mitra. I just got an e-mail from a subscriber who said your grandmother column was 'pure crap.'"

Hmm. Might it be Adi? She dropped on a chair facing Robert's desk, not sure what to expect.

"His grandmother sleeps seventeen hours a day, complains that he neglects her, and when he brings her presents, grouses about how cheap and tasteless they are," Robert said in a light tone, as he read from the screen. "What a silly idea to celebrate the cranky old hags of the universe. He asked us to terminate you."

She asked, with hope in her, "Did you like my column, Robert?"

"As a matter of fact, I did. You're still a bit formal, but you obviously have interesting ideas. Readers like me, who've never thought of helping their grandmothers, or other deserving persons in their lives, are inspired by you."

Mitra offered him an appreciative glance, felt a smile flicker inside her.

Robert leaned back in his chair, asked Mitra how she got started in this business, and she was only too happy to tell him. In turn, she asked Robert how he got into editing from crime reporting.

"I lived in Phoenix when I was a crime reporter," he replied. "Phoenix is the capital of KFR—Kidnapping for Ransom. The first time I followed a KFR incident, I started out with only bits of information and kept adding to it until I could see my way around. Ultimately, I traced the criminals behind it. I loved the work. Then I moved to Seattle and could only get a position as an editor." His eyes filled with sadness. "Tell me about what's going on with your missing friend."

Mitra took him through everything that had happened since they had last spoken, emphasizing her arguments with Adi about the ransom letter. Robert took notes in a notepad. Going through the details made Mitra so sad that at one point she stopped speaking.

"You all right?" Robert asked.

He walked over to the office break room across the hallway and returned with two glasses of water.

"Your friend's case is an interesting one," Robert said. "Eventually, I'd want to write about it for the paper."

"I appreciate all your help."

They schmoozed for awhile, unusual for Robert. He was trying to brighten her mood, she supposed. She asked him about his garden, if he had gone back to it.

His eyes sunk deeper under a jungle of eyebrows, even as the customary rain cloud returned to his face. He seemed to be asking: Why go so moony over plants? Why go so moony over anything? We all know life is one lick of punishment after another. He looked depressed, stayed silent.

She noticed a fancy gold-toned business card engraved with a dancing figure on the desk. Another glance revealed the card was from Caribe, the new Caribbean dance hall and bistro just up the street from the newspaper office. The man did have a weakness. Might this be the place to take him out to dinner, to show her appreciation and become closer friends? Imagining him slightly inebriated, twisting, undulating, and perspiring on a smoky dance floor, she couldn't help but smile to herself affectionately.

Belatedly, remembering her client appointment, she scrambled to her feet. She was already fifteen minutes late. She thanked Robert for the books. "And, with you helping me, I no longer feel like I've reached a dead end."

"Take care, Mitra."

She strode out, listening to a whistling tune from an adjoining cubicle and observing a butterfly kite hanging precariously from the ceiling. In another ten minutes, she reached her client's house only to have the doorbell unanswered. How much the recent events had changed her work habits. She'd never missed an appointment before. *Oh, Mitra, how could you do that? Don't you understand how much reputation counts in this business?*

On the way home, she stopped at Cinema Books on Roosevelt. The clerk she'd seen speaking with Adi earlier in the day stood at the cash register.

"Hi," she said brightly to him. "I saw you talking with my cousin earlier. Do you remember him? Do you know what he likes to read? I'd like to get him a birthday present."

"Oh, yes, I remember your cousin. I helped him. He bought a bunch of books. I'll show you the big book he wanted to buy, but couldn't. His credit card didn't go through. He paid cash for the other books."

They walked to the shelf together. The clerk pulled out an oversized book titled, *Bollywood: Now and Then* by P.R. Rashid.

According to the synopsis on the book jacket, the book concerned itself on the history and current state of the Bombay film industry: "Everything you ever wanted to know about Bollywood."

Back to her house, Mitra phoned Detective Yoshihama and recounted the details of her encounter with Adi outside Cinema Books.

"So you suspect a film connection?" he asked, his voice going deeper, indicating he was taking her suggestion seriously. "That's most interesting."

"I was never much for Bollywood movies," she replied, "but I'm going to read every word of this book."

TWENTY-FIVE

AROUND TWILIGHT, Mitra got into her Honda and headed to Grandmother's, turning on classic rock for company. She glanced at the rear-view mirror and saw a white Datsun pickup truck behind her.

Only seconds before, she'd seen the truck parked in front of her neighbor's Tudor. But now, drawing into the 45th Street, she noticed the truck again behind her car. She wondered with a chill if the pickup could be following her. She took several lefts and rights and lost it, only to meet it coming back toward her in the opposite lane. Trembling, she took a look at the driver. Aged about fifty and possibly of Eastern European descent, he had a Baltic gloom hanging over his face. She checked his license plate and memorized the number: 666-ZVZ.

Upon reaching Grandmother's house, she parked in front and again checked her rearview mirror, relieved not to see the potential stalker. She called Detective Yoshihama and reported the incident. He greeted her eagerly and said he would make a note of it, adding, "I'm driving to a gun party. A shootout has gone on earlier. Talk later."

For a moment Mitra forgot about her travail and wondered if he'd be safe. She hopped out of the car, walked along a cemented path, mounted the front stoop, and pressed the doorbell hard. Opening the door, Grandmother wrapped her in a hug, but made no comments about the rigidity of her body.

"Do you know I bought fifteen copies of the newspaper yesterday, the entire supply, at the corner grocery store?" Grandmother said. "The Vietnamese owner asked me to autograph a copy for her. 'Grandmother's Day—what a fabulous idea,' she said."

Mitra glanced at her, then at the window, the pickup still on her mind.

"Anything wrong?" Grandmother asked, her face shadowed by concern.

"Someone's been trailing me today. He looks kind of creepy."

"You know that doesn't surprise me. You're being shadowed for a reason. If it continues to be that way, report it to the police, will you?

"I've already called Detective Yoshihama."

"Does it ever happen when you're out with Ulrich?"

"No." Mitra's stomach clenched, as she heard Yoshihama's advice in her mind: *You might want to consider staying away from him.* "Actually, I haven't seen Ulrich much lately. I feel secure when he's around or when I go some place with him."

"When a woman really wants to feel secure, she chooses a man who's more open about his background." Grandmother paused. "I don't want to interfere and I've seen him only once. I only know what you've told me, but if you'd care to hear what I think—there are those who are the marrying kind and those who aren't. He looks like a drifter to me."

Grandmother—why did she have to be so stern-eyed and so judgmental? "We're enjoying each other for now," Mitra said. "I'm almost thirty, but not in a hurry, not thinking long term."

"So they all say."

"What are you really worried about?"

"That you'll make the wrong decision. Like me. That you'll latch on to someone and not be able to let go. Find out more about that guy, will you? He's trouble. And, I might as well share this with you. Yesterday, early in the morning, I saw him parked in front of my house. He was talking to himself. He saw me come out to get the paper. I'm sure he recognized me. And I believe he knew it was my house. I got back inside and locked the door. When I checked through the window a few minutes later, he was gone."

Mitra found herself crumbling inside. How would Ulrich ever find out where Grandmother lived? Had he been going through Mitra's stuff? Might there be something wrong in his psyche?

"I'm sorry," she said, "if he's scared you. He's never acted that strangely with me."

Tampopo, their feline friend, stalked in, brushed against Grandmother's leg, and purred. Her forehead creased, Grandmother said, "Much as I don't want to pile on you, I found this little devil rolling around the flowerbed you worked on so hard."

Mitra took a shaky breath. "What? Why did you let her loose? Let me go see."

She rushed out the back door, Grandmother following, and headed straight to the flowerbed. Street light illuminated parts of the bed. It appeared as though it had been ravaged by a storm. The cat had dug up the soil and made a salad bar out of the tender seedlings. More than half the bed would need to be replanted. She shook her head and said to Grandmother that next time she'd spread bark mulch, scatter prickly pine cones, or throw crushed red cayenne flakes to discourage her frisky friend.

Tampopo strolled toward the lanky nicotiana plant in the far corner of the yard. About two feet high, it was already blooming red. Mitra and Grandmother followed Tampopo who leapt toward an unseen insect.

"Believe it or not, she doesn't bother the nicotiana," Grandmother said. "Could it be because it's related to the tobacco family? I, too, hate cigarettes, but love these flowers. They start smelling heavenly at sunset, almost like jasmine. They come into their own after dark."

Even though Mitra's concerns about Ulrich hadn't been resolved and they hadn't agreed on how to cat-proof her yard, they were back to their common ground: flowers. This could be Grandmother's way of extending an apology about her earlier observations on Ulrich. The sweet fragrance of nicotiana had certainly revived Mitra.

"They're a hummingbird magnet," she said. "Wait till they return from the south and you'll see."

Then she remembered that hummers were among Ulrich's favorite birds. Aware that Grandmother mistrusted him, Mitra swallowed.

TWENTY-SIX

TWO DAYS LATER, Mitra's search for an art-deco planter for a client took her to a local mom-and-pop gardening shop in Fremont. Even here, she looked for Kareena, as she did everywhere. Then she came back to herself and told the store clerk what she needed. The clerk rummaged around in her inventory of containers, setting aside an iron kettle, a terra cotta elephant, and a faux Grecian cement pedestal. It appeared she was out of stock in the style Mitra needed.

Out of the corner of her eye, she noticed a familiar figure at the cash register. It was Detective Yoshihama, casually dressed in a faded red sweat shirt and jeans. She studied him more closely, which she hadn't done when he'd come to her house. He was probably in his mid-thirties, on the cusp of the settling-down age. Minus his bulky jacket and cop badges, he appeared smaller, just another shopper engaged in mundane chores, attractive nonetheless.

She didn't need another man in her life now. Oh, no. She had Ulrich. Still, she admitted to herself, Yoshihama had an appeal. She kept watching him. He spoke with the store clerk in a quiet confident manner, both smiling.

After paying for his purchase, Yoshihama walked out of the store. She, too, hurried outside and tried to draw his attention. But by then, he'd gotten into his SUV and pulled out of the curb. She ran to her Honda parked half a block away and started following him, taking a right, then two lefts. She didn't quite want to do this: she'd been followed recently and that had threatened her. Yet, given that she wanted to speak with him in person urgently, there was no other choice. He parked in front of a house, hopped out, and climbed up the front steps.

She parked her car across the street and surveyed the house, a nondescript pastel-yellow 1920's craftsman, set back away from the sidewalk and elevated. She closed the car door and crossed the street, dodging a white Datsun truck whose driver refused to slow down. She wondered for a moment if it was the same pickup that had followed her the other night.

She bounded up Yoshihama's front steps and halted on the concrete pathway leading to the front door of the house, alert to the fact that she was invading his private space.

Her eyes swept over the large square lawn to her right. A conscientious gardener could nurture this lawn into a thing of beauty, but Yoshihama hadn't done much. A volunteer lobelia waged a losing battle against an army of purslane. The grass resembled an aging flower child's unapologetically long, unkempt hair. Cheerful, yellow, "Aren't I pretty?" dandelion blossoms punctuated the grass.

Pruning shears in his hand, Yoshihama studied a cherry tree at the far end of the lawn. He reached for a branch, then stepped back. From the looks of it, the tree had received only limited attention in recent years. It hadn't been properly pruned. The branches crisscrossed, robbing air and sunlight from each other.

"Good morning," Mitra called out.

Yoshihama turned and their eyes caught. It took him a split second to place her. Then he answered, "Ms. Basu," in a cheerful manner. "Taking a break from reading books about Bollywood?"

Mitra smiled, as she walked toward him. "Actually I was running an errand down the street. I always check out people's yards—professional curiosity, I guess—and saw you working. You have a potentially nice space."

"Thanks. I think." A strand of unruly hair curled at the side of his neck. He looked toward a starling perched atop the tree.

"Is that a cherry?" A question she didn't really need to ask but, hopefully, it'd keep the conversation going to the point where she could enquire about Kareena.

He nodded. "In the last two years, I have gotten maybe four or five cherries each spring. I can't figure out what's wrong."

She stole a glance at his hands. They were soft and smooth unlike hers with their calloused palms. His shears had rust on the cutting edge.

"If you prune it right, the tree will give you more fruit and it'll live longer. One of my clients has an Asian pear in her backyard. It's quite prolific because of the care it gets."

"You're a professional gardener, as I remember," he said. "This is my first attempt. So, how would you prune this one?"

She went over the basics: aim for an open center to admit sunlight and improve air circulation. Prune the crown low for easy harvesting. And be sure to use quality shears.

"That sounds like it'll take me hours," Yoshihama said.

So far he hadn't uttered the word "we." She assumed him to be someone who lived alone, liked his privacy, but was overwhelmed by the demands of property maintenance. "You have a backyard, too?"

He smiled into her eyes. "Would you like to see?"

He turned and started on the path toward the back of the house, brushing past a lobed-leaf hydrangea bush hanging far beyond its optimal space. She followed, watching his long strides.

Yoshihama turned. "Forgive the mess. I've been busy at work lately with a couple of complicated drug cases. It's been a month since I've mowed."

He had, indeed, let the yard go. A gigantic pine blocked what Pacific Northwest gardeners cherish most: natural light. English ivy had smothered a wooden fence and destroyed its planks. Some rotten boards had fallen over onto a flowerbed that ran along the fence. The bed was an eyesore of crown vetch, originally intended as a ground cover. An invasive variety of mint was sprawled on the ground everywhere she stepped. She had, however, seen worse. Her adopted grandmother's yard, when she first got the assignment, lurched to mind.

He was studying her, as though to check how horrified she might be. "At least you haven't fainted."

She would be thrilled to beautify this plot of land, if she ever had the chance. Drawing in a pleasant expression on her face, she said, "You know, you could have a great yard here if you clean out the ivy jungle and take out the pine. I can see deciduous shrubs on the right, minimum-care perennials like daylily and bleeding hearts on the raised bed, a honeysuckle bush in that corner for lushness and color."

He managed a small smile. "A spade, a roto-tiller, muscle power, and hundreds of hours, huh."

He steered her toward a tidy cement patio, the yard's only redeeming feature. "Would you like to have a seat?" he said eagerly, as though wishing to prolong this visit. "Do you have time?"

She risked a glance at her watch and pulled up a chair from the patio's wrought-iron dining set. He took the other chair.

"So do you take on projects like this?" he asked.

"Yes, but you might want to see some of my work first. Recently, I planted a garden for Glow Martinelli, my adopted grandmother. Her plot isn't much bigger than yours. I'm sure she wouldn't mind showing it to you, if you call her ahead of time."

He asked for the particulars. "I'd like to see it."

She noticed a gaudy mass-market paperback lying on the patio table. The cover showed an elaborate office desk, a reclining woman in a corporate suit with buttons popped off—no undergarment from the looks of it—and a fully dressed male executive leaning over her. She glanced at the title: *Between Five and Seven*. Bold letters at the top proclaimed it as the third title in the "Boardroom Romance" series.

This detective read romance novels? She wouldn't have guessed it. It could also be that he kept his emotional side well hidden when on police duties.

She raised an eyebrow. "This looks interesting."

His face flushed. She'd embarrassed him. "Oh, the cover is misleading," he said. "This author puts more energy on the characters, less on the plot. You see, as a detective, I like to study the idiosyncrasies of human behavior, to deduce what a person's real motives are from what he says or does. I also read partly to escape."

She recognized his flimsy defense and glanced at the lurid cover once more. Flipping to a pink bookmark, she noticed flamboyant character names such as Orianna and Lance, put the book down, and nodded seriously.

"I'll pick up a copy," she said. "For my mother who lives in Kolkata. She zips through at least three books a week. She calls them her bon bons. She's a careful reader, likes to get involved in the nitty-gritty. It's the smallest acts, she says, like how a man ties his shoe laces, how he counts money, or how he dumps the newspaper into the waste bin that reveal his character. She also says women are in the habit of noticing minor flaws in a person's actions that add up to major issues."

"Quite so. I know a woman detective back east, a romance reader who uses tactics like that. She's one of the best." He paused. "I also read a ton of foreign newspapers on the Internet. *Hindustan Standard* is my favorite paper. It's idle curiosity, but I like to keep up with international crime stories. Robert and I have that in common."

"My mother also reads *Hindustan Standard*."

He went silent for an instant. "Would you like some tea, Ms. Basu?"

"I'd love a cup. You can call me Mitra."

"And you can call me Nobuo."

She detected a subtle cheer in his voice, as though he'd wanted to be on a first-name basis all along, and nodded. With a spring in his stride, he disappeared inside.

Might he be trying to hit on her? Certainly, he was handsome. But she needed to swing her focus back to the business at hand: Kareena and her well being.

Nobuo came back and set down two tall slender glasses filled with ice chunks and clear red liquid. "It's rooibos, intense like black tea, but totally herbal."

She took a sip, found the vanilla fragrance quite agreeable, then drank deeply, only now realizing how thirsty she was.

He held his glass eagerly, as though wishing to hold on to this moment. "I've come to the conclusion that women are miniaturists. They notice small brush strokes. We men can get fixated on our career, economy, stock market, and baseball, and miss all except the obvious and the tangible, the big blob of color on the canvas, if you will. We miss the subtle shades of a sunset, step on wildflowers, forget family birthdays. I am trying to learn the small brushstrokes, but that takes time. I figure it'll take us men a few more centuries to catch up with women—if we ever do."

"Listen, I know you must be growing tired of me asking the same question. But have you come across any new information about Kareena?"

"As a matter of fact, yes. But Mr. Guha requested that I don't speak about it. Hasn't he told you?"

"Nope." When did Adi tell her anything? She was only his wife's best friend and sister, though he was unaware of the sister part. "Do you mind telling me?"

"Ms. Sinha is okay. Airline records indicated she took a direct flight from Vancouver, B.C. to Kolkata about two weeks ago. We don't know her exact destination in Kolkata."

"She's alive? She's free? You're sure of that?"

Nobuo shrugged. Mitra gripped the edge of the table. So her sister had betrayed her. "Kolkata? She's not from there. She's from Mumbai. She's never mentioned having any relatives in Kolkata. Did she travel alone?"

"She reserved only one seat. The charges showed up on her credit card statement."

"Have you closed the case?"

"No, it's still open. I can't be completely certain until I talk with her. Yesterday, I got a call from a woman in Maui. She's been missing for a month. 'I'm fine,' she said. 'Don't tell my husband I'm here.' I assured her I wouldn't, and closed that case." He looked down at her empty glass. "Would you like a refill?"

In her bewildered state, thoughts racing in her head and colliding, Mitra could only nod.

"Just give me a minute." Nobuo grabbed the two glasses and headed for the kitchen. She heard the sound of the refrigerator door opening and then a pouring sound.

So Kareena had voluntarily left. But why did she fly to Kolkata, of all places?

Nobuo placed the filled glasses on the table. She caught his eye. "What if someone stole Kareena's identity and bought a ticket with her credit card? Have you called the Kolkata police, by any chance?"

"As a matter of fact, I'm in touch with Kolkata's Lal Bazar Control Room. They've gotten two photographs of her in different locations in Kolkata. Mr. Guha has positively identified the woman in the photos to be his wife."

Mitra sat rigid, unable to process the information. "She had to have a reason for walking out. And there had to be a reason for the money demand, whoever might have sent it."

"The note could have been forged."

Her voice rose slightly as she thought out loud. "I thought I knew Kareena."

"People aren't always who we think they are. I often hear things like what you just said, Mitra." Nobuo's expression hardened; his voice carried a tone of certitude. "'My son couldn't have molested that child.' Or 'My daughter has never touched a drink.' Or 'My husband couldn't possibly have cleaned out his company's bank account.' Multiply that by a few thousand and you'll understand why I have a job."

"But we're not talking about a potential criminal here. My friend is a highly respected domestic violence counselor. She goes out of her way to help women in distress."

He gave a fraction of a nod. "Yes. I know of at least one battered woman who wouldn't have survived without Ms. Sinha's intervention, which makes me even more curious about her."

She stared at him. "Curious?"

"Let me tell you something about myself, if I may. My father wanted me to join his export-import firm. I declined his offer politely and respectfully and joined the police force instead. I didn't do it for the adrenaline, due to my interest in psychology, or because I have a criminal mind. The police have the highest rate of getting injury while on the job. I'm simply interested in figuring out why normal people, sometimes knowingly, make serious mistakes. What were they thinking? I wonder."

"Kareena wants to be happy and loved. Who doesn't? Granted, she's made a mistake by walking out and not telling anyone, but there has to be another story here."

"Have you ever known people who look for love and happiness in the wrong places?" Nobuo said delicately, shaping the words love and happiness in his mouth gently.

"Could you elaborate on that?"

He stared at the ivy cascading over the fence. He was probably ready to resume his afternoon chores and didn't want to discuss the case any further. "All I can tell you is that Ms. Sinha went away, but she's all right. That'll have to be enough. Mr. Guha doesn't want sensitive information about his wife or the ransom note released to the public."

Mitra slid out of the chair and bumped the table, rattling the spoons and glasses. "Thanks for the tea. I'd better be going."

She stepped off the patio. He walked her around to the front of the house, then to the sidewalk. She could feel his gaze on her back. Thanking him again, she plodded downhill to her Honda. The cold hard metal of the car keys shocked her skin. Once ensconced in her vehicle, she found even more dreariness settling over her. What was she to believe now? That Kareena just left without saying goodbye to anyone? That the ransom note should be forgotten?

Regardless of her actions, Kareena was her sister, her family.

The only solution was to fly to Kolkata.

But Mitra couldn't afford the steep airfare or to take time off her business.

A truck edged up alongside. Oh, no, that driver again. He might have been following her all morning. Why hadn't she spotted him before? Her mind ran fast, while her fingers on the steering wheel froze.

She'd better not show her fear. She made a face and looked defiantly into the driver's eyes. Oh, no, this was a much younger man driving a Toyota, with a child in the backseat. His face wore a scowling mask of impatience, a daddy looking for a parking space. She started her car and eased out.

She heard a car engine. This time it was the Datsun pickup going in the opposite direction, with the same driver.

They exchanged a look. His cold, mean eyes bore into her. "Count your breaths, Miss," he seemed to be saying.

TWENTY-SEVEN

HOW NICE OF VEEN to call to say she'd returned from India and that she wanted to meet Mitra for dinner. A few minutes before leaving the house, Mitra drifted to the living room and touched the wisteria blossoms flowing pure and white out of a vase on the accent table. It was as though she could feel Ulrich's lips, shoulders, and hands. A sigh came out of her. They had so much to talk about. She'd called him several times in the last few days and he'd finally left a message on her voice-mail yesterday. The message was in German, puzzling her even more.

She picked up the receiver, punched his number, and this time he answered in person. To hear his hello gave her a thrill and a shot of uncertainty.

"Where have you been in the last few days?" she asked, her voice creaking with anxiety.

Sounding a little agitated himself, he replied, "Save your questions for another time, Mit. I'm just fine. I'm busy right now."

Hurt and confused, managing a shallow breath, she said, "Sorry to have called at an inconvenient time."

Abruptly, he hung up.

Mitra arrived at Nana's Soup House to find Veen and Jean already claiming a table. Both of them looked more cheerful than they'd been lately, as to be expected on day twenty-three. Their warm welcome help Mitra settle down. She ordered her favorite baked potato soup. As soon as she broke the news about her chance meeting with Yoshihama a day earlier and his latest report on Kareena, they perked up.

"Yoshihama is right." The mirror-embroidery on Veen's sleeves glittered in the light. "Kareena has made a mistake. Of course none of us is infallible."

Mitra inhaled the starchy fragrance of her soup. "Seen Adi lately?"

"Yes," Veen said. "A neighbor complained that Adi wasn't maintaining his yard, like Kareena used to do. Our neighbors are really conscious about property value. Yesterday, I went to check out Adi's yard when I thought he wasn't at home. It was a mess. Garbage, broken branches, dandelions. The rosemary bush has grown unwieldy. Shit, Adi caught me snooping around. I doubt he'll ever share any information about Kareena with me. Oh, this might be news to you, Mitra. I found out from a mutual colleague that Adi's selling his business."

Mitra put her spoon down. "Selling his business? But that business is his life."

"He's apparently in a 'cash-flow squeeze.' Maybe he's trying to raise money to pay off the rest of the ransom."

"I wonder why the ransom demand would still have any force if Kareena has left on her own."

"The answer is obviously in Kolkata." Veen said, drawing the bread basket closer. "Should one of us go there, locate Kareena, and talk some sense into her head?"

Jean shook her head. Her twisted hoop earrings caught the light and shone. "Without an address or phone number," she said, "how will we find her in a city of twelve million? It's like losing an earring in a haystack. That actually happened to me once, believe it or not, with my favorite teardrop-shaped one. Never did find the darn thing."

"I can't afford the airfare to Kolkata," Mitra said. "I didn't win the bid I made for a huge commercial garden project."

"And if I ask for any more time off from work," Veen said, stirring her cardamom chai, "they'll fire me on the spot."

Their dessert order came. Jean took a bite of her peach crumble and asked for details about Mitra's tea with Yoshihama. Mitra obliged.

"That dude is hitting on you," Jean said. "I can tell from what you said that he's on the make. He's not a cop twenty-four hours a day. He asked your help in pruning his cherry tree? That's as good a line as I've ever heard. Ulrich has competition."

Mitra sighed, recalling the earlier phone conversation with Ulrich, short and abrupt, too painful to dwell on. She switched the topic by mentioning her planned little foray to Adi's house in his absence.

"Would this Sunday morning be a good time for that?" she asked Veen.

"Yes, that'd be perfect timing," Veen said. "Now that the weather is getting nicer, Adi's golfing every Sunday morning. He leaves home early. I think he gets a cup somewhere first."

Just the piece of information Mitra needed to make her next move. She thanked Veen and pushed away a slice of upside-down pineapple cake, her mind occupied with a plan for Sunday.

Upon returning home, she found a message from Ulrich on her voice-mail. Breathlessly, she listened, not knowing what to expect. He'd apologized for being rude on the phone earlier. "I wasn't quite myself. I hate myself for it."

Continuing to listen, she could hear the pain and torture in his voice, which gradually gave way to a warm intimacy. Cheerfully, he reminded her of their Sunday morning plan. The masculinity, the sense of protection he often exhibited showed itself as he said, "I'll pick you up from your place at 6:30, my wisteria." My wisteria—she liked the tender way he said it. He concluded by saying, "I'll wait for you somewhere and get you back home. Please forgive me. I love you."

TWENTY-EIGHT

WITH A GLOVED HAND, Mitra punched the keys to open Kareena and Adi's house and waited. The ivory-toned Victorian glowed bluish in the morning light. The garage door creaked open with a pained protest, as though stricken by the heart-splitting comings and goings it had to bear in recent weeks.

Mitra looked around and noticed a slight movement of the window drapes of a house across the street. Could it be a nosy neighbor or vigilant block watcher observing her surreptitious entry? No, she reassured herself, it was only 8 A.M. on a Sunday.

Besides, Mitra hadn't left a car parked out front to draw attention. Ulrich, who had dropped her more than a block away, was sitting in his cold vehicle, clutching a warm cup, and frowning at the newspaper headlines. Despite his serious doubts, he'd given up his Sunday slumber and accompanied her.

Mitra entered the two-car garage. Adi's Volvo was absent. He was playing golf, she assumed. Kareena's Jag, painted a British racing green, sat alone. The door was open. How like Kareena not to keep it locked, this expensive machine.

She opened the door on the passenger side and slid into the seat. Rifling through the glove compartment, she found a bottle of aspirin, three pairs of sunglasses, a map of Seattle, a pair of suede gloves, two candy bars, and a "Wish you were here" postcard from Molokai, initialed J.

Who was J? It was not Jean's handwriting.

Stop daydreaming, Mitra, gather whatever information you can quickly, leave no trace, and clear out.

The floor and the dashboard were bare. Mitra slipped out of Kareena's beautiful machine, shut the door, and entered the kitchen, taking a tentative step on the terra-cotta floor. A stained wine goblet sat on the French-blue limestone countertop.

She walked to the white memo board hanging on the kitchen wall. Thumb-tacked with miscellaneous notes, the memo board was the overscheduled couple's Command Central, possibly also their way of keeping out of each other's hair. She read the dentist's reminder card, the recycling truck's schedule, an "I luv you" proclamation in Adi's script and "Where the hell is my camera?" in Kareena's scribble.

Mitra entered the bedroom. In the darkness, a band of clothing on the floor snagged her foot. She flicked on a table lamp. The white light threw the surroundings into clear relief.

The master closet door was ajar. She opened it wider. Fifteen or so of Kareena's outfits hung on a rail. There was the peach sleeveless shift, the mandarin-collar jacket with gold buttons, and the two-piece knit in lemon yellow.

The room was hot. Adi had left the central heating on. Feeling suffocated, Mitra took off her cardigan and tied it around her waist.

She examined Kareena's ebony dresser drawers one at a time, sifting through scarves, lingerie, belts, and hair ornaments, taking care to return each item to its proper place as she went.

Next to the flower-appliquéd brassiere and panty sets there rested a handkerchief collection. As Mitra lifted a lacy hankie in a lily-of-the-valley pattern, a seductive scent of Indian *attar* floated over her. She fingered through each hankie's layers, folded it, and put it back in its place. At the bottom, there rested a letter, written in a natural colored sheet, and folded in half. As she picked it up, the letter slipped and fluttered to the floor. She stooped to pick it up.

She hesitated a moment, then curiosity overcame propriety, and she unfolded the letter.

Dated several months ago, it was scribbled in poorly written Bengali. Adi couldn't have been the sender. For all his shortcomings, he was well educated.

> *My beloved Karu, my thousand-and-one light, the brightest diamond in the universe, the sole reason the sun rises, the moon becomes full, and the nightingale sings*

Mitra's mind went numb and her heart silenced a beat. Karu: an endearing diminutive for Kareena. No one called her that, except this "poet," as far as Mitra knew. It wounded her to stumble upon such a vivid piece of evidence of Kareena's other existence.

The "poet" was clearly unschooled. That was evident from the archaic expressions and spelling errors in Bengali.

Mitra read on:

> *How much longer will you keep me waiting? I can't stand it that you're not around. I leave my mobile on twenty-four hours for your call. I can still feel your kiss on my skin, your touch on my thighs. I am counting the days, my love, until we can be together again.*

Mitra wanted to scream at Kareena. How could you do this? You're sophisticated, educated, and brilliant, and you fall for this schoolboy trash?

Why was Mitra being so critical? Because Kareena hadn't confided in her? What right did she have to judge this letter-writer, someone she'd never met? Maybe he had offered Kareena what she'd needed. Besides, in romance, as in war, you were allowed to be unfair, the use of effusive language being the least of anyone's concerns. Maybe he had fulfilled some fantasy of hers. Or maybe she just wanted to escape an unhappy, abusive marriage.

Mitra let her eyes run over the page, then skipped down to the signature at the bottom: Jay.

Mitra stood still. Kareena really *was* having an affair. But Kareena was her sister, her family. She must continue to follow her.

Mitra folded the love letter, placed it back in its place, and shut the drawer with a jerk. Adi, most likely, had read it. How had he reacted? Had he broken out in anguished sobs, Adi who was always right, always in charge? Adi who had everything but that which he craved the most, his wife's love?

Mitra mounted the stairs to Kareena's study. Dazed, she sat at Kareena's workstation, pulled open the mobile file pedestal, and flipped through the hanging folders: statistics on abused women, transcripts of phone conversations with clients, health insurance statements, and utility bills.

She walked her fingers through the back of the central drawer. There lay a small yellow memo pad with violet grid lines. Graffitied all over on an inside page were the initials J.P.B. in Kareena's stylish hand, as though it were a mantra she meditated on.

Who was J.P.B.? The Jay who wrote the love note? The one who'd sent the postcard from Molokai?

Could this be the self-styled actor Kareena was last seen with at Soirée? Could he be a film actor? Mitra had seen Kareena's fascination with Bollywood films, her way of losing herself in the make-believe world.

A car door slammed near the front of the house and Mitra's heart leaped to her throat. *Stop dallying. Except for the ransom note, you got what you came for. And Ulrich is waiting for you.*

Mitra descended the stairs, passed through the kitchen, and slipped out of the garage. Once out on the sidewalk, she took up the stride of a speed walker. A faint blue morning light filled the street. As she rounded the corner, she spotted a familiar steel gray Saab waiting at the pre-arranged spot. She clambered into the passenger's seat and gave a sigh of relief.

Ulrich raised his eyes from the paper. "You okay?"

She nodded. He started the engine. Belatedly, she noticed she didn't have her cardigan on. A chill rippled through her. Oh, no.

"My cardigan," she said, "I had it wrapped around my waist. It must have fallen off in the garage when I ran out. I have to go back."

Ulrich glared at her. "Are you sure? I don't think you should go in again. Someone might spot you."

And indeed Kareena's friendly neighbor, Sylvie, was at the intersection. Dressed in an edgy orange scarf and a plum windbreaker, she power-walked. Her poodle scampered along behind her.

Forget about the sweater for now. "Let's go," she whispered to Ulrich

Mitra hated to think of leaving without the sweater. Adi would, for sure, notice an unfamiliar piece of clothing invading his garage. And, if he did, he might connect Mitra with it. He could turn her in to the cops.

She mentioned this worry to Ulrich, as he hustled out of the parking space. "Adi's so out of it, he might not notice," he said.

As he drove through the neighborhood streets, she remained silent, but mulled the matter over in her mind. Finally, she said, "I'll have to go back for the sweater some other time."

His car shot out on the highway. Face taut, he said, "Mitra! Think twice. Don't be foolhardy. You mustn't go back. Do you hear me?"

The speedometer was hovering around 75 mph. "Could you please slow down?"

She glanced at him. Face flushed and posture stiff, he maneuvered the vehicle through an ever-shifting pattern of vehicles. This was the fourth time he'd become exasperated since they'd met. They could easily have talked it out. Where did this temper stem from? Why did his mood change so often? A taxi jumped in front of them. Ulrich muttered expletives under his breath in German, but slowed down.

In a few minutes, as they got off the highway, Mitra cracked the window open. The wind lashed at her cheek. A flapping red banner, like a warning, stuck out from the back of a truck overloaded with metal pipes. Mitra felt fractured, as though the wind streaming by had swept away a piece of her, never to be recovered.

TWENTY-NINE

SEATED AT HER DESK on the same morning, Mitra got down to her immediate task, to figure out who JPB was. She Googled "Bollywood" and the initials "JPB."

Lo and behold, there popped up before her the color portrait of an actor, hunky and leering, his shirt open to his navel.

She jerked up straight in her chair. Facing her was the *jhola* man she'd run into first at Soirée, then outside Sabnam's Sandals.

She kept searching and stumbled onto more articles. Jay Prasun Bahadur had become a romantic idol in the small regional film industry in Kolkata shortly after Mitra had left India. Within a few years, he began to bag roles in Bollywood and became a national icon. His adoring fans touted him thusly:

"JPB is all natural, muscled, and feral."

"He portrays a country boy with 'poetic accuracy.'"

"He plays God Rama. He's our hero. *Jay Bahadur ki joy.*" Long live Jay Bahadur.

Mitra now had even more reason to sit down with her newly purchased title, *Bollywood: Now and Then.* She pulled the book from the bookshelf and hurried through the pages containing biographies and color shots of film stars of yesteryear, eventually reaching a chapter titled "Money and the Mafia." Her eyes became riveted to the page.

Indian banks hadn't traditionally lent money to the Bollywood film industry, as it wasn't considered a legitimate business. How unfair, Mitra thought, even though she wasn't much for films. Unfortunately, this arrangement led the Bombay film industry to seek film financing from the mafia. Mafia? Mitra hoped that Jay wasn't mixed up in any organized crime.

She read on.

The mobsters would loan money to film makers at a high interest, as high as 50%. They would want their payment, of course, but also a cut from the movie stars' salaries, profits from the overseas markets, and even rights to the film music. They also wanted to see themselves portrayed in films in a noble light.

It rushed back to Mitra, the extravagant gangster film she'd watched with Kareena, in which the gang lord was a heroic character. Also charming and nice-looking, he was saved at the end. With an uncomfortable feeling rising in her, Mitra closed the book, put it aside, and made a few discreet phone calls to friends who were well versed in Bollywood movies.

Within minutes, her cellphone chimed: Jean was returning her call. She religiously rented Bollywood DVD's from R & M Video and Spice Center and had much to report.

Jay Bahadur, the actor, could dance, Jean confirmed. He won hearts and pocketbooks. Now in his late-thirties, he had had many liaisons, none permanent. His leading ladies had complained about his groping and other indecencies, even drug orgies. Jean believed these stories were nothing but jilted lovers' attempts at revenge.

According to Jean, for years, schoolgirls had squealed with delight and broken out a sweat as they watched his hip-gyrating dance sequences. Career women would bribe youngsters to stand in the ticket line for them at his film premieres. His face would regularly grace the covers of film magazines. In recent days, however, Jay Bahadur's popularity had spiraled downward.

"The fizz is gone," Jean said. "His wattage is the lowest ever."

Most tellingly, film magazines had stopped reporting dirt on him. And so Bahadur was desperate to regain his status. His finances weren't in the best shape, but he still lived in a twenty-two-room mansion in Kolkata and entertained fabulously.

Kareena would revel in such luxury, Mitra thought. Diamonds and sequins, cocktails and ball, A-list invitees—that was Kareena.

"Of late," Jean said, "Jay Bahadur has turned to making films, not just acting in them."

"So how does he raise money for his projects?" Mitra asked.

"I don't know," Jean said. "I'm only a fan. I should say I was."

After thanking Jean and finishing the conversation, Mitra printed several photos of Jay Bahadur, scrolled through more screens, and read additional postings. One entry suggested that Jay Bahadur displayed abusive behavior on screen and off. He'd punched an inquisitive journalist in the mouth during a film premiere, but somehow managed to escape a jail sentence.

Well, anyone could write about anything on the Internet.

The phone rang, startling Mitra, and she lunged for it. Mr. Shah, a community elder was responding to her voice-mail message.

"People love the person Bahadur plays in the movies," Shah said in a light tone. "Recently, he did God Rama in a dance film based on *Ramayana*. Doesn't that make him worthy of worship?"

"I don't doubt he's popular and he plays God Rama convincingly, but what can you tell me about his character?"

Shah barked out a laugh. "Why are you so interested, young lady, if I may ask?"

"I'm doing a research project," she fibbed.

"Another lovely girl doing another research project on the handsome lady killer from Bollywood."

Mitra nearly fell back in the chair hearing those words, but kept on listening.

"Bollywood seems to be taking America by storm. People in my office ask me if we dance all the time in India—at home, in the midst of traffic, at the car rental, on top of K2. Well, if it weren't for my seventy-year-old joints." His laugh ended in a cough.

His humor didn't touch Mitra. Mentally, she went over the recently acquired facts. Jay Bahadur, the dancer, starred in either romantic or religious films. He couldn't possibly have anything to do with gangster movies or crime lords. What might the connection be, if any?

"How much of the stuff you read about Bahadur should you believe?" she asked.

"I'll give you my two cents worth. JPB does indeed have killer instincts. I see murder in his eyes. That's what I hear about him. Did you read about the Ray murder case in *Hindustan Standard*? The famous throat-slashing? It happened four years ago. Horrible. Most horrible. Black money. Dirty dealings. You name it."

"I don't know much about that case." If truth be told, she'd never even heard of it. "I left India right after high school. I wasn't interested in Bollywood then."

"I've told you all I know. Have you seen any of Jay Bahadur's films? In Totem Lake Cinema in Kirkland, they show first-run films from Mumbai. Keep an eye on the listings. In case, a film by Bahadur shows up."

"I sure would check that out." Mitra thanked Mr. Shah and hung up. She knew her next step; to call Robert and share this information with him. Robert was going to open his own investigation. But she didn't have his home phone number, and this being Sunday, she'd have to wait.

So first thing the next morning, she called Robert and went over what she'd learned, finishing with: "Have you ever heard of the Ray murder case in Mumbai?"

"I vaguely remember it," Robert said. "I was still living in Phoenix and writing about crime then. Let me dig into it a bit more, make some calls, and I'll get back to you."

Mitra must take Robert out to lunch. She'd been thinking about that for a while. Now that he'd been doing all this extra work for her, she felt even more eager to do so.

Two hours later, Robert phoned her. "Indian mafia runs the B-town film industry," he said. "That's common knowledge. Here's what I found out about the Ray murder case. Manu Ray, an up-an-coming actor, was assassinated because he wouldn't share his film profits with the mobsters. He was Jay Bahadur's competition as a lead actor, and their rivalry had been widely reported. Of course, it's not Bahadur who did the job, but rather a hit man from the Mumbai underworld."

"Why do you think Bahadur was involved?" Mitra asked. "If Ray was assassinated because he wouldn't share his film profits, what does that have to do with Bahadur?"

"Well, there was enough evidence that Bahadur wanted to get rid of Manu Ray. There was bad blood between them."

"If so, why wasn't Bahadur arrested?"

"From what I've read, the British took away the Indian concept of dharma—rules of proper conduct—which had been around since the days of *Vedas*, and gave India a penal system. Unfortunately, that legacy, that penal system, is in tatters."

Mitra liked the education on Indian criminal law she was getting on the phone from Robert, but her mind stayed with Jay Bahadur. She repeated her question. "So why didn't Bahadur get charged with a crime?"

"Indian criminal law tends to favor the accused," Robert replied. "You can get away with murder, and many do. The courts are terribly backlogged—about 50 million cases are pending. It'll take half-a-century to get through these, not counting the ones still being added. Bahadur has some important connections, which probably have saved him. He got off scot-free when he should've been locked up at least as an accomplice."

"How sure are you of his guilt?"

"I saw somewhere that a journalist in Kolkata is putting together the evidence, so the case can be reopened. Although I've never met this journalist, I've sent out an e-mail to him. See what I get as a response."

Mitra shook her head, thanked Robert, and asked him to call her back if he received any new information. Kareena might have tumbled into a dangerous situation, with far more at stake than she'd bargained for.

THIRTY

THREE DAYS LATER, Mitra parked herself at her kitchen table, art paper and colored pencil within easy reach. She envisioned a trellised garden for a picky client who had a narrow plot facing a parking lot. A honeysuckle vine would twine a tall support structure and obstruct the undesirable sight. Wisteria would frame his window densely to create the illusion of fullness and texture. Mitra sketched a fan trellis, a window, the vines, as well as a wall of foliage to soften the scenery.

She went to visit the client and showed him her vision. He liked it. She got the bid, money she badly needed, and started clearing the plot out right away. In the afternoon, she returned to her house, positioned herself in front of the computer screen, and caught up on her e-mails. Odd, there was nothing from Robert asking for her column. She'd neglected to start on the column, having spent all her time on this new client. She could still get it done. Nor had Robert gotten back to her with more news on Jay Bahadur.

She should call him. After some pleasantries, she'd apologize for the delay and ask for a day's extension. Then she'd spring her offer of treating him to a lunch or dinner this week.

Peering through the window, she saw a dreary April sky, with no wind to disperse the leaden grime. It would help to have a hint of sunlight filter through the dense cloud cover. Two men walking down the block in opposite directions passed each other wordlessly, without even a glance, although neighborhood custom would dictate at least a nod of acknowledgment. The weather must have imprisoned both within their solitary selves, although it hadn't done so to Mitra. After working outside much of the day, she was in good spirits.

She approached the telephone. The box emitted its telltale intermittent beep, and the message light blinked red-orange. Two messages were waiting for her, one from Grandmother asking if Mitra would like to come over for dinner this evening. "Haven't seen you much lately," Grandmother had said. "Nothing fancy, but we'll have ourselves a soirée."

Happily, Mitra called her back and left a message accepting the invitation.

She pressed the message button again. It startled her when Robert's voice boomed out. They must be on the same wavelength. The message had come in at ten o'clock.

"Hello, Mitra." Robert cackled. "Today's my birthday, but I'm working at home. Thanks for the lead."

Had she heard him laugh? That was unusual for him. She replayed the message. Yes, it was a hoarse laugh. She punched his number and waited for him to grab the phone. The voice-mail clicked on after several rings and segued to a gruff, "Leave me your name and number."

"Robert, this is Mitra. Happy Birthday! How about having dinner with me tomorrow night?"

She hung up. Within a few minutes, the phone gave a trill. Grabbing the receiver, she made a quick guess as to who it might be and uttered a big-hearted hello.

She was surprised and a touch embarrassed when Mary, Robert's assistant, offered a subdued greeting. "I'm afraid I have bad news." The voice was soft, fading, teary.

Mitra gripped the phone. She had had plenty of bad news lately. How much worse could it get? "What is it?"

"Robert took his life this morning."

Impossible. This didn't make any sense. What did Mary say? "Robert?" Mitra stared blankly. "But why? What happened?"

"He didn't show up for work and didn't call. His next-door neighbor suspected something was wrong when he saw lights on. Robert was careful about turning off lights when he left his apartment. The neighbor's dog had been barking off and on most of the morning. Finally, the man contacted the superintendent who used his master key to get in. They found him in his bathroom. Blood all over. It was ghastly. His depression got him."

Mitra couldn't trust the floor she stood on, nor did she hear the rest. Robert's last recorded remarks still echoed in her ears. "I'm puzzled," she said. "Robert left a message on my phone this morning. He didn't sound depressed at all."

"He also left a message for his sister, although nothing out of the ordinary."

For a few seconds Mitra couldn't speak, as though words didn't exist for her. She only heard the screeching sound of a car outside. Suppose she'd taken Robert out to dinner sooner. Suppose she'd been home this morning to take his call. Could she have made a difference?

"Did he have any family other than his sister?" Mitra eventually asked.

"He was divorced, a loner, loved his job. He'd been depressed ever since he and his wife split four years ago. He had no close relatives nearby. His parents are dead. There is only his sister. She'd asked him to relocate to Los Angeles, thinking the lack of natural light was aggravating his condition. Seattle's such a suicide-prone city. But he wouldn't budge. We all knew he had a problem, but no matter how much we tried, none of us could reach him. He was a private man." Mary paused. "We're planning a memorial service. I'll let you know as soon as the arrangements have been made. I have to call other freelancers now."

It took Mitra half a second to realize Mary had hung up. She sagged and leaned her forehead down to her knees. After a while, she raised her head and stared outside. It was beginning to get dark. The streetlights twinkled. She sent Robert a wish: may his soul meet with peace. She visualized him basking in an aura of white light in a high spot, taking his solitary journey, away from his troubles.

It reminded Mitra that life was fleeting, that she must act upon the present moment, and that there might not be a moment to act upon tomorrow, if she waited. Kareena stole into her mind. In a flowing *salwar* suit and T-strap shoes, she walked along a noisy Kolkata boulevard. Despite the wave of faces around her, she saw no one she recognized. Mitra imagined Kareena longing to pour out the history of this past month, the fear and pain bursting through her. Mitra felt even more compelled to reach her.

She'd do it. She'd fly to Kolkata. She'd stay as long as necessary to make contact with Kareena and warn her of the prickly path ahead. Even if Mitra's finances didn't justify the trip, she would take it.

Breathing deeply, she contemplated her arrival. Kolkata—noise and dust, twisty alleys, impossible traffic, and still with scenic beauty and friendliness. Would Kareena gasp in amazement when she saw Mitra in the midst of such chaos and beauty? Would she want to empty out the contents of her heart and say, "Let's go sit and catch up?" With warmth and only the tiniest touch of chiding, Mitra would convey her concerns: *How could you leave your best friend imagining the worst for so many weeks? Don't ever go missing on me again.*

She phoned Detective Yoshihama to commiserate.

His voice heavy, he answered. "All the 'should haves' I've been thinking about the last few hours. I should have stayed more in touch with Robert."

"I'm still wondering about the message Robert left me this morning. Something about the lead I gave him." A sense of fear set in Mitra's body. It felt as though her heart had been drained of vital fluids. "What if he hadn't committed suicide? God, what if someone tried to shut him up for good, made it seem like a suicide? He was a former crime reporter, after all."

"There'll be an investigation. We're waiting for the coroner's report." He paused. "Would you like to have coffee with me early next week? We can talk about it."

"Sorry, I can't." She filled him in about her plan to take a trip to Kolkata. "Robert's death has done it for me. I don't want to lose another friend."

For a nanosecond the detective stayed silent. "At least you're doing something positive." He wished her a bon voyage, adding, "Record any conversation with Ms. Sinha, will you?"

Mitra got off the phone. Belatedly, remembering Grandmother's invitation, she picked up her car keys. Within fifteen minutes, she arrived at Grandmother's house. Grandmother opened the door and said brightly, "Hello, dear. Come in."

Grandmother's composed, beatific expression calmed Mitra, at least temporarily. She mumbled a greeting, as she stepped in and followed Grandmother to the living room. They sat on either end of a suede sectional couch. Mitra's gaze fell on a shadowy corner where a baby spider plant rested.

"Are you all right?" Grandmother asked.

Grief gnawed at Mitra's stomach as she brought Grandmother up to speed on the news of Robert's suicide.

"I'm so sorry, Mitra."

Mitra reminisced about Robert, all the ups-and-downs she'd experienced with him in the early days, and how they were getting closer. She finished by saying, "How do you know when to take better care of your friends and when to leave them alone?"

"Well, your friends do what they want to do." The nasal quality in Grandmother's voice was more pronounced, a sure sign she was drifting into a melancholy mood. "It's their life, after all. We're just bystanders."

"My work's cut out for me. I can't be a by-stander anymore. I must fly to Kolkata."

Grandmother leaned across. "Kolkata? But why?"

"Robert's friends, including myself, didn't reach him," Mitra said. "I want to reach Kareena before it's too late."

Grandmother fell back on the couch. "Doesn't she have relatives in Kolkata?"

"No, she has no family there."

"What about that actor you were telling me about?"

"I get conflicting stories on him. I won't tell Kareena how to run her life or anything like that. I want to be there in case she needs someone to confide in. Who better than me? And, to tell you the truth, there could still be a chance of foul play. Not everything is making sense. Maybe her actor-lover kidnapped her. Maybe it's the Stockholm syndrome—she's joined her kidnapper. I don't want to see her being victimized."

Without hesitating even for a fraction of a second Grandmother said, "Let me buy your ticket."

"Oh, no, I can't let you do that."

"Listen, you've spent many more hours in my garden than you've billed me for. Don't think I haven't noticed it. And you've told me yourself that lately you've taken on far fewer clients than you did in the past. Let me do this for you."

She kept insisting. Mitra finally agreed.

"I'll be happy to mow your lawn," Grandmother said. "I'll get your mail, water your plants, whatever else you might need done around the house."

Mitra promised to write down instructions on how to take care of her plant babies and explain them to Grandmother before leaving for Kolkata.

Grandmother put an extra color in her voice as she said, "Let's have dinner."

They both retreated to the dining room. On the table, Grandmother spread white carryout cartons with red dragon images and spilling with soba noodles. A mélange of smells and rich appetizing colors surrounded Mitra. She felt hunger pangs. Grandmother arranged tiny plastic take-out cups of sauces—soy, chili, vinegar, and rice wine—well aware that Mitra liked to season her meal in her own particular way. They progressed through the layers of scallions, carrots, celery, and noodles, talking about this and that. At times, Mitra went silent, grief overtaking her. Soon their plates were bare. They lingered in the companionable stillness.

As Mitra helped collect the dishes, she peered into grandmother's garden now deep into the shadows beyond the circle of light cast by the floodlight above the deck.

The evening had set in. There was no color anywhere.

Returning home, Mitra had barely stepped on the porch when her gaze fell on the bunch of wisteria that sprayed out of a vase placed near the door. Oh, Ulrich had stopped by. How terrible; she'd missed him. He'd left a sweet note on a post-it stuck to the door, saying, "Mit, my darling, call me when you can."

Glancing at the white purity of the flowers and placing the vase on the coffee table in the living room, Mitra forgave him for his mini-absence. She called, but no one picked up the phone. She recorded a message on his voice-mail about Robert's suicide and her sudden decision to travel to India. "Come over soon. I want to see you before I leave. And thanks for the flowers."

Surely, he would return her call, probe further about her trip, challenge her impulsiveness, and try to slow her down. He called her "Hurry Meister."

Tonight she could use cheer, slowness, and the warm cocoon of his arms.

THIRTY-ONE

OUTSIDE MITRA'S WINDOW, the sky resembled an unlit charcoal oven. The drizzle continued. "Gray as Granny's picture album," intoned the weatherman on the television news hour. "And it's getting just as old," he added, referring to the long stretch of overcast weather, dismal enough to dampen even the sunniest mood. Around here, Mitra reminded herself, the weather-induced malady wasn't called by its full name, Seasonal Affective Disorder. Rather, it was appropriately called SAD.

The India trip was coming up in a matter of days. The message Mitra had left on Ulrich's voice mail about the trip had gone unanswered. She wouldn't press him, however. Since Robert's death, she'd decided to go easy on her loved ones.

It was late enough for her to give dinner some thought, though she didn't relish the prospect of preparing a meal. She peeked inside the refrigerator only to find a useless assortment of ingredients: stale potato bread, a jar of stinky old garlic pickle, and a bottle of celery juice.

Through the sound of rain on the roof, she heard the doorbell screeching. Ulrich stood at the door, one eye swollen, with a blue-black smudge under it.

It was as though someone had squeezed all the comfort out of Mitra. "Uli, what happened?"

Unshaven and uncombed, his face damp from the drizzle and scruffy in a worn crew-neck pullover, he stood in silence. He looked nothing like the man she'd gotten close to, and that knowledge came like a blow. He bent and touched his lips to hers. The taste—a musky sweetness—was pure Ulrich.

She pulled him inside, wrapped her arms around his neck, leaned her head against his chest, smelling the drenched alpaca of his sweater and listening to the discontent beating of his heart. Noticing scrapes on his knuckles—swollen purple mounds—she winced.

She stepped back and appraised his face more carefully. "What happened to your eye?"

"I had a disagreement with a colleague."

Didn't Nobuo say something about Ulrich being arrested? Was this incident something similar? Her gaze fell on a tear at the neck of his sweater. He seemed self-absorbed, not noticing her reactions. They walked through the entryway into the living room where he claimed his favorite end of the couch and she took the other end.

Staring at his face, she asked, "A disagreement? Is that how you got that injury?"

"*Ja*. One thing led to another, and we got into a fight." The injured eye threw off the symmetry of his features. "It's okay between us now. I'm stronger than that bastard, even though he's bigger. I did more damage."

She shivered. "How badly did he get hurt?"

"He'll be okay."

"Did the police—?"

"Don't mention the police to me. I despise them."

Perhaps noting the freaked-out expression on her face, he made an effort to smile through his dry cracked lips. "All that's over now, Mit. I understand that you don't care for fights, but sometimes a man has to defend himself."

Something in his tone of voice made her cringe. She might as well be direct with him. "Where have you been the last several days?"

"Do you know that house up in Ballard?" he asked and she nodded. He'd boasted about the "redemption" of the 1905 single-family dwelling with which he'd been entrusted, Mitra recalled. "I took it apart, with the help of a few other workers, and put it back together. You should see it. We're almost finished. The windows, siding, floors, and plumbing have all been redone. We're painting now. This past week has been extremely busy. I'll have to show you one of these days what I did."

She nodded her assent, her watchful gaze on him. There must be more to his story and she'd somehow get to it.

Silence darkened between them until he finally said, "I got your message. What is this thing about you going to India?"

She related to him her findings in Kareena's house and all that had transpired since.

"Your friend abandoned her husband and took off? She had a lover, you said? You've found some stories about him on the Net? " He laughed, if such a contemptuous sound could be classified as a laugh. "She didn't even tell you where she was going. Don't put a guilt-trip on yourself and try to find her."

Mitra had already chewed that matter to pieces. Still, his attitude slashed through her. "I want to make sure she's safe. I'm not sure if Adi ever physically abused her, but that actor—"

"If she's the kind of woman who abandons her mate, she's asking for it. Any husband or lover would be tempted to hit her."

Hit her? Mitra choked on those two words and was able only to say, "What?"

He caught himself and drew in a pleasant expression. "Oh, no, I'd never hit a woman." He shifted forward and slipped her a tiny kiss, but she didn't feel the usual swoon. "Who would help you in Kolkata?"

"I can count on a few people over there, like my mother." Actually, she wasn't sure about her mother, who might be ill.

He touched his black eye, as though it hurt.

"Have you been in fights before?" she asked.

He took a long pause. Looking away from her, he mumbled, "I haven't told you everything."

The crack in his voice disturbed her. "I need to hear it all."

"You remember my friend Klaus I told you about?"

She examined Ulrich's face, focusing her gaze on his good eye. "Oh yes, the bully, all the way through school, wasn't he? Later, you became friends."

"There's no such person. I'm Klaus. Everything I told you about Klaus happened to me. I changed my name when I came here."

Mitra looked down and smoothed the sleeve of her ribbed knit top. She'd been guarding her own secret involving a half-sister, but that seemed trivial compared to this. How much else about this man was a lie? Might he been hiding instances of emotional disorder? What had landed him in jail, if only briefly?

"I didn't want to use the name my parents gave me," he said. "Let me go back to the beginning. My father was a government official in Germany. We lived almost too well for the salary he made. Even as a child I picked up on that. I wondered how we could afford a fancy BMW, Rosenthal china, wine receptions for large groups. And still my parents acted angry, crazy, depressed. You know about the collective German guilt about the Second World War, don't you?"

She nodded uncomfortably.

"They took pleasure trips to Milan and Paris to forget their unhappiness. They'd leave me alone in the big house with a servant, like I didn't matter to them. My head would pound. I'd cry until my voice was choked." He paused. "It came out a year later that the money for our extravagant life came from embezzled public funds. Father was found guilty and sent to prison. We lost our house, our social position, my childhood."

"How old were you then?"

"Seven. Even a seven-year-old knows when something terrible is happening. After my father went to prison, my mother was devastated. Her tongue got sharper. She called my father names— when she was talking to me. I began to think that since I was his son, I must be damaged, too. The *ehrfurcht*—honor and fear—I felt for them, especially the honor part, went away. I got in trouble in school, bringing shame on my family. I wanted to study medicine, but my grades weren't good enough, and that was yet more shame."

"You managed an elevator business in Germany, didn't you?" she asked, nurturing hope that he hadn't lied about that, too.

"*Ja*, but I lost that job when I punched a salesman in the mouth. The *dummkopf* didn't follow orders." He described the scene: two angry bodies bump into each other, punching and clawing, blood and sweat mixing, crashing into furniture. Eventually one prevails and the other one lies on the ground moaning.

Why did he have to describe the scene in so much detail? With an edge of frustration in her voice, "Did you try therapy?"

He swiped a hand over his blond curls. "You name the therapy, I tried it. Finally, my counselor suggested working with plants. He found me the position of a field hand with a commercial farmer in Holland. I moved there to plant bulbs."

"You planted bulbs?"

A wistful quality edged into his voice. "*Ja*, I was a tulip apprentice." In recounting the episode, he described a place where the sky was smoky gray and hazy, where daylight had a thin watery consistency, and the wind punished. He turned the heavy soil, smelled the fresh earth, tuned in to nature's rhythm and became still, like a poet with the beginning of a couplet. The owner, a farmer lady, had a sweet freckled face peeking out from under a head scarf. Her hands were large and sturdy. Shortly after planting the last bulb, he left Holland. He wasn't making enough money. He promised to the farmer lady he'd be back for the next planting season. In his dreams, he revisited the field where silky blossoms in red, yellow, and purple flirted with the spring breeze.

His fingers drifted across Mitra's hand in a cool touch as he continued. "The first time I met you, I noticed your hands—rough, dry, working hands. Immediately, I thought of that farmer lady. I remembered standing in that field, earth on my boots.

"That evening, you talked about your small business and your plants. I could see how lovely and unspoiled you were. These days, everything is rotten inside and covered up to look good. Just being around you these last few weeks, Mit, has made a huge difference in my disposition." He gazed brightly at her. "You said your tulips had died. Perhaps we'll plant new bulbs together this fall?"

Digging in the rich earth and basking in the company of greenery might soothe Ulrich's grief about his past and his family troubles. Wistfully, she nodded and pictured their planting session. This was how it'd go: trowel in hand, he'd move about her yard, his face and mood brightened by the natural light, dark impulses tempered by the touch of the gentle soil underfoot. She'd open a box of bulbs. But the scene vanished.

"Why did you decide to emigrate to the U.S?" she asked.

"To go back to my studies. To get a silly degree. But being in a classroom makes me want to jump out the window."

"It's okay not to go to college."

"It's *not* okay! Working in construction is not high status work. It makes me angry to think that's only the job I can get."

She saw the despair, the self-pity that surfaced on the wrinkles of his forehead. "Uli, Uli . . ."

"I want to beat my head against my apartment's chintzy wall. And, no matter how hard it gets, you can't admit you're suffering. We Germans bury so much inside."

"You've left that life behind. This is America. Here you can get help. Here you can have a fresh start."

"Every morning, I wake up in Germany. I want to hear the language, see and smell German things. God knows, I miss real German bread. *Schwarzbrot*. And I'd never have believed this, but I miss *ordnung*, everyone knowing their place and what to expect from others."

He sank back onto the couch, like someone exhausted after a brawl. "Sorry, didn't mean to unload so much on you. I'm not—what do you call it—as belligerent as I used to be, as Klaus used to be."

She didn't hear the rain any more. The Ulrich she cared about was so different from Klaus, his *doppelganger*. That man was a completer stranger to her.

"Do your parents know about your new life?" she asked. "Have you tried to reconcile?"

His eyes darkened with hatred. "No. They're pathetic old people, drunk most nights, waiting for a slow death. I'd just as soon they were gone from this planet."

His fingers drifted across her hand in a leisurely touch. She snatched her hand away.

Voice strained, possibly from confessing so much, he asked, "Would you like to go out for dinner? I'm famished."

Her hunger had dwindled, leaving her with deep weariness. "I'd like to take a rain check. There's only three days before my trip—lots to do."

"You're really taking that trip?" His fingers caressed her cheek. "You're insane and adorable."

He didn't get her reasons at all. She sighed in disappointment. "Why, yes, I am taking the trip for Kareena. To make sure she's not in any danger."

His body stiffened. "Do you want to know the fucking truth? That time when I met your friend at Soirée, she flirted with me. She would have gone to bed with me."

Why had he lied to her about that before? Or was this current version a lie? Where in his mind did lighter shades of truth start blundering into an opaque distortion? "Really? Just flirted? That's all you did?"

"Lots of women find me attractive."

She sat quietly, uneasily for a second. She needed to see if he could tell the truth about anything. "Have you ever been arrested by the police? Have you ever been in jail?"

"What's that got to do with anything? You ask strange questions." He paused, as though to make light of her queries. "No, I haven't. Don't mention the police to me." A thick silence swallowed them until he stared at her lips and said, "Are you sure you don't want to go out to dinner?"

She shook her head. She was so sure that it tormented her. Making a move to rise, she said, "I better start packing."

"You're going to leave me and go to India?"

"I'll be back as soon as I can."

He straightened, thumped his feet on the carpet, and started toward the door. "You don't love me."

He sounded childish, selfish, suffering from separation anxiety, like Klaus. "Uli, Uli."

He rushed through the door, slamming it after him. She ran after him, but to no avail. Standing on the porch, she watched the streetlight reflect yellow on his blue pullover. He hopped into his Saab. The car roared, accelerated away from the curb, and disappeared into the bleakness of the night.

Muted sounds drifted from the neighboring houses: a baby howling; another car speeding, a dog whining. She felt her heart dividing at the thought of Ulrich's rage, his time in jail for reasons unknown.

After shutting the door, she reflected on his insinuation about Kareena's flirtation. How far had it really gone, if at all?

Then there was the fact that he was Klaus. *His emotions ran every which way,* as he'd once said. *He couldn't control them.* She shivered again. No one seemed to be who she believed they were.

THIRTY-TWO

AFTER SPENDING MOSTLY a sleepless night replaying Ulrich's visit, Mitra felt a pang of fear as she rolled out of bed. A warm familiar face had become an illusion. A lover had morphed into a stranger with aggressive tendencies. Ulrich didn't at all understand the reasons for her trip. And he'd confirmed that neither he nor Kareena were the people Mitra thought they were.

Outside, the day emerged from its dark shroud. Mitra worked on her travel shopping list for a few minutes. What gifts should she buy for Mother? She picked up the phone and punched Mother's number. How much she wanted to hear her soothing voice.

"Ma, I am coming home on Monday."

"You're coming home?" Mother exclaimed, a spark of joy in her voice. "Oh, my precious. I can't wait to see you."

"Apparently, Kareena is in Kolkata. I'll look for her."

"My, that's a surprise. I hope the weather doesn't slow your search. No one has seen such a scorching spring. The gods are not kind to us. I drink fifteen glasses of water a day and still I'm thirsty. It's impossible to get around in Kolkata in the best of times, and now we have days like a furnace in hell."

"After the cool spring we've had here, I'd appreciate hot weather," Mitra said. "I'm going shopping shortly. What can I bring you besides novels?"

"Nothing, nothing. I have all I'll ever need. You just get yourself over here safely."

Mitra kept pressing until Mother said, "A box of truffles—I want to give them to the children in my building. Nowadays, they go for chocolate more than sandesh and rosgulla." She paused. "My neighbor's ten-year-old boy snaps fabulous photos with his camera. I have never looked through a camera lens."

"I'll bring you a digital point-and-shoot camera."

Mother laughed, her laugh edged with a wistful note. "I'll ask Naresh to pick you up."

"Naresh?"

"You'll enjoy meeting him, my neighbor who lives on the top floor of my building. He's like a son to me. Isn't Naresh a nice name? Naresh is young, unmarried, and looks a little like Jawaharlal Nehru, half Kashmiri and half Bengali. He has no vice other than eating out too often."

Mother was already trying to fix her up with a prospective husband, and Mitra would try to get her to back off for now. "There's no need for Naresh to meet me at the airport. I have an early arrival—I'll just take a taxi." She paused. "I have a boyfriend here, Ma."

Mother's tone became alight with interest. "A new boyfriend? Is he Indian? Is he coming with you? Are you two serious?"

The details of last night were still too fresh in Mitra's mind. Her voice faltered, as she said, "No, he isn't coming with me. He's German. We're just dating."

"You don't hear the *shehni*?" Wedding music.

"Neither wedding bells nor *shehni* tunes—I've been preoccupied lately."

"Well, I'll call Preet and let her know you're coming. She's pregnant again, with her second child." This was Mother's way of pointing out what Preet, a high school friend, had achieved and she hadn't. Once again, Mother had erased her daughter's accomplishments from the chalkboard of life with a sweep of her hand.

"Preet—yes, I'd very much like to see her."

"It's about time you got reacquainted with your birthplace and your old friend." Mother sniffled.

Mitra got the impression Mother wasn't feeling well. Still, when they bid goodbye to each other, Mother sounded more cheerful than in their recent conversations. A rush of excitement ran through Mitra, as she got busy updating her shopping list. The list overflowed with trifles that Mother, a charitable soul, might want to give to her neighbors: fountain pens, games and puzzles, photo frames, and candles. What about Preet, a high school friend Mitra hadn't seen in ages? She, a young mother focused on the needs of her son and unmindful of her own, might appreciate a few luxuries—

perfumed soap, stationery, and a home facial kit. And Mitra mustn't forget picture books for her son.

Remembering Detective Yoshihama's suggestion, Mitra added a digital voice recorder to her list. It excited her to think she'd hear Kareena's voice again.

A question seized her mind: without an address or phone number, how would she find Kareena in Kolkata?

There was one person who might be able to supply her with that information, a person she must visit, even if she still suspected him of wrongdoing.

THIRTY-THREE

UNDER FAST-FADING DAYLIGHT, Mitra parked her Honda in front of Adi's house. Dropping in unaccompanied on him wasn't without its perils and she dreaded the prospect. However, she'd have to take this risk to solve several puzzles before she flew to Kolkata two days from now.

If she'd consulted with Veen before this visit with Adi, she would have growled. "No, Mitra, don't go to him, you'll get nothing but grief," and would have tried to talk her out of it.

Had Adi, by now, noticed her cardigan on the floor of his garage? If so, what had he done with it? Or to her good fortune, did he still walk around his house as oblivious as he was before Kareena's estrangement?

Adi was apparently at home. Lights in the living room shed a pale aura on the white curtains on the bay window. Mitra surveyed the front yard. The greenery looked withered, as though Kareena's absence had disrupted the spontaneity of nature.

Stepping into the entry porch, Mitra pushed the doorbell. The cold evening air hit her face and momentarily hampered her breathing. The door opened with a jerk. She jumped back involuntarily.

Adi's eyes flashed both surprise and annoyance. Their gazes locked just below a hanging petunia basket. For an instant, neither of them could summon a greeting. Her eyes ran over his lightweight black t-shirt. Just below the glaring company logo of his software company, Guha Software Services, a slogan screamed: *Save Your Business Soul.*

"What are you doing here, Mitra?" Adi said in a nasal voice. He coughed deep in his lungs, his face flushing like an autumn maple leaf.

"Just happened to be in neighborhood. Looks like you have a cold."

"A touch of bronchitis," he said. "Got it playing golf. Can't seem to get rid of it. I'm resting, cooped up here."

"I'll be happy to make you a pot of tea. That might help break up the cough."

Adi's face softened. "Come in."

Stepping aside, he opened the door a little wider and she walked in. Precious little had changed in the passageway or the kitchen since she had been here. The mail basket still overflowed. An old note in Kareena's handwriting was affixed to the memo board tacked to a wall. The smell of furniture polish lingered in the air, indicating the cleaning lady still did her job.

The thermostat ought to have been cranked up, but everyone knew that Adi was impractical about daily living, even if he had fallen ill.

"I'll make the tea," Mitra said.

"Let's wait a while." Adi gestured toward the living room. On the coffee table sat an open laptop, a wine goblet, a remote control, and a Kindle. Mitra crossed to a plump club chair, the one close to the door. Adi offered her first a glass of Chateau Ausone and then orange juice, both of which she refused.

He slumped down on the sofa, reached for his glass, and leaned toward her. "So what are you doing in my neighborhood?"

"I'm off to Kolkata to visit my mother and thought I'd stop by before I leave."

Adi's face turned ashen. He stayed silent.

Most of Mitra's Indian acquaintances would have jumped in with: *Could you carry a gift for my auntie? Otherwise, I'll have to pack the darn thing, fill out a customs slip at the post office, wait in line, and hope it arrives in one piece. My auntie will surely ask you to stay for dinner.* Adi did not.

His face, so introspective, so lacking in his typical predatory alertness, struck Mitra as odd. Bereft of his throne, his script, and his restless gaze, he seemed half the usual Adi.

Slumped in his chair, seemingly weak and broken, he asked, "Did the detective tell you she's in Kolkata?"

The best defense, Mitra figured, was to be bold. "That's not the main issue. I think we both have a vested interest in Kareena's welfare."

"Look here—my throat hurts if I talk too long." The strong downturn in his sentence indicated he was starting to bridle again at her interference. After a pause, he added, "Mademoiselle Basu, Kareena happens to be my wife. Our marriage is a private matter."

"Did she leave you? I can't imagine how devastating it must be for a DV counselor to be married to an abusive man."

Adi stared hard. "Okay, you've said your piece. If you want to know the truth, here's how it actually went. A wife becomes bored with her loving, faithful, hard-working husband and decides she needs a little thrill. She starts flirting with men. She starts coming home late. The husband finds out, asks her to stop."

"And he 'straightens her out?'"

"Things are seldom quite that simple." Adi's voice thickened. "Suppose the husband tells the wife he loves her, he'd do anything for her, and it is for her sake he gave up his family. They'd tried their best to stop him from marrying her."

Mitra inspected Adi's face. His eyes were soft with anguish. He wasn't lying.

"She keeps defending her right to see whom she pleases," he continued. "She's been faithful to him a long time, but not any longer. She calls him dull. Her extravagant taste is the only reason she's stayed with him. Finally, the husband can't take it any longer."

Mitra could still picture Kareena's bruised forearm. "Yeah, right. It's the woman's fault. She pushed his buttons. How do abusers get away with such rationalizations?"

"Let me tell you the rest. He leaves town for a week. The wife goes to visit her lover during that weekend, comes back with bruises on her arm. Apparently, he has a temper. She defends him. She says things happen in a moment of frustration."

"You're trying to tell me that those bruises were someone else's doing?"

"Yes. Do you think she would have taken any beatings from me? She'd have called the police and they'd have picked me up."

It struck Mitra, the irony: Adi would rather be portrayed mistakenly as an abuser by Mitra and possibly other community members than someone left behind. With a pained expression, he turned to the empty wine goblet poised in his fingers. His fixation spoke of loneliness, desolation, and lost time.

Mitra found herself swollen with doubts. Kareena had never shared her contempt of her husband with her. If what Adi said was true, that is.

Adi began coughing, the sound ragged. He flung himself up and lurched toward the kitchen. She glanced at the window as a wave of light from a passing car broke against the glass, reminding her she needed to get out of here soon.

An incident from the past floated back to Mitra: the occasion of her twenty-eighth birthday. She and Kareena had driven to Spice Route, a popular Indian hangout. Adi was waiting just outside the restaurant entrance on that chilly evening, cradling a pair of purple-and-white orchid bouquets. Smiling gently, he presented a bouquet to each of them and wished Mitra many happy returns. With delight and gratitude, she accepted the exquisite flowers, but noticed Kareena frowning over hers.

"Orchids make me sneeze," she said.

On that day Mitra had noticed Kareena's petulance, her lack of appreciation for her husband's sweet gesture.

Sitting in Adi's living room, Mitra fleetingly saw that both the parties were at fault.

Adi reentered the room, tissue in hand, and dropped back into the sofa, harder than necessary.

"I still need to go to Kolkata and see if I can find her," Mitra said. "From what I hear, Kolkata has changed a lot. I wouldn't know where to start. If I'm going to have any chance of tracking her down—"

Adi rearranged his feet. "Go to the Gariahat shopping area. She probably hangs out there. Try some private restaurants. She goes to exclusive places—I don't know any names. I trust you'll keep all this to yourself? This is for her security."

Gariahat—at first Mitra had a hard time believing Kareena would spend time in such a congested section of Kolkata. Then again, the area boasted shopping bargains. Kareena took special delight in finding them. Mitra now had a location to scout.

The mention of the word security, however, had alerted her and reminded her of another issue. "Have you paid the rest of the ransom?"

Adi wrung his hands, avoiding her gaze, and she wondered if he wasn't purposely holding back. After a moment he said, "Do you know what my biggest regret is? I was too driven, didn't spend enough time with her, didn't show her my love often enough. She wanted a kid. I said no. I wasn't ready. She asked again. I still said no. Now I'd like to have children, I very much would. You know what I mean? I did it all wrong."

Poor Adi—he was stuck. He'd tried to buy Kareena during their marriage, and now he was still trying to buy her back. And for all his faults, he had standing in the community. If all this ever got out, it would drop a truckload of shame on him.

Mitra's heart wavered—was Adi the victim of Kareena's betrayal, or had he driven her away? She was no longer sure.

"I wish you and I had gotten along better," she said, "talked more, shared more."

"I called my family yesterday," Adi said. "Finally, after a decade, everyone spoke with me. My mother asked me to come visit her in Mumbai. My kid sister, Malti, wants me to meet her new husband. I never told you about her, did I?"

Mitra shook her head.

"She's eight years younger," Adi said in a hurt voice. "We used to quarrel a lot and, of course, being older, I always won. When we talked yesterday, she said exactly what you just said. I wish we'd gotten along better. I wish we'd talked more."

A queasy guilty feeling gnawed at Mitra. Perhaps she'd judged Adi too harshly, without realizing he was going through so much stress. "What will you do now?"

"I'll be a nomad, a desk-less person for a while. Then I'll outsource myself somewhere. It's time for me to move on. I'll have to put all this behind me and turn over a new leaf. Is that a good aphorism for a gardener?"

Mitra smiled a yes. Now that he'd opened up, he might appreciate the irony of the secret she'd suppressed from him: Kareena was her half-sister. She and Adi were related, after all.

Was now the golden moment? In Adi's face, she read pain, confusion, and resignation.

Some things, like fallen leaves, were best burned in a fragrant fire.

She drew herself up from her chair.

Adi glanced at her and held his lips tight, as though stifling a thought. "Wait just a sec."

He returned and handed her a shopping bag, with a flourish. "I think you left this here."

A row of pewter buttons protruded from a camel-colored cardigan. Mitra felt a flush on her cheeks. However fond she was of this sweater, she would never wear it again.

"Thank you," she mumbled and started toward the door, turning and apologizing for any possible inconvenience and expressing wishes for his speedy recovery.

He followed her, maintaining a respectable distance. As she reached her car, she heard the torment of Adi's coughing. She turned and took one last look over her shoulder. Although he should really be inside, there he was, leaning over the railing, his shirt billowing in the cool evening breeze, the front door wide open.

"Mitra!" he called out to her, with the tiniest glimmer of hope in his voice.

Clutching the car key, she took a few steps closer to the balcony, and looked up at him.

"If by some stroke of luck you do find her, will you tell her . . .?" His voice caught and he turned.

She could finish the rest of the sentences for him: *I still love her. I always will. I'll be waiting.*

She stood solemnly, realizing what it must have taken for him to admit to his feelings, given the fact that Kareena had strayed.

She heard the door slam. A yellow streetlight illuminated the block ahead. She waited a moment, got in her car, then turned the key in the ignition.

THIRTY-FOUR

LAST NIGHT, tossing and turning in bed, Mitra had again craved Ulrich's touch, even though it had been three days since she'd seen him. And the moment she woke this morning, her travel day, he floated to her mind.

She'd taken a shower and scrambled into a blue skirt and a matching travel blazer when Mary phoned from the newspaper. As they exchanged greetings in a somber voice, Robert's unseen, substantial presence seemed to hover over them.

"You can take a little more time with your next column," Mary said. "We're doing a whole page story on Robert in this Thursday's issue." She gave Mitra the exact date when she needed to e-mail the column.

Mitra could hardly believe it. They still wanted her as a columnist? "Well, I'm off on a trip, but taking my laptop with me. I'll meet the deadline."

"You should know Robert thought highly of you. Recently, he'd put in a few good words about you to the management. They'd like to make you a permanent columnist. Keep this to yourself for a few days. You'll get an official call and a letter."

Mitra should have been dancing. But there was heaviness in her stomach, and grief hardening behind her eyelids. She still had a hard time believing that Robert wasn't around. He'd puzzled her, but she had a deep regard for him. He'd left her with this gift, one she cherished. And it was because of him, she was flying to India.

Just as she finished the call, her phone rang again. "You won't believe this, Mitra." Veen said, "Adi's missing. I'm spooked. He hasn't shown up at his office for two days, hasn't called his assistant, either. Do you have any ideas?"

It took Mitra several moments to process the news. "No, I saw him just a couple of nights ago. We had the best talk we've ever had. He seemed sad, but other than that, he seemed okay. Could he have gone to his beach house?"

"He never goes there during the week."

Mitra glanced out the window at her driveway and glimpsed Grandmother alighting from her car. She'd arrived on time to give Mitra a lift to the airport. "I'm sorry, but I can't talk any longer," Mitra said to Veen. "I have a flight to catch. Let's stay in touch. Be sure to call me at my mother's in Kolkata if you hear any more about Adi."

Minutes later, Mitra and Grandmother cruised down Interstate 5. Finally this trip was becoming real to Mitra, as real as the snowy peak of Mt. Rainier etching its presence on the horizon. But she felt no joy. She reflected on Adi, a new-found sympathy in her heart for him, and a gloom settled inside her. What could possibly have happened to him? For sure, he'd looked depressed on her last visit, but she hoped he wasn't suicidal like Robert.

With the traffic slowing, Grandmother said, "Oh, I should tell you. Nobuo Yoshihama dropped by yesterday to see my garden on your suggestion. He liked the 'hot' color scheme. He said he was seeing your *mind* at work. We had tea. You have to get to know him a little bit to see what an interesting young man he is. And steady, too. We talked for over an hour. He asked about you."

Nobuo Yoshihama, the cop with soft eyes. Mitra turned the name over in her mind. A plane buzzed overhead. Up the hill, she could see the airport gates. Soon she would be flying away from here, away from her troubles. She needed a break. God, she needed a break.

THIRTY-FIVE

MITRA'S PLANE TOUCHED DOWN at Kolkata's NSC Bose Airport. It was early morning. She found the joy of returning to the landscape of her youth tempered by fatigue and dehydration from long hours of air travel, as well as her fears for Kareena's safety. Once finished with customs, she walked outside, stepping as though into a sauna bath. Crows flitted about in the lingering fog as the sky freed itself from darkness. Feeling it was going to be a scorcher, she peeled off her single-breasted blazer.

A friendly-looking cab driver, no more than twenty years of age, clean shaven and wearing well pressed clothes, flashed a smile at her. "Taxi, Madam?"

She nodded and climbed into the passenger seat of a yellow-and-black taxicab and recited her mother's address. The taxi cruised along a main boulevard. She noticed the dusty roads, flowering Bengali script on the doors of businesses, a sprawling banyan tree that stood as strong as a house. This early—it was only 7 A.M.—the roads belonged to the sweepers, day laborers, delivery men, and lost souls.

A cacophony of cars honked one after another, then in unison, and the noise jolted her off the seat. Turning her head, she saw a mini-temple on the sidewalk. A young girl with clasped hands offered her silent prayer to a statue of God Shiva. Many a parent here followed the time-honored custom of instilling a wish in their daughters' heads: deliver me a husband like God Shiva. Without realizing it, Mitra had brought her hands together.

They passed by a crane-less construction site, with two women swaying beneath baskets of bricks on their heads. That reminded her of Ulrich, he of the strong hands and muscular physique, a construction worker. She remembered his eyes, which were pale or intense green depending on his state of mind, his high cheekbones, and a disturbed forehead. A flutter of uncertainty and pain rose inside her. At the same time, she couldn't help but dwell on the fact that the sight of women doing such demanding physical labor would have brought a chuckle to Ulrich's lips.

New buildings dazzled Mitra at every turn. Where had that boxy computer university come from? And the jungle-like park with the floral arch entrance? What had happened to the makeshift sidewalk stalls? On a second look, she discovered that they'd been replaced by a multi-storied shopping complex. A billboard on the front promised prosperity: Buy more. You'll go to heaven. There you'll meet five friends.

Mitra sighed deeply. She'd be at a loss how best to proceed in a town no longer her own. The mythical sanctuary she called home, one she'd believed would withstand time, had disappeared.

The taxi driver veered off the main artery and negotiated a maze of twisty, unfamiliar streets. Startled, she asked, "Where are you going?"

"Please, *barodidi*, leave the driving to me." The driver addressed her as an older sister, as was customary. His hair was rich ebony; so were his eyebrows. He wore a flimsy white short-sleeved shirt, an indication of how high the day's temperature would rise. His arms, exceptionally long and thin, were sturdy on the wheel.

"I'm the best cabbie in town," he announced. "I can sense from kilometers away where the traffic is piling up. I know the city, as well as you know your mother's face. Truly, they call me 'Driver Maharaja.'" The driver king.

Should she believe him? This trip was taking longer than expected. Mother must be pacing between her drawing room window and the front door, listening to every footstep, her anxiety level gone to condition "yellow." Then Mitra caught sight of a prominent sign on the back of a lorry, "Drive and let drive," and chuckled.

"We call this 'Lorry Literature,'" the cabbie said.

They emerged onto a lightly traveled section of the main thoroughfare, bypassing what must have been a congested area. So far, he'd made the right navigational decisions.

"To where do you belong?" the cabbie asked.

"Seattle, but I grew up here. I'm here to join a friend." She spied an opportunity to pursue the age-old system of getting a fix on

anybody in any town: enlist a cab driver's help. And so she decided
to be open with him. Besides, this level of sharing was common here.
"Actually, she's missing. But I expect to run into her."

"She must be eager to see you, too. Always hang on to your friends,
bandhu, because they're God Krishna's best gifts. My grandmother say
that."

"How true," she said, enjoying his cute grammar. "Have you
ever taken fares to the mansion of Jay Prasun Bahadur, the actor?"

"I haven't, but one of my co-cabbies might have." He turned and
gave her an odd look. "You obsess with him?"

"Oh, no, nothing of that sort. My missing friend and Bahadur's
girlfriend might be the same person. Her name is Kareena. She's
attractive, medium height, and wears sunglasses even in the rain."

"Sunglasses?" the driver said. "Who she hide from? Herself?"
He laughed, turned to catch a glimpse of her and, as he noted the
gravity on Mitra's face, his voice became serious. "Sorry, didn't
mean to offend. I try my best. I know how this city work and I have a
mobile phone. Give me a day or so and I find out JPB's current
girlfriend's name."

The taxi glided through an intersection and entered a residential
district. It teased her, the colorful houses, a tangerine one with a blue
door, and a salmon-tinted one with curlicue grill decoration. Driver
Maharaja pulled over to the curb in front of a five-story, pink-
washed, Indian-style apartment complex, Mitra's old home.

Standing on a second-floor balcony strewn with flowerpots, a
woman in a sari shrieked down at a man on the sidewalk. *"Mixing
water with the milk again? Cancel my delivery."*

The milk-man grimaced, mounted his bicycle, and pedaled out
into the road. This much was familiar. Then, gazing across the street,
Mitra looked in vain for the elderly biscuit-wallah's stall. She still
could visualize his *khadi* cotton vest, muslin dhoti, out-of-fashion
Nehru cap, and his aloof demeanor. His motto would be mirrored on
a banner: "Right Belief, Right Knowledge, Right Conduct, and Right
Refreshments." He had been a proud veteran of India's freedom
movement. His stall had been taken over by a clothing store. Mitra
missed his white cap and prattling on about the glories of the past,
and even his stale biscuits.

Her attention shifted when Arnold deposited her luggage at the entrance, with a thump. "My name is Ashish," he said, "but friends call me Arnold. Guess why? I'm ambitious like, you know, the other Arnold. Someday I emigrate to California. But, if not, I at least like to be elected the chief minister of this state. But no scandals though." He pressed a business card in her hand. "Welcome to Arnold's Private Investigation Bureau. Me, your sherpa, can escort you wherever you wish to go, safely and in record time. I dress up in a fancy uniform if you like. Privacy assured. Confidentiality maintained. Satisfaction guaranteed. And smiles plenty."

Any old dented taxicab could transport Mitra from one Kolkata neighborhood to another. Kareena, however, would have enjoyed the company of this flamboyant driver.

Mitra tipped him amply. He smiled big, the kid, as he waved goodbye.

Entering the foyer, she headed for the hallway on the left, which was every bit as dark and humid and as pungent with cooking smells as she remembered it. She knocked at a familiar door. A baby howled inside. Was it the wrong flat? But no, #12 was where her mother resided.

A door opened from the next apartment. "*Esho, esho*," Welcome, welcome. Mother ushered Mitra in #14. Mitra could only smile, overwhelmed as she was by emotions, in seeing her mother after twelve long years. Thin and crushingly tiny, Mother wore a gleaming white sari. Her face still resembled that of an artist's clay figurine, with polished eyebrows stretching out in wide curves, the eyes underneath them at once deep, large, and wide. Her nose was tiny, like an afterthought, and her full lips existed in perfect harmony with the rest of her features. If there were any wrinkles on her forehead, she wore them well, as recognition of her struggles.

Mother gave her a quick tour around the flat. Mitra saw that it had a similar layout to the one in which she'd grown up: bedroom, kitchen, and combined living room and dining area. But this one was newly remodeled and decorated more luxuriously. If anyone were to ask her, she missed the humble old place, one scented with childhood antics.

"You didn't tell me you were moving," Mitra said

Mother examined her fitted black top and denim skirt. "It's been three days. Only yesterday, I invited the priest from the temple to come and do a *grihapravesh*. You remember the worship ceremony for Lord Ganesh to bless the first entry into a new home, don't you? The priest recited *slokas* for an hour to keep the evil spirits away."

"You didn't move for my sake, did you?"

Mother wiped her eyes with the back of a hand. "You're coming home after such a long time. I wanted to make your stay comfortable."

Mitra dropped her luggage in a corner, bent at the waist, and touched Mother's bare feet in the time-old gesture of respect for one's elders. Mother waved her hand over Mitra's head in a blessing, known as *ashirvaad*.

She wouldn't spoil this beautiful moment by speaking about her mission to find her half-sister.

THIRTY-SIX

MID-DAY, Mitra sat at the table. Mother served her yellow dahl, silky rice, and a glistening heap of greens. Just the first few bites of her mother's cooking nourished Mitra emotionally. Mother brought up the topic of Aunt Saroja's death.

"I couldn't attend her funeral," Mother said. "I don't like to fly. But her cousin who lives here arranged a special *sradhya* ceremony so her soul will attain tranquility and I went to that."

Mitra put her fork down. "I still can't believe she's not there."

"Don't stop eating." Mother pushed a side dish of eggplant toward Mitra, confiding that the purple rounds had been painstakingly fried according to a well-guarded formula.

Mitra lifted a slithery blackened sliver and bit into it. Greasy, charred, and oh, so slimy, the repulsive taste took her back to bad days in childhood.

"You're still a finicky eater," Mother said.

The submissiveness of Mitra's youth had vanished. "I no longer take a big lunch, Ma."

"But you should." She reminded Mitra that one's digestive power was at its peak in the middle of the day, an ancient belief she'd grown up with and which had served her well. "Naresh, my upstairs neighbor, works as a supplier to fancy restaurants. He *loves* my eggplant *bhaja* at any time of the day. He can finish a whole platter by himself."

Mitra would have been more than happy to share with Naresh her portion of the eggplant. Then her mother's words snagged on her brain. If Naresh worked as a supplier, he might have connections to fancy eateries patronized by local celebrities. "Any chance of meeting Naresh?"

"I'll ask him to come over." Mother paused. "How's your German boyfriend? Will he be calling you?"

Obviously, Mother has misinterpreted Mitra's reason for wanting to meet Naresh. She took a bite of the eggplant skin and tasted its bitterness. "He might. Or we might e-mail each other."

Mother excused herself to take her medicine. When she returned, Mitra asked, "You've never talked much about your illness, Ma. What did the doctor diagnose?"

Mother began to clear the dishes with steady hands. "Don't make so much fuss over me," she said in a low voice.

"I worry, Ma. I worry about you all the time."

"I'm just fine." Mother's voice crackled with curiosity, as she added, "You said on the phone your missing friend Kareena is supposed to be here. So what prompted your stylish friend to set her golden feet down in our humble city?"

"Her new love interest." Mitra dribbled out a few details about Kareena's supposed entanglements with actor Jay Bahadur, her voice sounding paper-thin to her ears. She could tell from Mother's occasional, contemplative "hmmph" that she was affected by this new development.

"Well, it's going to be a bit of a challenge to search for her among our fourteen million residents." Mother's spectacles slid down her nose. "And her film-star boyfriend will complicate the search. Do you know he lives in a high-fenced mansion guarded by a *darwan* and a Doberman? I doubt you would be able to go within a hundred meters of it. Your friend could have saved you from misery if she had just picked up the phone."

This reality check with Mother, after a twenty-two hour flight, was like descending through a mine, the atmosphere in each level thicker and more suffocating than the one above, discovering precious objects, but with an apprehension of being buried.

Mitra's grim silence didn't inhibit Mother. "And why do you have to carry the whole load of tracing her?"

Outside the window, sunlight radiated through the feathery foliage of a neem tree casting a latticed pattern on the sidewalk. Kareena's betrayal—how that ate away at Mitra. And yet there was a part of her that insisted on reuniting with her sister.

Mother was staring at her. Mitra wished she could reply with an open heart. But then Mother would be outraged. Her tone indignant, she'd rail: *this friend of yours is my beloved husband's child with that whorish actress? You want to welcome her to our family? Have you no consideration for my feelings? And even when you feel betrayed by her?*

Mother gazed into Mitra's eyes, her expression softening as though she sensed her daughter's anguish. "Now it's time for you to take a nap. Use my bedroom. I have the bed specially made up for you."

"A nap? No. I'd like to be out and about."

Mother raised a school-teacher finger. "My silly girl! Don't go out in this heat. Chill! Listen to your mother, will you?"

"Okay, Ma."

Mother's gaze glistened with the satisfaction that her little girl was about to be safely tucked away.

"We'll talk about your friend later," she said. "Meantime, I'll sit with a novel I borrowed from the library."

Stepping into the bedroom, Mitra shut the door and turned on the ceiling fan. A pigeon fluttered outside the window, as if not sure whether to return to its nest on the roof or soar up into the open sky.

A side table held the silver Fuji camera that Mitra had given her mother. On the far side of the bed, there stood a dresser strewn with a comb, a jar of Pond's Cream, and a photo gallery. Mitra drew closer. She hadn't seen these framed pictures of her father exhibited like this before. She'd have to make copies for her album in Seattle.

In a black-and-white shot from his college days, her father appeared as a cultured young man clothed in a light shirt and dark pants, his face luminous. How old had he been then? She did the arithmetic in her head. He was about eighteen. In the next image, accentuated by a wide mahogany-stained frame, and older by more than a decade, he faced the camera as an office clerk in a traditional white *dhoti*. Character had etched itself on his sad lips, hollow cheeks, and deep-thinking eyes.

Staring at the picture, Mitra could now see the resemblance between her father and Kareena, as though a fog had just lifted from the landscape. Look at that fluff of hair above the short forehead and the dome-shaped eyelids. Gazing into the gilded mirror, Mitra saw her thick hair rising from the same forehead, but didn't find similarly shaped eyelids. Scrutinizing the entire photo collection from many angles, she concluded that Kareena resembled their father more than she did. In the last picture, Father, then in his thirties, beamed from beneath a bushy moustache and a broad genial smile. If her head ever whispered any doubts about Kareena's lineage, they'd been vanquished by these photos.

Mitra moved away from the dresser. She couldn't help but go over the first and only conversation with Mother about Dimple Sinha, Father's first wife. Mother would like nothing better than to forget the second-rate actress of yesteryear. Blessedly, Mother didn't know Kareena's last name: Sinha.

Even if Mother stood face-to-face with Kareena and experienced her sunlit personality, she might not be willing to embrace her into their family. That'd take time.

Mitra heard footsteps. Mother might push the door open, peer at the untouched bed, barge in, and catch her not taking a nap.

She crept into the cool low bed, stretched out, and covered herself with the soft, elephant-print spread. The whisper-quiet ceiling fan whirled at full speed. Her stiff back welcomed the horizontal comfort. She lay awake.

THIRTY-SEVEN

AN HOUR LATER, Mitra strolled down Gariahat market where a feeling of festivity prevailed. Stalls lining the sidewalk offered a dizzying assortment of goods. She spotted scarves, contraceptives, leather sandals, candles, and regional newspapers in all thirteen languages. The air brimmed with a brew of gasoline and diesel exhaust, mitigated by the fragrance of jasmine from flower stands. Kareena loved to amble around shops. She'd be amazed by the finds here.

Although dressed in a cap-sleeved gauzy shirt, jeans, and sandals, with her hair pinned back, Mitra found the afternoon heat biting her skin and high humidity sapping her strength. A blond tourist just ahead of her glanced about in bewilderment. He might have been wondering if a gigantic clearance sale was going on. But Mitra knew from experience this was just another afternoon in Gariahat.

The throng moved along the sidewalk at a leisurely pace, too leisurely for Mitra's Westernized temperament. A glimpse of a denim boutique, and she was dazzled by the shades borrowed from the sky in all its many moods. Seated on a stool at the store entrance, a sleepy clerk saw her eying the merchandize and flagged her down.

"Why don't you come inside and have a look, madam?"

"I'm from the States. We have plenty of jeans back there."

"But *we* make your jeans. Our factory mass-produces them on a twenty-four-seven schedule." He flashed a self-satisfied grin and pointed inside. "Why not buy direct and save? I'll offer you a most reasonable price. Would you care to join me for a cup of tea?"

Standing on the sidewalk, Mitra was crafting appropriate words of refusal in her head when a buzzing blue-and-white motor scooter on the road brushed her back from the curb. She stood for one trembling moment, watching the slowing scooter, unnerved by the near miss, and shaken by a vortex of wind. The leather-jacketed man on the driver's seat had a *jhola* on his left shoulder. Behind him was a helmet-less woman, her arms around his waist. Could it be? Seen from behind, it was the same head, shoulders, and back. Could it be? The purple *salwar*-suit would be Kareena's style.

Mitra had found her. Her heart palpitated; her body was electrified. She stood on her toes, raised an arm, and called out, "Kareena!"

The scooter thundered away. Mitra rushed after it in a near-daze, even as it dipped out of sight, only to collide with an elderly man.

"Didn't God give you eyes?" he said in a voice seething with anger. "Are you drunk?"

She offered apologies, then pushed on through the crowd. She looked to the distance to the wave of purple. It vanished, it mocked.

THIRTY-EIGHT

LATER IN THE SAME AFTERNOON, standing by the kitchen counter, Mitra watched Mother as she tossed chanachur on the stove, her spoon sliding across the wok-like *karai* with a rhythmic scraping sound. The air in the kitchen throbbed with the perfume of red chilies. The nut-and-legume mix would complement their afternoon tea perfectly.

Mitra experienced a residue of sorrow on her palate from spotting Kareena earlier today and not being able to get hold of her. But then she remembered another option.

"Ma, is your neighbor Naresh coming over?"

"Tomorrow." Mother looked amused. "Not soon enough? Have you forgotten? You can't be in a hurry in Kolkata. This is now a tech hub, but we still have an eighteen-month year."

Frustrated, Mitra switched the topic. "Did you finish the novel you read last night? How did you like it?"

Mother set bone-china teacups with an orange-flower motif on the table. She opened the refrigerator and got out a platter of fresh pineapple slices. "The first twenty pages were beautifully written. It got boring after that. I know how to spice it up a smidgeon."

"I know you do. All the books you've read, if you lined them up, they'd fill this flat, this entire building, and overflow into the street all the way to Hazra."

Mother tossed the brownish mixture on the stove faster and faster. She inspected her fingertips, examining if spices had discolored her nails. She did this when she needed extra time to ponder.

"I don't just read them," Mother said. "I rewrite them in my mind, play with the plotline. For instance, this situation with your friend—it needs a fresh look, an alternative plotline."

"Are you saying you're going to help me, Ma, with fresh ideas?"

"Yes, I am. I haven't done much for you. I sent you away at a young age. Now I want to be there for you." She took the cast-iron *karai* off the stove, her hands quaking and veins protruding with the weight. "So, do we have a case together?"

Mitra leaned forward and extended a hand toward her. "Yes, Sherlock, we're partners."

Mother cracked a smile, a rare big one, and grasped Mitra's hand. "I already have so many ideas. But I might not tell you everything ahead of time."

She slid a gold-rimmed porcelain teapot to the center of the table. They grabbed two chairs. Mother poured with care, a full cup for Mitra and a half cup for herself. "As a starter, we could catch a Jay Bahadur film this evening."

"You mean something of his is playing?"

"Yes, a film that opened a short while ago. He produced, directed, acted, and wrote it, not all of it well. The film, *She's a Cutie*, has bombed. Even though the title is in English, it's been shot entirely in Hindi. It's showing in one theater only. Would you like to see it?"

Mitra nodded. She clued Mother in about Arnold, her "sherpa" taxi driver. Never mind his high-pressure sales pitch, maybe she should hire him for their evening out.

"The subway would be better. You breathe less polluted air. But I'll let you hire that character." Mother rose. "Oh, I just remembered, I have to call my *dhobi*. Excuse me a moment." She disappeared to the living room, leaving Mitra wondering why she had to call her laundryman.

Mitra picked at the snack mix. Mother returned and slid back into her seat. "The *dhobi* will be here shortly," she said. "He's delivering clothes next door. They all have cellphones now."

"Why did you need to speak with him?"

"He lives near Sonargaon. I saw in a magazine interview that Jay Bahadur was born in that village."

"Where is it located? Is it one of the more prosperous villages?"

"It is north of here, about an hour's train ride. Prosperous? No. They don't have enough plumbing, only a few television sets, no street light, and you can't find pure water. Kids quit school by Class Eight and go to work in the fields."

"How can the *dhobi* help us?"

"Believe it or not, he doesn't just wash clothes," Mother added. "He has other talents. He used to be a gossip reporter for a film magazine. You'll hear the details directly from him. Speak with him and establish a rapport. He'll open up with you, since you're from America. He loves Americans."

Mother excused herself and went to the bedroom. Mitra gathered her sweat-stained travel clothes. Hearing a pounding at the door, Mitra went and asked who it was.

A man hollered, "The *dhobi*, madam."

Mitra pulled the door open and assessed the man standing there, balancing a bundle of wrapped clothing on his head. Neat and restrained in appearance, with shining olive-black eyes and weathered brown face, he was dressed in a short sleeve shirt. He looked to be pushing the half-century mark, yet his eyes were full of mischief. She waved him in.

"Namaskar." He folded his hand at chest level in traditional greeting and smiled through his *paan*-stained ruby teeth. Tattooed on his right arm was the word "Om." His frosty-white shirt contrasted with his walnut complexion and scratched hands. "I understand you want some detective work done."

Mitra stared. In her childhood, the laundrymen, mostly illiterate villagers, quietly hustled from door to door, picking up and delivering bundles of clothing, and that was all they were expected to do. This man spoke perfect English. She could see his keen, laughing eyes peeking out from under his turban.

Motioning toward a couch, Mitra said, "Would you like to have a seat?"

"*Dhobis* don't sit." He smiled again. "That's our job description. But I'll answer your questions."

"What can you tell me about Jay Prasun Bahadur? He comes from your village, doesn't he? I need news."

"*Nischoi, nischoi.*" Sure, sure. "I don't generally ask why someone wants to know about someone else. I'm an equal opportunity provider of news, you might say." He paused. "Bahadur's cousin used to play carom board with my wife's niece. I'll give you more news, but only if you entertain me with an Indian accent."

"Indian accent?" Mitra was taken aback. "What do you expect to hear? Pali? Sanskrit? Urdu?"

"Just joking, ma'am." He looked embarrassed, realizing he had crossed a line. "Give me two days. I'll bring you the lowdown on Mr. Bahadur straight from the lady constable in my village and my relatives."

"You continue to do that type of work on the side?"

"Oh, yes. I might appear dumb, like a tree, but I still have important connections. Those mother-fucking criminals have run me out of my job as a reporter, but I'm still the go-to guy for the cops if they want any intelligence about any celebrity who has relatives in nearby villages."

"I wonder if Jay Bahadur has ever gone against the law."

"Since you ask . . . just the other day, I saw a police newsletter which reported that Bahadur was caught boasting on tape he had connections with the Kolkata crime syndicate. The tape was made by security officials four years ago. I don't have the article, but ask your friends. The name of the newsletter is *The Criminal Mind*."

"Are there likely to be charges against Bahadur?"

"That's possible. We call it a 'cognizable offense.' That means a policeman can arrest a suspect without a warrant in the case of a serious crime." He paused. "Do you have t-shirts that need washing, ma'am? Americans always bring t-shirts with jokes and slogans on them. My two young helpers like to read them. It improves their English."

With quick steps, Mother came to greet him. The *dhobi* passed her the laundry packed in a tidy bundle and gathered Mitra's clothes. At the end of the transaction, Mother slipped a wad of rupees onto his palm. She added, "I've included a good *bakhshish*." Gratuity.

He stared at the colorful bills. "Anything for you, Mata-ji, and your lovely daughter." He addressed her as his respected mother. "This'll pay toward my daughter's dowry." He bowed, said "Om," slipped out the door, and disappeared.

"Can we really trust this 'Om' guy?" Mitra asked Mother.

"Oh, yes. I trust him. He's been washing my clothes for ten years. You can't keep a secret from your *dhobi*. Your clothes give it all away."

In the next half-hour, sitting by the window, Mitra flipped through the glossy colorful pages of the *FilmDunya* magazine, occasionally raising her eyes and musing about the information received from the *dhobi*. Mother dusted and rearranged items on an S-shaped shelf, often glancing in Mitra's direction. A smell of old books overcame Mitra, like memories intruding.

She put the magazine aside, unable to concentrate any longer. "Your *dhobi* seems pretty clever," she said. "What if he makes up stuff and wants more *bakhshish* from you?"

Mother shook her head. "I don't just look with my eyes, I look with my experience. I can tell by the flicker of someone's eyes what they're up to. The *dhobi* will be more than happy to tease gossip out of his peers. Everyone is interested in stories about people of status higher than their own. The village folks fill half their plate with chanachur, the other half with gossip."

"You trust gossip?"

"Of course. Gossip is the newspaper of small communities. Any tidbit of gossip about that young devil is gold. He's your friend's destiny. We need to know about his daily routines and his vices. Does he walk his dogs every morning? Does he have a weakness for a particular brand of wine? How does he treat his staff? Better yet, how does he treat your friend?"

"The more I hear about Bahadur, the more worried I get about Kareena."

"Our infamous actor probably has multiple faces." Mother's eyes shined. "He shows whichever one is appropriate for the situation. Last week, I delved into a book on Cubism and got a feel for what being multi-faceted means. We'll deconstruct Bahadur and your friend, like a Cubist painter does with his subject."

Mitra wished she could rejoice in her mother's new zeal, but inside she was rattled. "I just want to see Kareena, not pick her or her man apart." She became silent, feeling hopeful one moment and doubtful the next.

"Don't look so unhappy, my dear," Mother said. "In all my years, life's storms have come and washed away what little amusement I had. I always told myself the weather would clear up. Even if it didn't, the sky would at least be different. Hoping for the *different* is what keeps you going." She looked toward the bedroom, to the digital clock visible from here. "You haven't worn a sari in awhile, have you? Did you pack any? We still dress up to go to the cinema."

Mitra peered down at her jeans. She didn't have a sari collection anymore—she'd sold them in the auction to pay for the reward for Kareena's safe return—but she'd be embarrassed to admit that to Mother.

She shook her head. Mother gestured with a hand. "Let's go see what I have. I'm so glad saris are one-size-fits-all. How convenient."

In the bedroom, Mother opened an ancient steel trunk. They sorted through layers of silk, cotton, crêpe, georgette, and chiffon, saris and matching blouses, pulsating with colors, patterns, textures, and artistry. It was partly Mother's trousseau and partly an heirloom collection. Mitra chose a hand-painted Chanderi silk in *mehendi* green, drawn by the fabric's lullaby quality. She wrapped it around her.

Once dressed, Mother radiated dignity in her white cotton sari woven with tiny silver stars. She draped the sari train modestly over her chest.

In the mirror, Mitra looked a trifle burdened by the layers. "Do I look fat, Ma?"

Mother stole up behind her. Wisps of curly hair fanned her forehead. "No, dear. As you get older, you don't see the younger you so clearly. You create a forest of sorts inside you of different identities, the way you act, what you think about. Then, as the years pass, the forest gets denser and foggier. Wait till you're my age. You'll search for the young soul you once were, happy to just catch a glimpse of her. You won't think you're fat. That's my long winded way of saying you look beautiful."

Mitra heard a bang at the door and checked her watch. This must be Arnold, with his taxi. They reached the door. Mother veiled her hair and smoothed the front pleats of her sari. Her scrubbed face had a healthy sheen. She appeared confident, a woman on a mission. Mitra was pumped up, too. Who knew if she'd succeed or not, but at least this remarkable person would accompany her on her journey. This glowing woman was the mother she had always wanted.

THIRTY-NINE

WHEN THE TAXI ARRIVED at a busy intersection, Arnold managed to squeeze through a tight spot. The driver of a Maruti stuck his head out the window and yelled: "*Shala, dusman,* idiot."

Arnold, unfazed by the insults, turned round to face Mitra, his eyes and hair glistening in the sunlight peeking through the window.

"Got news for you, *borodidi*. I asked my cabbie friends about Jay Bahadur. Most of the time, he has his own Mercedes and a chauffeur. He also rides a scooter. But occasionally, he hires public taxis. His latest girl friend's name is Kareena Sinha—that much I've gathered."

A blast of afternoon wind whipped through Mitra's plaited hair. Her voice rose in excitement. "I'll hire you for the week at double your rate, if you can take me to her."

"Oh, no. Your humble "sherpa" is not allowed to pull into Bahadur's driveway. His armed guards shoot at me. This is Kolkata. We don't always have the means to do what we want to do, you see. Did I disappoint you? Our streets are not paved with gold, like they are in Mumbai."

"The gold," Mother said, "it's in your heart."

"Are you a poet?" Arnold asked.

"Not in this life," Mother replied, "but the next."

Arnold pulled to the curb by a busy sidewalk. "Light House Cinema is just ahead of you."

On the marquee stood a life-sized, hand-painted portrait of a by-now familiar man in a dancing pose. Mitra and her mother entered the huge cinema hall five minutes before the start of *She's a Cutie,* and found it nearly empty.

Mitra settled into her seat, her mind humming with anticipation. What was it about Jay Bahadur—the king in Kareena's life—that turned the female mind to mush, even though he reportedly had underworld connections and possibly faced criminal charges?

The lights went off, the screen stormed with color, and the hall throbbed to the beat of high energy music, a tie-in of jazz and raga. Jay Bahadur materialized, dancing fast and fluidly, as though the ground were a silk rug under his feet. Legs loose, spine flexible, he skittered into new positions, seldom offering the viewer's senses a rest. His natural rhythms, always sensuous, occasionally suggestive, created a feeling of breathless intimacy, as though he was dancing just for the person who was watching him. Mitra found herself more engaged than she'd expected.

In another rich-boy-meets-poor-girl story, the film took Bahadur to Mumbai, with its beaches, bustle, and business deals. He met the heroine in a call center, courted her on the weekend on a silver mountaintop, then by a preternaturally blue lake and, finally, in a garden ablaze with red flowers, with techno music always swelling in the background.

As she watched the actor, Mitra finally grasped why Kareena had fallen for him. He danced with wild abandon, a forest fire. She had rhythm and motion and grace locked in her. He set Kareena's spirits free.

After nearly three hours, the credits rolled. Mitra looked sideways at Mother who held an expression of satisfaction on her face.

"That was an eyeful and earful," Mother said. "Jay Bahadur is wild. He reacts from his guts, jumps into a new situation without thinking."

In other words, Mother liked him. They stepped out into the evening, a humid one. A street tabla player tapped out a tune. Still hearing the movie's musical score in her head, Mitra swayed to his rhythm. Arnold waved at them from the opposite corner and hustled them back into his taxi. Mitra noticed her mother was shivering. Her lips pursed, she had little tremors in her body. She confessed she didn't feel well and once in the back seat rested her head in Mitra's lap. Holding her hand, keeping her gaze fixed on her, Mitra worried that her visit had strained Mother's delicate constitution.

As soon as they reached home, Mother turned the fan on, put on a thin cotton nightgown, and collapsed on the sofa. Her doctor had prescribed her medicine—that was about all she would reveal. Mitra suspected from the symptoms of chill and fever that Mother had caught malaria, and asked if she should call the doctor's office.

"No," Mother said. "Go to your room and get some rest."

This current episode of Mother's illness must be due to the excitement Mitra had caused. Why had she gotten her involved? What if Mother fell seriously ill?

Mitra retired to her room, dark save for a pleated-silk table lamp casting a feeble light. Staring out the window into the sultry blackness, she felt alone. Young Bengali voices in the corridor outside interrupted her train of thoughts. She had to pay attention to understand the words of a language once as close to her as her breath. Once again, she woke to the reality of Kolkata: the press of humidity, the unfamiliar rhythms, the sounds of a language as close to her once as her breath and now an exotic music. She felt homesick for Seattle—her friends, her garden. How was Grandmother coming with her plants? Had Veen heard anything about Adi? Had he returned? Was he safe? If Jay was involved with the Mumbai mafia, had they taken Adi? Mitra's stomach did a flip-flop. Should she call Veen to get the latest news?

No. That might wake Mother, who was a light sleeper.

Snatches of a silly song from the film swirled in Mitra's head:

> *Yes, you're the one for me*
> *Why do you go away?*
> *Darling, what keeps you away?*

The song was mindlessly romantic. Ulrich flashed into her head. What might he be doing now? It would be morning over there. In work clothes and boots, hair tumbling over his eyes, he might be laying the foundation for a new house. As she imagined the details of his face—high cheekbones, a troubled forehead, eyes going lighter or deeper depending on his mood—she shifted and twitched. Like a picture swinging from its wire on the wall and not quite returning to its familiar position, in danger of toppling.

Now that she was sure Mother was sound asleep, Mitra decided to look some more for Kareena. She left the house, hailed a taxi, and went to a busy shopping area, Dakshinapan Shopping Centre, where she knew she could find a phone kiosk. Her cellphone didn't work here.

She located a phone kiosk, but on second thought decided not to buzz Veen. It was too early in the morning over there to call.

The evening air was smoky with cigarette smell. The crowd seemed exuberant, everyone except her. A large family, chatting loudly, passed by. A street dentist shouted a "Hello, Miss," his tool kit on display next to his chair. She waved his offer away.

For a long time she checked every store, every alleyway, every passing face, looking for someone who wasn't there.

FORTY

"I'LL LET YOU AND NARESH get better acquainted." Mother said and bustled off toward the kitchen, the keys tied to the train of her sari jingling merrily with each step. Earlier she'd said that she was feeling better and her cheeks had, indeed, regained color, but the doubter in Mitra remained concerned.

Sitting on the sofa, Mitra evaluated Mother's friend from an angle. Older than her by at least seven years, he had even features and smelled of cheap cologne. His hair was flattened with pomade, as though he didn't want to offend anyone with a misplaced curl. He struck her as the kind of nice controllable bachelor that elderly ladies fawned over and young women considered dull.

She wanted to jump right to the Kareena issue, but that wouldn't be proper. She should get to know him first. "Ma talks a lot about you."

"I've heard a lot about you, too. When you form an impression about another person before actually meeting them, you're never sure how that'll turn out."

What did he mean? That she wasn't as pretty as her mother? That her ribbed cotton tank and velour drawstring trousers were inferior to a queenly sari? That she didn't wear a kilogram of gold to trumpet her socio-economic status?

"You're a supplier for restaurants?" she asked.

"Yes. My business is doing well. Restaurants are the new 'temples,' you see. Young people open their pocketbooks in restaurants like the older generation used to do in temples to make offerings to gods. We're a young nation. Half our population is under the age of twenty-five. Our GDP is growing at the rate of eight—no, make that nine percent—a year. Even our beggars are smiling."

Mitra listened to the boring talk, knowing how much Indians loved to discuss current state of things. For Mother's sake—she might be paying attention to them from the kitchen—Mitra must at least appear to be making friendly contact. "Of course, I see signs of progress. But I think things can move a little faster here."

"You have complaints?" He lifted a brow. "Most foreign-returned Indians do."

He didn't understand her, a frustration. "I didn't come here to complain. I'm here to find my friend."

She heard the sigh of a sari, as Mother rejoined them, balancing a tray on her hand. The tray held *chai*, eggplant *bhaja*, and *sandesh*, a combination that smelled oily, spicy, and delicious.

"Nobody can make these *bhajas* like you, Mashima." Naresh, suddenly cheerful, addressed Mother as aunt-mother, an appropriate term, given the neighborliness of this city.

Mother leaned forward eagerly and pleasantly, her attention on Naresh so complete that she had forgotten her habit of checking everyone's plate. They bantered for a few minutes, making it transparent they'd formed a loving mother-son duo. Like an odd third party, Mitra fiddled with the teacup in her hand and sank into the sofa to listen and observe. She took a bite of an eggplant *bhaja*, and concluded she still hadn't acquired a fondness for it.

Mother threw a glance at Mitra, then turned to Naresh. "Did you have a chance to check out that private restaurant?"

"Monopriya? Yes, I talked to one of the cooks. Jay Bahadur has been there with his new girlfriend, Kareena." Naresh lowered his tone. "She's pregnant."

The news jarred Mitra. She set her cup down.

"He made a starlet pregnant some years back. That was a scandal." Naresh waited a beat and smirked. "Charming as he is, Jay Bahadur is a has-been, a *badmaish*." Rogue character. "He dances his way out of things."

Her mind in uproar, Mitra stood up and slipped into the kitchen. They hardly noticed her departure. She drank down a large glass of water, all the more determined to have a rendezvous with Kareena. Meanwhile, the flow of words between Mother and Naresh continued.

"What days and times," Mother asked, "do they show up at that restaurant?"

"The cook isn't allowed to give out that information. Manopriya is very private. The owner, Keshav Khaitan, wasn't there when I stopped by."

"I'd heard gossip that Khaitan has a 'heavy weight on his head.'"

Mitra strolled back, plopped down on the sofa, and asked, "What's this 'heavy weight on his head?'"

"'Heavy weight' means pompousness," Naresh said. "Pompous, he is. Even if I were to talk to him, though, I doubt he'll divulge any gossip—he's particular about protecting the privacy of his exclusive clientele. He has all sorts of measures in place. His doorman was once a champion boxer. And he'll let someone in only if he recognizes the face and only after checking against a register. They don't want photographers sneaking in."

"Mitra just wants to meet with her friend," Mother said. "Couldn't she be let in through the back entrance?"

"I suppose," Naresh said mischievously, "a dishwasher could be bribed—"

"Bribed?" Mitra interrupted. "In new young India, you still do business the old corrupt way?"

Naresh laughed through his milky white teeth, half-embarrassed. "Just joking, ma'am." His expression turned serious.

"A long weekend is coming," Mother said. "We could offer the dishwasher a little something to buy chamcham sweets for his kids."

Naresh wiped his hand in the napkin in one quick jerk. "You should be the one negotiating with the restaurant, Mashima." Naresh fixed his attention on Mitra. "There is another alternative. Do you know a VIP who might be able to make a reservation for you?"

"I just got here," Mitra mumbled, feeling somewhat defensive. "I don't know anyone."

"Oh yes, you do." Mother said. "Your high school friend, Preet. She's married to a big shot in the local government. Today, I phoned her to let her know you've arrived. I'm in frequent touch with her. She's not back yet from her vacation, but I caught her aunt on the phone. I told her why you're here."

Mitra's heart skipped a beat or two. They had an ancient saying here: Whatever is heard by six ears doesn't remain secret for long.

"Ma, what are you thinking? First the *dhobi*, then Preet's aunt. Rumors could fly. Jay Bahadur and Kareena could go into seclusion." Belatedly, she recognized the shrillness in her voice, and that mortified her.

Mother, a hurt look on her face, got up and scrambled toward the bedroom. The black border of her white sari slashed the air.

Naresh watched her until she was out of sight. Then his gaze slid back to Mitra. His disbelieving expression seemed to say: *you speak to your mother in such a disrespectful tone?* But all he actually said was, "You want to meet up with your friend that badly?"

Somewhere in this apartment building, a practiced hand plucked a sitar, gentle tones that resembled a deeply emotional human voice. Mitra closed her eyes for a second. She was trying her best to adapt, although not terribly successfully. She was searching for a friend who might not even want to be found, who might have intentionally abandoned her earlier life, including her friendship with Mitra.

A neighbor clattered up the stairs. Something came to Mitra. She would stick to her plan.

"I'm sorry to get everybody upset," she said to Naresh. "But my friend might be in danger."

"If she were a friend of mine, I'd try to keep her away from Jay Bahadur. It's like jumping into fire. You follow? It's madness. More than one starlet has regretted it." Naresh paused and checked Mitra's face, then continued with: "I'm sorry. I don't mean to scare you. You're a guest of India. It's our duty to see that you have a pleasant and worthwhile stay here."

"Guest? This is my home—I grew up in this building."

Naresh got up, without meeting her eyes. "I must go now."

Mitra shot to her feet as well. Naresh opened the door, then faced her. "I'm happy to finally meet Mashima's daughter."

"I hope I didn't disappoint you too much."

"Not at all. I'm happy to be of help."

"Could I request you to bribe that dishwasher, if that's what it takes?"

"Yes, sure, but it has to wait a couple of days. I fly to Chennai this evening to attend the opening ceremony of a new hotel run by a friend. I'll be back in a day or two. I'll contact the dishwasher and report back to you. I know you're wondering why it couldn't be any sooner. It's our Indian time, you see. *Achha, ashi.*" I'll visit you again.

He pressed his palms together in a gesture of farewell, conveying peace and blessing, and Mitra did likewise. She left the door open a little longer to listen to the plaintive melody coming from a neighbor's flat, someone singing, speaking of loneliness and grief.

She wondered what her sister was hearing just now. As she imagined her, Kareena appeared tense, disoriented, her cheeks marble hard. She was associating with criminals. She was in trouble.

Back to her room, Mitra picked up an issue of *FilmDunya* from a basket. Big headlines screamed about a marriage breakup in Bollywood's First Family.

She tossed the magazine back into the basket and covered her eyes with her palm. What if Bahadur abandoned Kareena, as he'd done with a former pregnant girlfriend? What would Kareena do then, with a child on the way?

FORTY-ONE

THE NEXT MORNING, Mitra woke late, showered and dressed, popped into the living room, and found Mother intent on the *Hindustan Standard*. Mother's fresh white cotton sari glowed around her. The air bristled with the scent of the hibiscus oil she'd massaged on her head. The ceiling fan whirred, sending forth gusts of air and teasing her curls.

Mother greeted Mitra, folded the newspaper, pointed to a stack of cleaned pressed clothes on a side table.

"The *dhobi* came by with your laundry and some news. Jay Bahadur is going back to his village for location shooting in less than a week. The villagers are planning a big reception for him. It is expected that your friend will accompany him."

Mitra pulled up a chair. "I must catch Kareena before she leaves."

"Here's another bit of news from the *dhobi*. He gets all sorts of inside information due to his job. This one's a bombshell and he's gotten it from Jay Bahadur's great aunt. Apparently, he had a vasectomy a few years back. It's not public knowledge. His aunt laughed at the idea that Kareena's child is his."

Mitra couldn't speak. How twisty it all seemed. "Either way," she said a moment later, "I'd like to speak with Kareena. Is Naresh coming back today?"

"Not until tomorrow, but he's been working for us. He called about an hour ago. Jay Bahadur's assistant made a reservation for two for this Friday evening at Monopriya. It's expected he'll have dinner with his girlfriend. Now the question is how to get you a reservation on the same date and time. Unfortunately, the dishwasher has refused the bribe."

"There has to be another way."

"Sit down, dear. There *is* another way. Preet returned my call. She's back and she wants you to give her a buzz."

"I can't wait to see her. Where's her number?"

"Here it is." Mother handed her a piece of paper. "I had a nice chat with Preet. She's missed you. The woman is seven months pregnant, but stuck at home all day pretty much by herself. When I clued her in about what you're here for, she said she'd be delighted to join in our mission."

"If she's that far pregnant, then—"

"She's bored, bored, bored and eager for our company." Mother's eyes sparkled. "What a sleuthing team we make—a gardener, a pregnant housewife, a *dhobi*, a "sherpa" cab driver, and a retired schoolteacher. We'll defeat that actor guy, get your friend out of his clutches, and put sense into her head." She paused. "Kareena is a fancy name, too fancy for my taste. I just can't get it out of my mouth."

FORTY-TWO

PULLING ON A PAIR of slim denim pants and a white blouse, Mitra recalled her high school years. She and Preet had been inseparable then. Preet was a good three inches taller and fuller of figure and her shrewd-eyed aunt always proclaimed she had health, *shashthya*. The older generation appreciated plumpness in women—a sign of a robust constitution and the ability to survive the ordeal of bearing children. The same elders had cast dubious glances at Mitra's matchstick body. But equally dissatisfied with their respective appearances, Mitra and Preet had commiserated.

A tinge of rivalry existed between them. Mitra was an exceptional student, at the top of her class, for which Preet envied her. She nicknamed Mitra "Bright Eyes," whereas Mitra called her "Rosgulla Face" because of her round face and sweet expression. Mitra would often announce her wish to go to college, get a job, make good money, and only then consider getting married. Preet had wanted to marry right after she graduated from college. Despite endless discussions, they'd never agreed on the merits of career vs. homemaking.

What would Preet be like now?

Within half-an-hour, carrying a gift, Mitra arrived at the shore of a popular lake in South Kolkata called Rabindra Sarovar.

On weekends, during their high school years, Mitra would slip away from her tiny flat and join Preet here. They'd sit on their favorite bench and chatter up a tempest. A bandana tied around his forehead, a vendor would cry in a nasal voice, "*Garam, garam,*" or "hot, searing hot," urging passersby to indulge in *jalebis*, crunchy, sweet-scented pretzel-like pastries haloed by sugar syrup. All too soon it would be dusk, *sandhya*, the time to slow down and meditate, as the sages had long proclaimed. Mitra would trudge back home.

Letting that scene fade from her mind's eye, Mitra took a closer look at the lake. Trees shimmered in the early afternoon light, kokil birds stared down at passersby from their high perches, and food vendors in dingy turbans hawked their wares. The place was just as she had imagined it.

"Mitra!"

She turned to see Preet approaching from the south end. Smiling, her eyes misty, Mitra embraced her. "Preet! Such a long time." A sense of joy welling in her, she couldn't finish the sentence.

"Look at you now." Preet's gaze held a loving light. "Hey, you're a different person, but slender as ever. The gods didn't intend me to be stick-thin. Or else they'd have handed me instructions."

"Shall we go find our bench?" Mitra asked.

They strolled down a trail, their eyes cast over the limpid waters, chatting about old times. Preet hadn't changed much. She had the same fair skin, the same broad forehead now brightened with a vermilion dot at its center indicating her married status, and the same shiny black hair pulled into a knot at the back. Pregnancy, however, had enlarged her already sizable frame, and she walked more slowly. Mitra could see that marriage and motherhood suited Preet. So did the blazing violet silk she had on, the luminous cluster of gold bangles, and the amethyst necklace.

A green coconut floated on the surface of the lake. They spotted their favorite bench under the flickering shadow of a banyan tree and walked over to it.

Preet settled onto the bench gracefully. "I didn't understand what life was about," she said, "until I got married and had a child. I don't have a long list of ambitions. I call it a good day if the floor is swept, my husband isn't too grumpy, and my son has cleaned his dinner plate. I hope you don't pity me for not having a career outside home."

"Believe me, I don't. We've made different choices. Seems to me you're where you belong in life."

"Frankly, Mitra, I've missed you—I cried for weeks after you left—but I think it was better for you to have made that leap. You walk differently. You speak better. And you're much more poised." Preet laughed, full-cheeked. "You used to be one clumsy girl."

Inwardly, Mitra winced. "I didn't plan my life, either," she said, "until I went overseas."

"I kept asking your mother about you. She wouldn't say much. She isn't like my mother, who keeps track of every move I make. Even now, when I go visiting relatives in another neighborhood, my mother

checks in to make sure I'm back safely. You know *mayer pran.*" A
mother's affectionate heart. "She shares everything with me."

The remark brought about a sense of soreness in Mitra. So far,
Mother had been reticent about her illness. Mitra wished to hear
more about it, wished to have more of her mother's "affectionate
heart," and trust.

"Now, tell me about yourself," Preet said. "I hear you have a
German boyfriend. Oh, *baba.* What is it like to be with someone from
Deutschland?"

"You end up learning Deutsch," Mitra said, with a smile. If only
she could confide in Preet that she missed Ulrich crushingly in all
she did. She ached for his presence, under dynamic daylight or
during static night hours. Wherever she went, she saw impressions
of his being—in a balcony, on the steps of a temple and right now
just beyond the iron fence of the park. Then she recalled the lies he'd
uttered, his mood changes, and his violent past and the bright
scenery dissolved before her mind's eye.

Then, noticing the seriousness with which Preet tilted her head,
"He's nice. We talk. We do restaurants. We dance. We share plans."

"Now that you're away from him, you're not sure?" Preet said
in a wary tone. She'd always been able to sense people's woes. "You
go back and forth? One minute, you're dying to see him, and the
next minute—"

"You seem to be speaking from experience," Mitra said in a light
voice.

Preet narrowed her eyes; there was tightness around her mouth
"My cousin's been in that miserable state for a month. She's
hopelessly hooked on a guy." She went silent for a moment. "Have
you done a background check on your German? I hear it's common
practice in the West. My cousin's detective agency handles that kind
of work on the side and it's one of the few agencies to do that."

Background check? Eyes lowered, Mitra shook her head.

It dawned on her that she was trying to show her relationship
with Ulrich in a softer light, as though trying to justify it to herself.
Hopelessly hooked. On what? A dreamy view of a possibly dangerous man?
Yes, that was her.

"I'd consider it an extreme adventure to date a man so different." Preet patted her sari folds. "I should take the dust off your feet in respect. My husband comes from a similar background to mine. We grew up five miles from each other. Still, we squabble. The other day we fought over which brand of toaster to buy. Can you believe it?"

Mitra touched Preet's shoulder gently. "Count yourself lucky."

"But—you look so worried. Your mother told me the reason why you're here. Is there any way I can be of help?"

"Yes. I need a favor from you." Surveying Preet's expectant face, she added, "I'd like to get a reservation in a private restaurant—Monopriya. Apparently, only VIPs can get in there."

Preet laughed again. "Is that all? I'm pretty sure my husband can take care of that. He has friends in prominent places."

From behind a pile of chilies, tomatoes, onions, and limes, a vendor pushing a mobile cart called out to them. "Ladies, nobody can make *ghughni* as well as I can."

"Some other time." Preet waved him away. She turned to Mitra. "Shall we go to my house and have lunch?"

"Yes, that'd be lovely. I have two other requests." Mitra mentioned the article the *dhobi* had suggested and asked Preet to locate it for her. "One more thing. This may sound strange to you, but do you have any DVD's of Dimple Sinha?"

"Let me think. I collect old Bollywood films that have been digitally mastered. I might have a copy of the one titled, Betrayal. Lady Sinha isn't in films any more. Why are you interested in her?"

A bicycle rolled by. The air Mitra breathed was stuffed with dust. "It's just for something I'm researching."

"Oh, those movies are campy. Lady Sinha always plays herself. She shows her boobs, changes into new saris and jewelry at every opportunity, sings naughty songs, does naughty things, and weeps to gain your sympathy." Preet stood up, her long earrings swaying. "I laugh when she weeps—oh, poor thing."

Mitra stumbled to her feet. Now she finally saw why Adi's family hadn't approved of Kareena and why they'd ultimately disowned their son when he married.

It was Kareena's mother—her reputation in society.

FORTY-THREE

THEY HOPPED INTO A TAXI and, within minutes, reached Preet's neighborhood. Under the burnished sun, an orange commuter bus rolled along the road, belching clouds of oily black smoke, blue letters on one side declaring, *Auspicious Journey*. Indians loved to decorate everything, even the public vehicles, with colors, designs, and inscriptions.

"Welcome to my humble *bari*," Preet said.

Her home was in a guava-tinted, three-story building from the colonial era. She unlocked the door to her first-floor flat, and they entered. The air carried a feeling of order. Mitra kicked the leather slides off her feet and parked them next to a toy truck.

A beautiful boy, about four years of age, rushed to greet them, his complexion a pleasant caramel-and-cream.

"You smell of rosgulla," Preet said to him. "Have you been snacking?"

He nodded. Mother and son embraced each other. The sweetness between them jarred Mitra. Thus far, she'd chosen career over marriage and family. She couldn't be sure if that had been a right decision.

"Hi, I am Sam. Pleased to . . ." It seemed Sam, whose full name was Soumyendu, was trying to practice his English, but had forgotten the rest of his speech. To save him embarrassment, Mitra introduced herself.

Sam listened, his dark eyes pooled with curiosity. Tall for his age, he wore baggy shorts that flapped around his slender legs. "Mitra-masi, how long will you stay here? My cousins from Australia spend a month."

Mitra couldn't help but smile. Deep inside her, she hungered for a child of her own, and this boy had made her desire rise to the surface. Before she could reply, Preet said, "Give Mitra-masi a chance to settle in first, then ask questions. Come this way, Mitra."

She led Mitra to her living room motioned toward a velvet sofa whose cushions were streaked with stunning mirror embroidery. As Preet turned on the white ceiling fan, the diamond ring on her finger glinted with pinpricks of light. From a gift bag, Mitra brought out a few cosmetics for Preet and a hardcover picture book on tree houses for Sam.

Preet looked delighted and thanked Mitra. Sam took the book with both hands, flipped through the pages, settled on a picture, and beamed. "Can I build a playhouse like this one on our palm tree?"

Mitra glanced at the picture of a wood structure bolted to a tree at a dizzying height. "You'll need a huge redwood for that," Mitra said. "I doubt you can find that here."

From the way his lips pursed, she could see that he didn't believe her. The concept of unfeasibility hadn't yet trespassed on his young mind. His gaze darted back and forth from his mother and Mitra to the tree-house book, then to his toy truck by the door, and he walked away.

Preet watched him with a bright gaze. "We're predicting Sam will be a newspaper reporter. He's inquisitive and he listens. He's been telling his playmates his auntie is coming from the States and his baby sister is coming from heaven. Did I tell you we're expecting a daughter this time? Just what I'd wished for. If I'm going to have a legacy, that'll be my little *memshahib*." Princess. "I'll dress her up and set her on her throne."

Mitra succumbed to a pang of envy. She felt lighter, lesser. Guilt, too, cast its shadow on her. Here was a friend she cherished, and she couldn't share her happiness as readily as she'd have liked.

Preet interrupted her thoughts. "Did you know that your mother came to see me in the hospital after Sam was born? She held him, sang to him, put a drop of honey on his tongue. We talked and talked. She said since she didn't have a son, which she'd always wanted, she was hoping to at least have a grandson."

Dreariness settled on Mitra's chest. "She wanted a son? That's news to me. I thought after my father's death, she didn't want the complications of children."

"Not only that, according to her, those were the times when woman were expected to have a male child. If they didn't have one, they were considered failures."

Mitra looked away. "Well, I must be a great disappointment to her, then."

A shadow of apprehension passed over Preet's face. "Hey, cheer up. You still have time."

Preet crossed to a display cabinet and plucked a DVD from her substantial collection. "Here's Dimple Sinha for you. While you're watching it, I'll go to the store across the street. Be back in a minute. My maid-servant will keep an eye on Sam."

Mitra dropped her head back against the sofa cushion, her thinking mechanism hardly at rest. The screen before her came alive with images of Kareena's mother. Dimple, the screen siren, played the wife of an auto-industry czar, having an affair with a wild-haired artist. Draped in velvet, with pinked lips and arms decorated with silvery glass bangles, Dimple was an older Kareena: the same walk, smile, hand gestures, and style of dressing.

Dimple and Kareena had the same voice and speech mannerisms, same penchant for luxuries. Was Dimple that selfish in real life? Or was she playing the villainess with gusto and believability, in which case she was merely a fine actress?

Sam sneaked in, scooted onto Mitra's lap. "She looks *lovi*. Yes, she looks greedy."

Dimple's on-screen husband came home, questioned her about how she occupied herself in the afternoons. She lied, fluttered her eyelashes, hummed a seductive tune, even shed a few tears.

Sam slid off Mitra's lap, saying, "Crocodile's tears," and promised to return. If only Dimple didn't resemble Kareena so much. Mitra would have laughed at Sam's comment and at the scene before her.

After a few more minutes, Mitra turned off the DVD player and stretched her arms. She'd seen enough of her father's first wife. A low-key man, he'd somehow been attracted to fanfare and flame.

She ambled to the window. A man pulled a wheeled cart glistening with a heap of green herbs. The sight transported her to misty monochromatic Seattle, to her yard and greenhouse. Soon it'd be time to cut back the rhododendron, trellis the flowering pea, and tend to the dahlia bush.

Preet bustled in, her forehead pearled with perspiration. She escorted Mitra to the kitchen, motioned toward a stool, and began slicing a mango. "What do you think of Lady Sinha?" she asked eagerly.

"She's not a bad actress. What is she supposed to be like in real life?"

"The real Dimple Sinha is reportedly far worse than what she portrays in her films. She's made a habit of what one film critic calls 'unfinished unions.' She marries, then dumps the husband before he can catch on to what a heartbreaker she is. It's like she throws her dolls away before they can break on her."

"Does she have children?"

"If she does, she's always kept them out of the public eye. At least she's done that for them."

Sam, riding a stuffed giraffe, jumped into the room. He gazed at his mother, then at Mitra, as if trying to assess to whom he should pose his next question. "Where is Seattle? I'd like to ride my giraffe to Seattle."

"You could fly there in a day's time," Mitra said. "But it's as different from here as a giraffe is from tiger."

Sam's dark eyes saddened. He parked the giraffe in the middle of the room and leapt into Mitra's lap. "You're not going back there, are you?"

Mitra leaned her cheek on Sam's cushiony hair. He reminded her, this treasured child, of the distinctness of her two lives, Indian and American, and how difficult it was to draw the halves closer. As with a broken mirror, the parts simply didn't fit; the views were distorted, dizzying.

"I'm having a great time with you here but, eventually, I have to go back." Mitra seemed to be answering his question, as well as her own. "My work's there. You go where your work is."

Her reply must have been too burdensome for his tender ears. Or perhaps he heard a familiar sound. He slipped out of her lap and bolted to the front door with a happy shriek, announcing that his father was home.

FORTY-FOUR

A DAY LATER, Mitra lounged in a woven chair on Preet's verandah. The temperature had climbed to ninety-six degrees. Two hand fans rested on the table. A crow cursed from a rooftop.

"You lucked out," Preet said, joining her, a peaceful but coy smile playing on her lips. With one hand, she adjusted her blue-print sari. Even in this blistering heat, she stuck with this voluminous garment. "My husband just called. He's made the restaurant reservation for you. Tomorrow evening at seven, just as you've requested."

Mitra nearly jumped out of her chair. "Oh, great. I can't thank you enough."

"Here's the clinker. It's a reservation for one. You have to go alone. The restaurant was completely booked except for a small table where they can seat only one person. It's reserved for a famous sculptor, an elderly gentleman who likes to dine alone. But he's on vacation this week. Your mother and I will wait for you in a chai shop close by."

Sam scampered in. The breeze puffed up the short sleeves of his checked shirt. "Mitra-masi," he asked shyly, "will you play the Alien Attack game with me?"

"In just a bit." Mitra proposed to Sam that they go for a ride in Arnold's taxi on Saturday evening. Afterwards, they could see the lights on the Esplanade and have ice cream. Jubilant, Sam ran inside, his sandals flapping on the floor.

Preet turned to Mitra. "Your taxi-*wallah* will also be available to drive you to the restaurant, I presume?"

"I hope so." Mitra borrowed Preet's cellphone and punched Arnold's number.

Arnold was happy to be of service. "I'll bring my friend's new Hyundai," he said, "just in case Miss Kareena needs a ride someplace. And I'll dress up like a chauffeur."

Mitra got off the phone. In this spacious courtyard, rows of palm and Ashok trees undulated in the light breeze. She noted concern in Preet's eyes. "What are you worried about?"

"I'll be right back. I have something for you." Preet went inside and returned with a few printed sheets which she pressed into Mitra's hand. "Here's a copy of the police newsletter you wanted. My husband and I have read it."

The pages had been culled from a quarterly newsletter titled, *Kolkata Police News*.

On top of the front page was the headline: Traffic Stats. Mitra's eyes skimmed the reports of Lane and Line Violations, Helmet Violations, and Road Accident fatalities. This was followed by a photo of a traffic constable helping a blind woman cross a busy intersection. Below that was the column titled Crime in the City. Mitra skimmed the top news items on this column. A college student had been beaten on the "N" Block of New Alipore at dusk by assailants with unclear motives. A young woman had been mugged on Hazra in broad daylight. Arson was suspected in a fire in an apartment complex in Behala.

As she flipped the page, Mitra's gaze fell on the heading, Citizen's Views. It consisted of a piece written by M. Palit, a journalist, and placed in a box.

> Did He or Didn't He?
>
> Although actor Jay Bahadur, the heartthrob of yesteryear, was never charged in the Ray murder incident, suspicions about him remain. Jay Bahadur supposedly has boasted to his cronies about hobnobbing with the Kolkata crime syndicate, particularly the Solsi Gang. A gang member, known by the initials A.E. allegedly masterminded the killing of the famed actor, Manu Ray.

Come to think of it, Mitra had heard of the city's gang activities from Mother. And she'd heard of actor Manu Ray from Robert. But no one had mentioned the gangster named A.E. How was Jay Bahadur linked to this?

Her stomach fluttering, Mitra continued.

A.E. was believed to have contacted Ray several times, demanding the world rights income from his latest box-office hit, in exchange for protection from future harm. According to sources, Ray repeatedly refused him. He was found, with his throat slashed, in his home on April 5.

Jay Bahadur, a school chum of Ray, is believed to have resented Ray for his rising fame. He is alleged to have helped the gang members gain entry to Ray's home. Bahadur's voice can be heard on a conversation with his cronies, including A.E. The conversations was related to the crime and recorded by security officials.

New evidence from Bahadur's account in the State Bank of India shows that his account was credited with three million rupees, believed to be "black money" received as payment for his part in the crime. The case may be reopened.

Mitra put the pages down.

Preet was watching her reactions. "Do you want to reconsider going? These people are dangerous. You don't want to get tangled up with them."

"I have come this far to see Kareena. She might not realize what she's gotten mixed up with."

Preet looked off to the distance, obviously plagued with concern, then turned when her maid, a young girl, appeared. Thin and straight as a bamboo pole, she'd wrapped her ponytail with a ring of jasmine blossoms. She served each of them a glass of fresh tamarind drink.

Mitra took a sip. The tart beverage was just the right refreshment in this scorching weather. Her mind went back to Kareena. What if she balked at Mitra's attempts to make her safe?

Mitra turned her attention to the courtyard. The sky breathed out a mouthful of wind. A swirl of dust followed. Straight and graceful only minutes ago, the Ashok trees bent down to the ground.

Mitra pushed the newsletter away. "I appreciate your help," she said to Preet. "There's much more to it than I thought."

"Your mother is showing a lot of initiative, by making calls and getting people together," Preet said. "It's really nice to see her up and about and excited, especially given her health."

Mother's health—the thought distracted Mitra. "Do you know what's wrong with her? She never talks about it."

"It's malaria."

"How do you know?"

"She told me."

Malaria, the deathly disease. For a moment Mitra couldn't speak. "She told you, but she wouldn't tell me, her daughter?"

"She doesn't want you to worry from afar. You see, after you left, your mother and I stayed in touch off and on. She knew we were close. Then I got married and had a kid. Once I became a wife and mother, she felt more comfortable confiding in me."

Mitra took an uneasy breath. "Malaria is not an easy disease to manage, not at her age. I should get back here more often to take care of her. I don't like the idea of her being alone."

"In case you haven't noticed, she's not so alone any more. You've met Naresh. She's like a mother to him. He lights up her days and, like a good son, takes care of her."

Mitra looked away to get a grip on her emotions. "I see." She gulped more of the tamarind drink and said lightly, "Some day I'll grow a tamarind tree in Seattle."

Preet broke out into a smile, as if happy to have the unpleasantness behind them. "In the meantime, why don't you wear one of my saris to go to Monopriya? Shall we take a look at my wardrobe?"

Watching her friend's benevolent face and gentle eyes, Mitra said, "I'm happy to give you joy."

The maid poked her head through the door and asked Preet a question about the night's dinner. When she departed, Preet said to Mitra, "When you have your own family, you'll see how many details you have to deal with. You *are* going to get married soon, aren't you?"

Mitra nodded, somewhat unconvincingly. Preet had an arranged marriage— arranged and blessed by relatives, whereas Mitra would have to find her own mate. And it couldn't be Ulrich. She'd have to break it off with him, knowing that would hurt. She'd have to start looking again. It wasn't always pretty out there.

"You'll make a wonderful mother," Preet said, oblivious to the jumble of feelings Mitra harbored. "I see how you relate to Sam. He's fallen for you."

In the bedroom, Preet opened the door of a lotus-painted armoire and laid her sari collection on the bed: light fabrics in bold colors; ice-cool neutrals, woven with stones. It took Mitra no time to choose a pale green number with a blue-gold crystalline border.

Preet insisted that Mitra do a dry run, and she obliged by draping the six-yard long fabric around her. Preet clasped an elaborate necklace of gold and ruby around Mitra's throat and pinned a pearl brooch over the sari pleats on her left shoulder.

In the mirror, Mitra found herself smiling out from yards of silk and gold, a cocoon of softness, refinement, and glitz, despite a slight bewilderment in her eyes. She couldn't completely believe all that was happening.

"Now, all I have to do," she said to Preet, "is run into Kareena at that restaurant and make it seem like an accidental meeting."

"Will it give her pause when she finds out how much scheming has gone into the *accident*?" Preet tested an assortment of sparkling green bangles, checking them against the background of Mitra's sari. Satisfied, she slid the stack onto Mitra's arm. "Have you practiced what you're going to say when you *accidentally* run into her and her news-making boyfriend?"

Mitra's bangles chimed. "The right words will flow, I'm sure."

FORTY-FIVE

AT THE ENTRANCE to a narrow lane, Mitra stepped out of Arnold's taxi and smoothed the front pleats of her sari. Mother and Preet wished her luck though the window. Arnold assured her he'd drive them to Time for Tea a block away, park the car, and wait for everyone to regroup there.

Mitra gave them a wave and walked down the lane, reading house numbers. On this clear evening, the stars shone like silver burst on a sari.

From inside the front window of a well-maintained single-story building, a doorman of indeterminate age, dressed in a muslin turban and beaded *chappals*, watched her.

A small tasteful sign on the door identified the place as Monopriya, "mind pleasing." Had she not been looking, she would not have found this private restaurant dwarfed by multi-story family dwellings.

If only she weren't so nervous. If only she didn't have to enter this fancy establishment alone. If only she had a guarantee that her friend would turn up.

As she mounted the stoop to the anteroom, Mitra nearly tripped on the front pleats of her slithery silk. She recovered and clutched her purse tighter. She could feel the digital voice recorder shifting position inside the purse.

Stepping forward, the maitre d' turned an appraising gaze at her. "Do you have a reservation, madam?"

"Mitra Basu."

He checked her name against a register, bowed deeply, and said, "This way, please," in a voice deep, rich, and calculated to intimidate.

Swishing her sari, Mitra trailed after him. A waiter, resplendent in a saffron uniform, appeared. He asked her to wait at the edge of the room, apologizing and saying that he was getting her table ready.

The long room had textured walls, gold tablecloths, and gleaming mahogany chairs, as ostentatious as a garden of gaudy silk roses. Tall red candles on each table threw mysterious shadows on walls decorated with paintings of pirates and ships. There were at least twenty tables, spaced far apart from each other, mostly occupied. Elegant hands gestured, diamonds refracted light, beverages glistened, and brilliant smiles acknowledged witty repartee, as though the room only permitted that which glowed and charmed.

At a table on Mitra's right, a man wearing a tweedy charcoal suit leaned intimately toward his lady companion, their conversation muted, measured. The woman wasn't Kareena. From a table on the left, just beyond a potted palm, there wafted fragrances of mace, clove, fine rice, and rose water.

Mitra took a few steps to the left, her ankle-strap heels digging into the cushiony carpet. She peered into a private room and studied those in attendance. A large family was holding a celebration of sorts. A man stood up, raised his glass, and offered a toast.

No luck.

Back to the main dining room, Mitra walked past a woman, swathed in a brocade sari in purple and sitting alone in a corner. Mitra was half-way across the room when the angle of a chin, as well as the pose of the rested hand alerted her. She turned and looked again.

Why hadn't she noticed her before? This woman *was* Kareena, not a look-alike, not a mirage. Her face was puffier, perhaps due to pregnancy. She was nursing a glass of water. She set the glass down and consulted her watch.

Yes, Mitra had found her dearest friend. After a month, and far away in India, in an exclusive restaurant. Even though her pulse raced, Mitra felt herself smiling. She'd finally succeeded in her quest.

Kareena picked up the napkin from her lap, pearl eardrops gleaming in the candlelight. Clearly, Mitra's presence hadn't yet registered.

It's me, Mitra wanted to cry out. *Remember? Mitra: Your chief ally and sister. Your bestie.*

She wove her way toward Kareena's table, her legs slowed by the sari.

A brushed shove against her shoulder made her stagger. She turned to face the culprit, the person in a hurry, one who had just sailed into the room. She could smell alcohol, cologne, and hair pomade.

She recognized Jay Bahadur. He pushed past her, peering over his shoulder and tossing a terse, "Excuse me." Clad in a striking white-and-silver *kurta*, he carried himself like a prince. Even without makeup and flattering lights and despite bloodshot eyes, he looked rakishly charming.

Mitra gripped the back of an empty chair to keep from stumbling over. Once steady, she watched this unworthy man pick his way to Kareena's table.

Kareena looked up at him, with her idol-worshipping eyes. As he leaned over to peck her on the cheek, he seemed to instantly re-mold himself from a discourteous drunk into a perfect lover. He eased into his seat, his princely aura and perfect posture remaining intact. He smoothed his *kurta* and took her hand.

Mitra lost her breath. She wanted to yell out to Kareena: *Your husband is waiting for you to come home. The police are looking for you. Your friends want to know why you don't call. And you've gotten mixed up with this crook?*

A diner at a nearby table gave Mitra a curious look. And yet she decided she must think this through. She stood frozen and watched the lovers from a few feet away.

Kareena smiled into Jay Bahadur's eyes. He whispered a few words. She laughed, a tinkling crystal peal. Mitra had never heard Kareena laugh so freely, so happily. She stroked the pleats of her sari on her left shoulder, causing a jangling of her bracelets.

Should she leave, Mitra wondered. Give her sister the gift of privacy?

Think again, Mitra. This is real life. You can't rewind it. If you walk away, that'll be the end of it. You won't be able to save your sister from any harm that might await her.

Kareena looked in Mitra's direction, casually, as though brushing her eyes over a stranger. Her fingers ran over her ring. How could she not recognize Mitra?

All right. Now was the time. Mitra strode to their table, heart leaping with both fear and joy. "Hi, Kareena."

Kareena raised her eyes, shocked and confused. Then her expression changed to one of recognition and happiness. She laughed, as though she couldn't believe what she saw. Eyes rounding in pleasure, she stood up in one swift move and grasped Mitra's hand.

"Mitra!" Her voice crackling with wonder, she engulfed Mitra in a tight hug. "What're you doing here?"

"I came here to see you."

It didn't matter how casual the words of their greetings were. Mitra felt in an instant as though she had regained that closeness she'd missed. A wave of relief coursed through her. Kareena was alive and in good spirits and happy to see her. That was all Mitra could hope for.

Jay Bahadur cleared his throat, a small ominous sound. Mitra took a step back. Her moment of elation evaporated. He looked at Mitra piercingly, raised an eyebrow, and signaled to a man on a nearby table. Mitra noticed the big, burly man, with eyes like a razor blade, a bodyguard possibly. He sized Mitra up at a glance.

Kareena swept out an arm. "Jay, darling, meet my best friend Mitra from Seattle."

Jay nodded at Mitra. His expression remained skeptical, but he said in a charming tone, "What brings you all the way from Seattle?"

Mitra fumbled for an answer. She mustn't rouse suspicion in Jay's mind, if she hadn't done so already. *Okay. There might be a way out here. Mention mother.* Indians generally respected their mothers. Any excuse about Mother would do. "I came to visit my mother. She's ill."

It must have temporarily satisfied Jay, for he mumbled a few words of good wishes toward Mother's health. The bodyguard, his eyes narrowing, listened to their conversation.

"May I have a word with you in private?" Mitra whispered to Kareena.

Kareena wiped her eyes with the back of her hand and said in a loud enough voice for Jay to hear. "Why, Mitra?"

"I must speak with you about my mother."

"I'll be back in a minute," Kareena whispered to Jay.

"Don't be too long, darling." Jay turned to Mitra. "We'll be waiting here for you," he said in a calculating tone that chilled her bones.

Mitra crossed the room, with Kareena behind her, and slipped into the Ladies Powder Room.

The pink wallpapered room was mirrored on three sides. Kareena and Mitra faced each other and their many reflections, a whiff of Kareena's perfume settling between them.

Kareena's pregnancy showed—a slight bulge under her sari. She put her arms around Mitra. They clung to each other for a long moment. As they disengaged, Kareena said, "What a wonderful surprise to see you here."

Mitra could feel tears accumulating in her eyes. "Thank God, I've found you."

"Is your mother really ill?"

"She has malaria, but mostly doing well. Listen, I came to see her, but I also came to look for you."

"You don't know how much I've missed you. I think about you all the time." Kareena choked, as tears streamed down her cheeks. "You left your job, your newspaper column, and your friends. You flew for twenty-two hours. All for your mother and me?"

Mitra rummaged her purse for tissue; so did Kareena. They wiped each other's eyes and laughed together. But Mitra couldn't suppress the upheaval of emotions in her. Nor could she disregard the fear and worry in Kareena's eyes. Something was not right. Despite being with Jay in this fancy restaurant, she looked shrunken and lost.

"What's wrong?" Mitra asked.

"Nothing's wrong. You, silly." The smile Kareena flashed seemed tentative. "I'm excellent. I can't tell you how much it means to see you again. How did you find me? It mustn't have been easy. And why?"

"Kareena, we need to talk. About everything. Why did you leave so suddenly, without a word to anyone? We were so close. What you did made me feel like I don't know you anymore."

"There's a lot you don't know, that I didn't tell you. I'm so sorry that I haven't called. I didn't mean to freak you out. Much has happened. Time just flew. And now I'm not so sure . . ." Kareena's voice tapered off.

"Did you hear what I just said? What happened to you? What could Adi possibly have done to make you ditch your life there?

Why did you treat me this way? I thought we were the best of friends. I deserve at least an explanation."

"It's a long story, too long to talk about here."

"Listen, I have a car waiting. We can go any place you like." Mitra raised a hand in assurance. "We'll drop you where you want to go afterward."

Kareena looked absent for a moment, as though considering what to do next. "Okay, we'll get together, but my chauffeur will drive me. Jay has ordered that I don't ride in any other car. With his status, he has to be careful." She paused. "How about meeting at Chitra's on Nutan Lane in an hour?" She glanced at Mitra out of the corner of her eye, but Mitra couldn't read her expression. She couldn't read her at all anymore.

"Could you give me your mobile number?" Mitra asked. "Just in case?" She got pen and paper out of her purse.

Kareena hesitated, then recited the numbers. Without delay, she slipped out the powder room door, her sari sliding off one shoulder. Her ornate sandals clattered; they didn't seem to fit well and her steps lacked rhythm.

Mitra stood for a moment, unable to shake off her uneasiness. The walls, that were so bright only a minute ago, seemed to be drained of their lustrous pink shade.

She hurtled across the dining room toward the exit, barely noticing what was ahead, and ignoring the curious eyes of the onlookers and the heated gaze of Jay.

The waiter's voice receded behind Mitra as she rushed out of the door. "Your table is ready, madam."

FORTY-SIX

AT THE CRAMPED NOISY FRAGRANT chai shop, Mother and Preet turned to look at Mitra. Bright ceiling lights magnified their wide-eyed astonishment. They must have been thinking: *Back so quickly?* A few patrons from neighboring tables stole glances at her as well. Whether they were staring at her sari or necklace, or perhaps her awkward entry, Mitra couldn't tell. She slid onto the hard bench next to Preet.

"How about chai?" Mother asked, with her usual wisdom and tact. At Mitra's nod, she placed an order with the serious-faced waiter, adding, "My daughter doesn't take any sugar. She doesn't like her tea too strong. And make that a big pot and extra hot."

A chattering group took the table next to them. Mitra was grateful for the bustle, so she could have time to think.

Preet stroke her hand. "You look lovely. I'm sure every head turned when you walked into that restaurant." After a pause, "Wasn't Kareena there?"

Before Mitra could answer, Arnold came through the door. From around the room, patrons' eyes were drawn to his white satin maharaja jacket, he, so obviously overdressed. He glanced at Mitra and grabbed a chair.

"Did you find them?" Arnold asked. "Or was our actor-friend with another hyper-model?"

Mother smiled at his mangling of the term supermodel. "Hush, someone could be eavesdropping," she said. "'The walls have ears.'"

Mitra whispered a few details about her reunion and impending rendezvous with Kareena.

At the next table, an elderly American man talked about flying a racehorse from India to the U.S. on a chartered plane. "Did the horse jump around and shake the plane?" a boy at the same table asked. "Did it have dinner and movie on the flight?"

Mother chuckled at their exchange. Mitra tried to join in the laughter, in a gesture of being part of the group, but couldn't make a sound. Kareena—was she okay? She looked so different. Would she show up at Chitra's?

"You're not going back to see your friend, are you?" Preet poured chai into Mitra's cup. "I don't think you should. Why don't I take us all out to dinner at the Empress? How would that be?" She said the chef there made sauces that were "diabolically tempting."

"I wouldn't want to ruin your beautiful sari with some evil sauce," Mitra replied.

"The sari is now yours." Preet took Mitra's hand in hers. "It's gorgeous on you."

"Oh, by the way, I forgot to tell you, Mitra," Mother said. "Your friend, Veen, called from Seattle last night. You'd already gone to bed. It slipped my mind this morning."

Mitra's jaw tightened as she recalled Veen's last words: *Adi has disappeared.*

It crushed Mitra, as she rose from her chair, to shatter the buzz of intimacy. "You guys go ahead. I have to call Veen, then meet with Kareena. Sorry, I can't have dinner with you."

Preet handed her a cellphone, saying, "Take this, since your cellphone doesn't work here. Just in case you need to call us."

"Shall I go with you and wait outside?" Arnold asked Mitra.

Mitra thought for a moment. "If you show up in about an hour, that'll do. But don't wait in front."

"Okay," Preet said. "We'll wait in an alley a block north of the shop. Just take a right when you leave."

Mitra thanked them and slipped out.

FORTY-SEVEN

IN THE NEXT BLOCK, Mitra located a telephone kiosk. It'd be morning in Seattle. Her fingers numb from anxiousness about Adi's status, she had to dial several times before she got the number right.

Veen answered at the first ring. "My God—I can't believe it. Yesterday, the police found Adi. He's dead."

Mitra strained to catch Veen's words. "What did you say? I can't hear you too well." Her voice cracked; hot tea swirled in her stomach.

"He's been murdered," Veen said, her voice turning hoarse. "Some hit man."

"Hit man?" Mitra stood there dumbfounded, as though blood had drained from her body, as though someone had erased all her knowledge, memory, and power of comprehension.

"Shit," Veen said. "I can't eat or sleep. I drink fifteen cups of tea a day and still I'm in a fog." She took a moment. "Are you okay, Mitra?"

"Can I ring you back?"

"Yes, let's talk in awhile. Meantime, you need to call Detective Yoshihama. He wants to speak with you urgently."

Mitra limped out of the kiosk, eyes welling with tears, her insides knotted, thoughts scattered. Hard to believe she was in such a state of shock for a person she didn't once care for.

She circled the block. Patches of dark shadows on the street obstructed her vision. Returning to the same kiosk, she dialed Yoshihama's number.

A sleepy voice answered.

"Mitra here. I've just heard about Adi. How could this have happened?"

"I'm so sorry." Yoshihama said. "Mr. Guha shouldn't have involved himself in the ransom negotiation."

Holding on to the phone box, Mitra learned some facts. Adi was found in Cowen Park. His throat had been slashed. God, the body had been chopped up. The tongue had been taken out. The cops had cordoned off his house. Yoshihama began providing more details— fingerprints, exact time of murder, the murderer being at large, forensic examiners working—but not all of it registered. Mitra stood in a dazed state.

"Seems to me this was an act of revenge," Yoshihama said. "The bad guys didn't get their loot quick enough, so they did away with Mr. Guha."

"But I'd heard from Veen that Adi was selling his business."

"Correct. We found a huge amount of cash in Mr. Guha's house. He was obviously getting ready to meet the rest of the money demand." Nobuo paused. "I've been consulting with the Kolkata police. Mr. Guha's murder is similar to a crime that happened over there several years ago. In both cases, the tongue had been taken out."

Mitra gave out a shriek. She couldn't speak for a moment. "Are you talking about the Ray murder case?"

"Yes, that's the one."

"I can't think straight . . . let me collect myself." Mitra paused. "I've found Kareena and made plans to talk with her shortly. Jay is with her. I'd seen him twice in Seattle."

"He must have been toying with the law enforcement. Criminals often do that, thinking they have the upper hand. Robert believed that."

Memories of Robert floated back to Mitra, scenes she wished hadn't happened. Weeks ago, seated at his desk, Robert had asserted his knowledge of the Ray murder case. Mitra had told him about Kareena's liaison with Jay Bahadur, and about the film book she'd bought containing details about the Bollywood mafia. Robert connected Jay with the mafia. Without Mitra's knowledge, Robert might have opened his own investigation, and which might have gotten him on the path of the assassin.

"Do you suppose there's a connection between the two murder-deaths, Adi's and Robert's?" Mitra asked.

"Yes, there are similarities in the physical evidences. Robert's killer might have made it seem like a suicide."

"And I suppose because Robert had bouts of depression, his friends and colleagues believed he'd taken his own life."

"Correct. Please be careful in Kolkata, Mitra. If Mr. Bahadur is involved with Mr. Guha's death and he suspects you know his past, then he may be a danger to you. I can't have you at risk that way."

Mitra heaved a sigh. couldn't leave Kolkata immediately. Wheels had been set in motion. "My work's cut out from here. I'll be back after I've gotten what I'm after. There are still missing pieces. I'm going to see Kareena now. I'll have to give her the news." Her voice faded.

As she bid him goodbye and stepped away from the telephone booth, a feeling of terror sprouted in Mitra's mind. She saw what she'd refused to see before, despite many warnings, like leaves gathering on a sidewalk and obscuring the pathway: Jay Bahadur and his criminal pals appeared to have collaborated in a case of extortion and two murders. They would stop at nothing.

Adi's sad face, his distracted expression, and the pain in his eyes hung before Mitra. He'd loved Kareena. He'd died for her. Justice was called for.

Which meant that Mitra would have to wring out the whole story from Kareena. However much that tore Mitra apart. However nauseated she felt. However much that affected their sisterly ties.

FORTY-EIGHT

UNDER THE NIGHT SKY Mitra walked the three blocks to her destination. Her sari and high heels hampered her movements, as did the unfamiliar sights: a row of electrical shops, a dairy outlet, an astrologer's cave-like den, and lots of alleyways. Most businesses had shuttered for the night. Still, Mitra stayed vigilant. She kept a watch over any pedestrian who happened to pass by, but they were few and far between. A uniformed policeman, a long bamboo baton in his hand, marched past, giving her a curious look.

She located Chitra's, a small upscale second-floor café, situated atop a bookshop. Entering, she saw Kareena, who occupied a large table, her hair glistening in the ceiling light, the purple of her sari contrasting with the white tablecloth.

Kareena looked up from the menu, her eyes sparkling, and acknowledged Mitra with a big "Hi."

Mitra grabbed a seat across from her. "Hey, this is just like Soirée." She considered it good fortune that their table wasn't within hearing distance of other patrons. "Remember how we used to share all that had happened to us during the week?"

"I miss it so much," Kareena said soulfully. "I've met lots of people here, but so far there's been no one to kick back with, like you."

A sullen white-jacketed waiter approached their table. Kareena ordered for both of them, which suited Mitra just fine. Glancing down, fiddling with the open purse on her lap, Mitra turned on the voice recorder. She bit her lip. How horrible of her, how devious to pretend to have tea with her sister, but actually try to make her spell out a secret story.

Kareena placed a bejeweled hand on the table. Gazing warmly at Mitra, she appeared more relaxed. "You've gone to a lot of trouble to see me. That means a lot. Had I known you were coming, I'd have arranged a party for you. But we're leaving town in the next couple of days. We'll stay in Jay's village for at least six months." She paused. "How are our friends in Seattle?"

Mitra filled her in with a rushed account of their mutual friends and the search party they'd formed. Kareena listened, a wistful light in her eyes.

"Can you tell me why you left Seattle without saying a word to anyone?" Mitra asked. "Your friends miss you. I'm sure your clients wonder about you."

Kareena appeared to search back to the past, her eyelids weighted. "I was getting ready to quit my job. Such depressing people to be around all the time."

Mitra seized the opening. "Was it because of Adi that you finally left? Was he mistreating you? Those bruises on your arm—"

The waiter placed a wedge of pound cake before each of them. As a child, Mitra had loved the dense, buttery moist, richly brown slices. Now she barely glanced at it.

"No, whatever else he is, Adi's not a wife-batterer,' Kareena said. "He's too chicken. But he hurt me, with his constant suspicion. You remember how you were concerned when a stranger stalked me on my way home once, creeping me out? You guessed it was the husband of one of my clients. Actually, it was someone Adi had sent. We got into a big argument over it."

"Was he trying to find out if you were sneaking out? That'd be like Adi, wouldn't it?"

Kareena stabbed her cake with a fork more aggressively than necessary. "Yes, I was seeing Jay."

"How did you meet him?"

"I met him in India during a trip almost two years ago. I'd gone to a movie premiere with a wealthy aunt who moves in high society. Jay had a starring role in the movie and a dancing role too. Could he dance! At the reception afterwards, we flirted. He called me the charmer, the angelic beauty, the glamorous. When I got back to Seattle, I couldn't get him out of my mind. He wrote to me and I wrote back—we exchanged many love letters. A month later, he came to visit me secretly in Seattle for a week. Three months later, he came again to see me. Our relationship started to grow serious." She paused. "One day I couldn't take it any longer—living with Adi, living a huge lie."

"Tell me more about your new love," Mitra said in a conspiratorial voice. "What's he like?"

"Are you jealous?" Kareena said jokingly, giving a short laugh. "I saw you deliberately bumping into him. He has millions of women fans, so I don't blame you. He has so much charm. He can win over anybody, although I've seen him get angry with the paparazzi, and it can get out of hand."

"Does he ever get angry with you?"

"He hit me once, missed my face, but my forearm—oh, that hurt. He swore in the name of God Rama, he'd never do it again. And he's kept his word."

A burst of laughter came from a nearby table, making Mitra realize how tense her face was. "I find it hard to believe you took abuse from a man, you who counseled battered women."

Kareena touched her diamond necklace. "The next day Jay came home with a dozen yellow roses and this necklace. He knelt before me, kissed my hand and feet, and asked for my forgiveness. He recited a poem he'd written for me. Have you ever seen the moon rising on the Red Fort on a summer evening in Delhi? If so, you'd know the feeling. I forgave him. We became even closer. He's my perfect match and there'll be no other from now on. He calls me his kokil bird, his brightest diamond, his sunrise. Our house is filled with music, dancing, wine, and poetry. We laugh so much. It's paradise."

Mitra stared bleakly at Kareena. Glamor, glitz, baubles, poetry. How long before her ill-gotten happiness evaporated? How long before the sand burned under her feet? How long before she followed her mother's pattern and left the guy or he dumped her?

"It's been a painful few weeks, trying to figure out what happened to you," Mitra said. "Now that I've found you, I'd like to fit the puzzle pieces together, put my mind at rest. Did Adi know your going-away was pre-planned?"

Kareena's eyes darted to the window. She launched into an explanation. Adi who knew about the affair from the beginning figured out what was going on. Even so, he contacted the police and reported her missing. As events unfolded, the police could have traced the lovers and arrested them. But Adi didn't want that kind of publicity to circulate the community—his reputation meant much to him. She finished by saying, "Adi figured out the rest, I'm sure, especially when he got the ransom note."

"Ransom," Mitra said, hiding her sarcasm, "that's so clever, Kareena, so cool." That was so terrible, she thought. "Whose idea was it?"

"Jay's. He has a lot of debt. He could no longer get any financing from his usual channels. With another movie in mind, he needed funds badly. I didn't have much of a savings, so I couldn't help him out. He said, 'We'll get money from your rich husband. How would that be?' At first I didn't approve of his plan. But eventually, I went along with it. Adi's loaded. And I'm sure he didn't want to get on the wrong side of Jay, knowing how powerful he was. We hid in Tacoma for several weeks, waiting to collect the money." She paused. "I'm so in love with Jay. I'll do anything—anything—for him. I've never felt this way about any man."

Mitra's eyes stung. She saw it now: Jay needed funds to finance his films and pay off his debt and so he and Kareena staged a kidnapping, demanding a huge ransom from Adi. Kareena had lied and cheated, all for a money-hungry gangster, however charming he was. This was not the same Kareena she thought she knew. Her obsession for Jay had changed Kareena's character. She was criminally liable as an accomplice to an extortion campaign. But Mitra had to keep her rage to herself. If her intentions were known, Kareena wouldn't continue to talk so freely. Mitra would lose a chance to record her statement in the voice recorder. And she wouldn't be safe in this restaurant or in this town. Jay would make sure of that.

"You're not eating?" Kareena asked. "This cake is delicious."

Mitra picked up her fork and shoveled a bite of cake into her mouth, but couldn't taste it. "How did it sit with Jay when Adi paid only half the amount?"

"He was furious. I don't know why Adi didn't pay the money. Did he not want me to come back? Was he just being cheap? Jay was on the phone with his buddies in Mumbai for hours, working on Plan B."

Kareena seemed to be justifying her declaration of guilt to herself as much as to Mitra. She had participated in a crime of extortion, even though she hadn't received the full benefit. How did a woman once cherished by all get knotted up in this mess?

The waiter refreshed their tea. "Adi went broke, I think," Mitra said. "I'm sure he meant to pay the rest."

"Adi, Adi, Adi. What's gotten into you, Mitra? Why are you so concerned about him? You didn't much care for him, as I remember. There's no Adi anymore. I've put the past totally behind me—I'm getting a divorce." She patted the proud round of her belly. "We'll raise our child in Jay's village in bliss. She'll grow up speaking Bengali."

Mitra glanced at the streetlight outside the window. "I worry about you, Kareena. How many lasting Bollywood marriages do you know of?"

Kareena tucked a lock of hair behind an ear. Her necklace glittered. "You're a sweet person, Mitra, but you seem to get tangled up in other people's affairs. You don't have a love life—that's why. You don't know how to give yourself to a man."

She'd hit Mitra at a tender spot. Mitra acknowledged the truth quietly and sat in a dreadful silence.

Kareena broke the silence. "Why are you acting like an amateur detective all evening?"

"Detective?" Mitra shrugged. "No. I'm still the gardener you knew. Hey, did you ever meet a German guy in Seattle by the name of Ulrich Schultheiss?"

Kareena startled. "Oh, he was just a play thing—you know what I mean?" She smirked. "You look so shocked. Why would I find an uneducated carpenter interesting for very long?"

Mitra saw the two faces of her sister: a kinder side that helped battered women; a dark secretive side that stepped out on her husband.

Mitra leaned back. "Never mind. Let me mention a number of worrisome incidents that happened to me in Seattle. I was frequently followed by a white Datsun pickup truck."

Again Kareena startled and paled. "Oh, Jay told me he was having a pest followed. I didn't know that—"

Leaving her sentence unfinished, Kareena turned her face toward the window. An uneasy silence dominated, as though a big hammer had just finished hitting a nail. The ceiling light washed the table's glass surface. It reminded Mitra where she was and the urgency of getting to the bottom of this.

She collected herself and caught Kareena's eye. "Oh, by the way, Adi wanted me to tell you he loved you."

Kareena frowned at the table. Despite her bright rouge and even brighter lipstick, she didn't look well. "You've seen him recently?"

"Yes, for the last time." Mitra's voice faltered. "I called Seattle just before coming here and got the news. Something bad has happened. Adi's dead."

Kareena raised her head. "What?"

"He was kidnapped," Mitra said in a teary, bitter voice. "An assassin killed him, just like that, and dumped his body in a park." It sickened her to continue. "The police don't know the motive. Like a movie script, don't you think?"

Kareena sat immobile, her face gray. In her mind, she probably saw it as a script from one of her mother's flicks—a married woman falling for a scoundrel, a batterer who was broke. To finance his habits, his directorial flops, their union, he demanded ransom money from the husband. Otherwise, the lover threatened, he'd go public with their liaison. He'd have the husband assassinated. In her infatuation, her love for the high life, she agreed with his scheme. The husband couldn't make the full payment and . . .

"The script ended with a twist," Mitra said.

"Adi—" Kareena choked and let the sentence dangle. Her eyes bulged in grief and panic. A single gray hair showed itself near her temple.

"It was his baby, wasn't it?"

Kareena didn't answer. She didn't need to. The answer was clear to Mitra.

She pictured Adi's sad eyes, the weariness about them. How happy he would have been if he were alive and received this news.

"Are you saying you didn't know Adi's life was on the line?" Mitra asked, angry at Kareena's naïveté, but keeping her voice level.

Kareena shook her head. After a while, she said, in a thickened voice, "Jay only told me he'd sent him a threatening note after a full amount had not been received. And I made the conclusion that was all that would be required."

Now that they'd talked and her fantasy was gone, Mitra saw her sister in her plain skin. Her chest ached with trepidation. She wanted to say: *You did all this for love— what you thought would bring you happiness. It's not working, if you ask me. There's still time for you to change your ways, dear sister.*

Mitra touched Kareena's hand. "Do you realize the trouble you're in? You're hanging out with criminals. They could kill you, too, if you cross them. Listen, don't go back to Jay. Come with me."

Her eyes unfocused, Kareena appeared to be processing the information. "I have to go now."

"Wait," Mitra said, "I've been dying to tell you something really big. Something that has changed my life. We're half-sisters. Aunt Saroja told me the whole story. We share the same father."

Kareena frowned, as though she'd just heard the most ridiculous piece of news. "What are you talking about? I need to go now."

A big bulky uniformed chauffeur, possibly also a bodyguard, appeared at the door. He signaled Kareena and favored Mitra with a glare.

Kareena rose, tossed a shawl over her shoulders, and took a tentative step. Mitra saw the tears streaming down Kareena's cheeks, running through her makeup. She didn't want to acknowledge the tight situation she was in, the bleakness facing her, or the hard edge of saying goodbye to a "friend of the heart."

If she let Kareena leave now, that'd be the end of everything. Their close ties would become a dot in the past. Their sisterhood wouldn't even be in the picture. Mitra jotted down Preet's cellphone number and Mother's address on a napkin, stood up, and pressed it into Kareena's hand. "Come to my mother's place tonight. We can hide you there. You can fly back to Seattle with me. If you want to break free of this life. If you want your child to—"

Kareena glanced at the napkin, folded it, and put it in her purse, taking time to do so.

"Please call me tonight," Mitra said.

Kareena turned toward the door.

"Kareena, please."

She halted and swiveled to face Mitra. A woman from a nearby table frowned at both of them.

"I'll stay up waiting for your call."

Kareena took a step, nearly tripping on the front pleats of her sari, and disappeared through the door.

"See you soon, sis," Mitra whispered, burying her face in her hands. If it had been hard for her to let go of a friend, she found it harder still to let go of a sister.

FORTY-NINE

MITRA EXITED THE CAFÉ. It must have been late by now, for all nearby businesses had switched off their lights. Her high heels hindered her movements, as did the unfamiliarity of this neighborhood. Feeling drained, she paused momentarily on the sidewalk and breathed the warm night air. No one was about. Occasionally, a car whizzed by. Kind of scary. Arnold and his taxi would be waiting for her somewhere in an alley a block away.

She was about to take the cellphone out to call Arnold when she noticed a handsome man, about 5'11", clad in an expensive black leather jacket, standing at a distance of few feet, in the direction she was going. A loiterer? No, he was dressed too spiffily. Should she go back inside the café and make her call from there?

The man nodded at her pleasantly, making her feel foolish. She needn't have been so paranoid.

The man took a deep drag on his cigarette, then tossed the cigarette butt on the sidewalk with a sudden force, and looked around.

His gestures startled her.

He whipped around, glared at her. She stiffened.

Run, Mitra, run.

But in these high heels? In this semi-darkness?

She cursed her stiletto heels and tried walking past him when he suddenly flew at her and tripped her. She slipped and tumbled on to the pavement. He stood over her, ready to strike again with a fisted hand.

"Who the hell do you think you are, Miss?" he said in a menacing tone. "How dare you step on my toes?"

"I did not step on your toes." She made a move to rise. "But I'm sorry if—"

"Now you'll be really sorry."

He kicked her. A pain shuddered through her body. Her stomach felt queasy. She closed her eyes, moaned, and gathered all her strength, ready to shout for help, but her voice was gone. She dreaded a worse blow, every nerve in full alert.

Without warning, she threw up all over his shoes. It poured out of her—the tea and the cake and all the grief. Even in her distressed condition, shrinking on the sidewalk, she couldn't help but notice that his black leather moccasins, new and pricey, Gucci possibly, were now soiled. His socks were drenched with vomit, too.

"You fucking shit," he hissed. He quickly stepped aside, shook his feet, and shook his head. "You've ruined my best shoes. I should send you to hell for this."

He was distracted. Now was the moment. Scooting into a seated position, she assessed her chances of escape. Could she run? No. He'd grab her again.

It flashed in her mind, the self-defense moves she had once mastered.

She stood. He grabbed her by the shoulders and twisted her around. With her bracing against him, he placed his hands around her throat from behind. His cold fleshy fingers squeezed her throat tighter and tighter, wiping out the lights as well as the darkness before her. She felt herself tilting, falling.

Fight Mitra. Kareena had advised her long ago. *Don't ever let a man harm you.*

A feeling of power surged in her, an animal power. She stomped on his foot with her spiky stiletto heels. Shrieking with pain, he let go of her throat. She slammed a knee to his groin, just the way she'd been taught. Then again with vigor. And one more time.

He hunched over, cupped his crotch with his hands, bared his teeth, and moaned. His eyes were closed.

Here was a break. *Be quick, Mitra.*

She took her shoes off, clutched them under her arms, and began to run. An uneven sidewalk, lots of potholes, unexpected loose stones. Her feet hurt. Her hand felt light. She'd lost her purse. But she had to keep going. Glancing behind, she saw he was staggering and lurching, just a few feet away.

He was getting closer. He stretched an arm out toward her; his eyes were on fire. She turned, drew nearer, and poked a finger at that fire.

He staggered, bent over, and moaned.

She ran down the block, shouting, "Arnold, Ma, are you there?"

A car honked. A familiar taxi pulled out of the alley and glided over to the curb.

Mother jumped out, closely followed by Preet, and shouted, "What's going on?"

Mitra, still panting, could only point to the assailant half a block away.

"That's a *goonda*," Arnold said. Thug.

Arnold started running toward the assailant, but Preet called out to him. "Don't go near him. He could have a gun. Call the police."

Arnold halted and punched keys on his cellphone. Mother snapped away with her new camera, shouting, "How dare you assault my daughter?"

The assailant looked up and straightened. "Fuck you, Mother," he shouted back. "Fuck you, fuck you, fuck you."

Mitra cringed. To insult her gentle mother with that kind of language? She spat on him.

Mother laughed and yelled out, "You fuck your mother? What a lovable son you are."

The assailant blazed a glance at Mother, pivoted, and limped in the opposite direction, mumbling curses as he went.

"Isn't he the jerk who played a bit part in *Cutie*?" Mother said, taking yet another shot of the offender in flight. "I bet either he's a buddy of Jay Bahadur or he was planted by him." She put the camera down and wrapped Mitra closer with an arm. "Are you okay?"

Mitra nodded, happy to be alive and exhausted from the excitement. How close she'd come to being seriously hurt. As she slipped on her shoes and steadied herself, the trio circled her, forming a shield.

"You're so brave," Preet said. "You fought that guy off."

"He's at least one and a half times your body weight," Arnold said. "He won't be able to show his face among his cronies."

"If it weren't for the self-defense class I took," Mitra said, "he'd have finished me."

"I doubt he would have had," Mother said. "We Indian women are strong. We have the tradition of great women like Sita and Savitri. Our best self-defense is our mental toughness."

Mitra dusted her sari off, but it was now smeared with dirt and her vomit. She walked back a few steps and recovered her purse, which was lying on the sidewalk. Thank God, the voice recorder was intact, as was Preet's cellphone.

"Jump in." Arnold opened the car door. "We need to get out of here fast. I don't like the feel of this street. Take it from me, Driver Maharaja. I smell bad things in the air."

FIFTY

MITRA'S THROAT FELT SCRATCHY, her eyes watered, her body burned and, with her knees buckling, she could barely walk when she reached home. After changing, she lounged on a recliner in Mother's living room. Preet and Arnold stayed with her for awhile, then said goodbye and left.

Mother pressed a cold compress on Mitra's forehead. "It's been quite an evening for you," she said. "Your forehead feels warm. Don't try to talk. We'll catch up tomorrow. But I forbid you ever to visit that friend of yours again."

Mitra couldn't stay silent. "It still feels unreal, seeing Kareena and hearing her side of the story. What a mess she's gotten herself into. I wonder if I could have done something more for her that I didn't."

"No, my dear daughter," Mother said. "You tried to save her, but she didn't want to be saved. She went astray. There's always a price to be paid for that."

Mother's phone trilled from the other end of the room. "I'll get it." She raced over to the phone and picked up the receiver.

Even in her distressed state, Mitra couldn't help but notice. Mother's face turned haggard as she listened, her expression one of disbelief. She hung up and stood motionless. She seemed to have lost her ability to speak.

"What's the matter, Ma? Who called?"

Mother didn't seem to hear her. She lowered her head. Silence thickened around her.

"Who was on the phone?"

"Arnold," Mother mumbled. She came over to Mitra and grasped her hand. "Oh, Ma Durga. Kareena—she is—dead. Car accident."

Mitra rose, then fell back against the pillow. "There must be a mistake. I want to speak with Arnold. Give me the phone."

"He's driving a passenger to the airport and can't talk. He heard on the radio that there has been a car accident. It involved the live-in companion of Jay Bahadur. Her chauffeur is in the hospital in critical condition."

"It's not true. Where's Preet's cellphone, Ma?"

Even as she said so, in her sinking heart, Mitra felt the news had to be true. Kareena—she was marked, being hunted. But why? There could be one reason. Jay had suspected she was going to cross him and that she'd decided to go with Mitra.

Mother handed Preet's cellphone to Mitra. Indeed, a message was waiting. It came only half an hour ago when Mitra was still fighting the assailant.

"I'm on my way, M," Kareena's voice said. "See you soon."

There was a rise at the end of the sentences, a spurt of hope. Her sister meant those words. She had finally figured it all out.

A deep exhaustion rolled over Mitra. "I can't handle it anymore, Ma."

Mother sat on the edge of the bed and placed a hand on Mitra's forehead. Her warmth and caring seeped through that touch.

Oh, God. How close Mitra had come to saving her pregnant sister, how pitifully close. It had slipped out of her hand, something most precious, and she couldn't stop it.

*   *   *

A day later, with Mother in a chair nearby, Mitra got her suitcase out. Much as she would have liked to stay longer, she'd decided to cut her visit short for safety's sake. Jay's thugs would want her dead.

As she began packing, Mother gave her more details about Kareena's death. Her chauffeur tried to avoid a lorry coming from the opposite direction, but couldn't. One report insisted his blood alcohol level was high. Kareena was taken by an ambulance to the hospital and pronounced dead on arrival. The person at the center of it all, Jay Bahadur, was in seclusion. His office had released a statement concerning his grief and his desire for privacy.

"How I wish I could have helped you more," Mother said.

Mitra shoved a toilet kit into her suitcase. "But you did help me, Sherlock. And I must thank you for it."

Mother waved a hand dismissively. "*Jaa.*" Don't mention it. "I must apologize to you for being so critical of Kareena. She was criminal and cruel, but she was your best friend. Who am I to judge? I'm not perfect, either."

Mitra laid her t-shirts and jeans over the heavier items. "You're way too hard on yourself. You have so much wisdom to offer. I hope someday I will be like you."

Mother peered at the basket of fresh marigolds blossoms Mitra had bought for her this morning. "You're young. Don't try to undo things. Live forward, make mistakes forward—even if you've lost your dearest friend and you're grieving."

"She was also my half-sister."

Mother nearly jumped from her seat. She looked fully at Mitra. "What did you say?"

Mitra revived a page of her family history, as narrated by Aunt Saroja weeks ago.

"That fallen woman was part of my family?" Mother said, her voice rising to the ceiling. "I wouldn't have ever wanted her sinful feet to darken my doorstep, no matter how much that might have meant to you." She choked up, rose, and hurried out of the room.

Mitra closed the suitcase and plopped down on a chair. Had she made a mistake revealing the family secret she'd been nursing for sometime?

A few minutes later, Mother re-emerged, her eyes brimming with regret. "Forgive me for over-reacting, especially when you're grieving. I didn't do much for you when you were little. And now that you've come for a visit after a long time, I shouldn't be yelling at you like that. Believe me, if circumstances were different—" She began weeping.

Mitra could have completed the sentence for her. She'd have welcomed Kareena into their family for Mitra's sake. Think of all the pride she'd have had to shed, the memories she'd have had to clear away, the sleepless nights she'd have had to endure. She'd have borne all that for her daughter's happiness.

Mother sobbed. Mitra rose and embraced her. She decided to keep silent about Adi losing his life savagely. Mother had had enough to cope with these past few weeks. Once back in Seattle, she'd write her a letter. For now, she'd tuck away that loss as a secret. Even if it burned inside her, as Kareena's memories did.

*   *   *

Arnold knocked at the door and said he was waiting outside with his taxi. Just at that moment, mother's phone rang. It was Preet and Sam.

Sam invited Mitra to his fifth birthday next year. "Mitra-masi, you must spend a month here." He wanted to build a tree house with her, and again play the Alien Attack game.

"I'll be back, Sam."

Preet came on the line. "I want to thank you," she said. "You've made me appreciate the life I have. What more can a friend do?"

Their eager voices stayed with Mitra as she cradled the receiver. At the door, she turned to face Mother. "I'll never be able to tell you, Ma, how much I love and admire you."

Mother pushed away a curl dangling over Mitra's eyebrow. They were even closer now. Ironically, it was Mitra's search for Kareena, not to mention her untimely death that had played a role in it.

"You've given me the incentive," Mother said, "to finally get out of this flat. This afternoon, Arnold will take me to Maniktola for a visit with your aunt Ranjana, whom I haven't seen in years. Of course, I'll take my camera with me. And I'll have Naresh put the pictures on his website, so you can browse them, too."

Mitra now knew what was going on with Mother's health. That secret would no longer separate them. And although her health wasn't in the best shape, Mother seemed content. She'd found what she always hungered for in life, a son, a Naresh. And as for their relationship, there would be letters and phone calls, reminding Mitra that she and Mother were still a big part of each other's life.

Mitra's longing for India would not go away either when she left its soil. India was another mother, at times nurturing, at other times indifferent. Mitra would love both from a distance, like an uninvited guest outside the door, forever wondering what it'd be like to step in.

She glimpsed Arnold down the hallway and slung her flight bag over her shoulder. In the moments it took Arnold to stow the luggage in the car, her whole visit shimmered before her. She said one last goodbye to Mother.

Mother gazed at her through watery eyes, touched her hair, and murmured a blessing.

"Come again next year," she said. "And bring another mystery to crack, will you?"

FIFTY-ONE

THE EARLY MORNING ATMOSPHERE was charcoal gray when Mitra landed at SeaTac International Airport. She caught a taxi home. It gladdened her that the ride took only twenty minutes. She unlocked the front door to her house and was happy to be back, anxious to get settled.

The message light on her answering machine winked. She pushed the play button, eager to infuse the air with friendly chatter. Adi had left two brief messages, each checking to see if she was back. She shook her head and replayed them, a voice she'd never again hear. She felt eerie.

The next four were from Veen and other friends, vibrant and newsy. The last one was from Grandmother, saying she was thinking of Mitra. One person simply hung up.

No message from Ulrich. He hadn't tried to contact her at all.

She strolled to the greenhouse, her first order of commitment. Although she trusted that Grandmother had taken care of her plants, she needed to verify that for herself. She hovered over the seed flats, breathing in the smell of rich moist earth and listening to the chirping of the birds outside. Petunias had sprouted, although as yet, the tender seedlings gave no indication they'd one day explode into a battlefield of burgundy. The stock starts had gained three inches in height. The verbenas appeared healthy, too, though a trifle less green than normal. She'd have hours of thinning, feeding, misting, and transplanting ahead of her.

As she stepped out of the greenhouse and entered the kitchen, it all rushed back to her, her dinners with Ulrich, the time they spent in her garden, and the flow of lust and friendship between them. Although it was over between them, she found questions popping up in her mind. Why did he have to lie to her about his brief fling with Kareena? Had he been in trouble with the police again? His mood swings—she must have a clear idea about that, too. She sought closure, but wanted to hear his answers. What if she dropped by to see him?

The very idea of resolving these issues charged her with new energy. She showered and changed into fresh clothes.

She knew he woke early. With traffic so light, it took her no time to drive to Ballard. She located his three-story apartment building, pushed the buzzer to his apartment, and waited eagerly.

He opened the door, his eyes red and dull. Dressed in a fleece jacket and heavy jeans, he appeared to be getting ready to go to work.

"Mitra, when did you get back?" The voice was different—less intimate.

"Just this morning," she said, noticing his stiffness.

"Come in." He didn't smile or kiss her.

She searched for words to justify her visit, but found none. The tiny studio apartment had a futon at one end and a couch at the other. A half-empty beer bottle sat on the floor by the couch; several empty ones cluttered a waste basket. A pile of hundred dollar bills rested on the coffee table. An empty pill bottle rested next to it. There was cobweb on one wall. A musty smell pervaded the chill air. The windows clearly hadn't been opened in awhile. An open suitcase, partially packed with clothes and a toilet kit, rested on the floor.

"Going somewhere?" she asked.

He looked away. They sat on opposite ends of the couch. It pained her to see how formal he'd become, how uncomfortable in her presence. He turned his gaze toward the suitcase. Their whole history seemed to have faded for him, a burnt-out fire.

"Was your trip worth it?" he asked. She could smell beer on his breath.

Her chin touched her turtleneck sweater. "Long story, a tragic one."

"You couldn't get your friend to come back, could you?"

For a moment, recalling Kareena, she couldn't speak.

"I told you not to go," he said. "Why didn't you listen to me?"

Her voice shook as she said, "Kareena is dead."

"I'm sorry." After a pause, "Why did you come to see me?"

A gleam in his eyes made her more uncomfortable.

"You came here to screw, didn't you? You're trying to forget the memory of your friend?" With a sudden force, he wrapped his arms around her and began fondling her breasts.

A pang of dread and disgust ran through her. She yanked his hand away and scrambled to her feet. "Stop it. I came here to talk."

He stood up, looked down at her from his full height, and roared with laughter contemptuously, as though he didn't believe her words. His laughter hit her so hard that she trembled. In this dizzying moment, under the unmerciful ceiling light, she regarded the strange new man before her, furious, looming, uncaring, and spiraling out of control.

How would she protect herself?

Get out of here, Mitra, fast.

She scrambled toward the door and opened it, jitters all over her body, cool air rushing in. She felt his presence on her back, as he pulled her toward him.

"You got away from me once—not this time."

"Let go!"

She shoved him on the chest. He barely bounced. She raised a knee. He slapped it down with a sharp blow. She shrieked. Then she remembered how much he hated the police.

"*Polizist.*" She shouted louder this time to jolt his ears even more. "*Polizist.*"

The police word bounced off the walls and floated out of the apartment, perhaps into the street. *Anyone out there?*

For a moment he seemed weak, unsure, and disoriented, as though he'd been slapped. His shoulders slumped, eyes showed confusion, and he looked toward the suitcase.

She wiggled out of his clutches. Her arm stiff as a rod knocked out a table lamp. It fell on the floor with a big crashing sound. He raised his eyes, mean and mad, but didn't have any fight left in him.

"Don't you dare move." She backed away toward the door. "Or I'll have you arrested."

He stayed riveted in that standing position, as though considering his next move.

Her heart lodged in her throat, she jerked the door open, and fled down the steps.

No sound of running feet behind her. Thank God. She staggered toward her car, trampling a few fallen wisteria blossoms on the sidewalk.

A cold wind lacerated the trees, but there wasn't enough oxygen to breathe. She started her car. Her eyes were dry. She didn't have any tears left.

Back to her house, Mitra paced from room to room, jumping at the slightest sound. Despite a perfect 68 degree temperature, the walls failed to enclose her in comfort. Her body ached; her mind churned.

She called Nobuo. Just to talk. Dispatch answered, this being a weekend. She decided not to leave a message.

Her mind went back to Ulrich, the intimate moments they'd once shared and her shattered dreams about a future with him. Soon enough the truth sunk in. He really wasn't Ulrich. That charmer didn't exist. He was a shadow-self. A shadow faded sooner or later. For all she knew he might even be leaving town for good. Perhaps it was for the best, she thought, pain pinching her throat. She wouldn't make the same mistake Kareena had made. Whether in the name of love or fantasy, wisteria or kisses, this one lesson forced its way into her consciousness. The lesson was written in blood, a gift from Kareena, who had paid for her mistakes with her life.

Mitra walked to the window, tugged at the curtains, and viewed the morning scene. Dewdrops glistened on the leaves of the plum tree. A bee sang around the sweet alyssum patch. The tulip bed was bare, as it had been since early spring.

She and Ulrich had never done any planting together.

It took Mitra several moments to feel the floor beneath her feet.

The fast-growing bamboo had spread. Its yellow-stemmed foliage leaned out, like an extended family welcoming her back. And, indeed, there was that call from Grandmother. She reached for the phone.

FIFTY-TWO

THE NEXT DAY, at about six P.M., Mitra pressed the buzzer at Grandmother's house and heard the chimes inside. The door was ajar. She slipped through. The room overflowed with aromas of ginger, lemongrass, and cardamom.

Smiling voices chorused: "Surprise!"

Veen swooped toward her, followed by the rest of the crowd: Jean, Sue, Sabnam, Carrie, the rest of the task force members, and other friends. So much comfort, such jubilance, such high feelings of returning to what was her home now. Mitra broke into a smile. She returned the hugs and pleasantries, but didn't catch sight of the instigator. How coolly Grandmother had said, "I'm having a few friends for dinner on Sunday around six. Why don't you join us?"

As Mitra worked her way through the room, well-wishers called out to her from all sides. From their sympathetic gestures, she got the impression that Veen had spread a synopsis of the tragic deaths—Adi's and Kareena's. Mitra could tell her friends sensed her grief, but had reached a silent agreement not to prod, at least not tonight.

The buzz in the room grew louder. A familiar voice floated above the hubbub of the crowd. "Hello, dear."

Grandmother made a majestic entry, clad in a kimono-style dress accented by a stone bracelet and earrings dripping with garnets. With her height and substantial weight, she resembled an elegant aging queen. She enveloped Mitra in a soft hug, released her, and wiped her eyes. She must have broken a pact with herself to keep this gathering a joyous affair. Mitra couldn't help but reflect on how you can be sad and happy at the same time, how so many moments strike a delicate balance between the two.

"My precious dear," Grandmother said, "I'm glad you've returned safely and in one piece. You hear of so many diseases one can get over in India. Did you suffer from the heat? Is your mother well? My, don't you look even thinner now?"

As she answered the questions, out of the corner of her eye, Mitra became aware of a guest being ushered inside. Nobuo Yoshihama. What brought him here? He seemed to be bearing a package. They exchanged a glance from a distance. He smiled warmly at her.

Why did her heart quicken?

"I invited him. He's a nice fella . ." Grandmother winked at Mitra. "Now I have something to show you in the garden."

They snuck out the kitchen door and stepped into the backyard. Moss had infiltrated the gaps between the flagstones of the walkway. In the dappled shade of late afternoon, the flowerbed pulsated with red, green, yellow, and blue. Grandmother shepherded her to the delphiniums, whose tall spikes were top heavy with lavender blossoms for the second time this season.

"See how gorgeous they are! And they're having a second fling!" Grandmother looked toward the patio. "Now that I have the loveliest garden in the neighborhood, I've ordered a set of French chairs. They'll be delivered before my birthday. And there's more good news. My granddaughter Isabel, bless her, is coming to spend two weeks of her summer vacation with me. I can't wait to get my two granddaughters together. The three of us will have to go out on the town."

Mitra smiled. It dawned on her that she'd finally put roots down, like that big leaf maple, deep and permanent.

"And Alice?" she asked.

Grandmother gazed off into space, the lines of her face reclaiming familiar territory through her beige makeup. Mitra regretted the insensitive question.

"My daughter—she was supposed to stop by Friday evening. I made a pot of her favorite bean soup. She didn't show. She didn't even call. Still, she's my little girl." A breeze flattened Grandmother's bangs. She sighed wearily. "You have to keep trying a little each day to let go."

"Each day," Mitra echoed. In her mind, she shut the gate to the past behind her with a click. It took her a few moments to return to the present, to become aware of the damp moss under her feet.

"Shall we go back inside?" Grandmother said. "I need to make the fruit punch."

"You go ahead. I'll be along in a minute."

Grandmother walked back into the house, tottering in her high heels.

Mitra stooped over the flowerbed, listening to the snatches of convivial chatter filtering through the window. She plucked a few tall grasses and stray buttercups that had established themselves at the base of a velvety coleus. She tossed them onto an impromptu compost heap that Grandmother had started in her absence. Blank spots stared up at her. She mused on what to tuck into next.

When she straightened, she saw Nobuo standing by her. Dressed in a black cashmere sweater and displaying a new haircut, he appeared as attractive as she'd ever seen him. Perhaps she was noticing him with a fresh pair of eyes.

With an approachable air, he asked, "How did things turn out over there?"

He listened as she briefed him on the headlines and the tragedy of Kareena's death. She suspected he'd gotten a summarized version from his contacts with the Kolkata police. Yet he listened with full attention, regarding her sadly, tenderly.

"You have to be careful," he said. "Those thugs are still on the loose, especially Jay Bahadur. You were the last to have a conversation with Kareena. They might be keeping an eye on you. I'll need all the details. Suppose we talk tomorrow morning at eight at your place?"

Mitra nodded and stiffened. The authorities were seeking truth and justice; the perpetrator was still at large. She would have to be courageous enough to share it all with Nobuo—about her sister, her lover, her accidental death, and the bits and pieces she'd gathered about Jay's entanglement with a murder case similar to that of Adi and Robert. She'd turn over the recordings to Nobuo. Her heart would split in pain, going over the incidents again, even as she sought a sense of closure.

They walked a few leisurely steps together. The magnolia tree, with its ivory pink flowers, arched over them. New branches had bloomed, hiding the old growth from earlier years.

"And oh, by the way," Nobuo said, "I have an update on Ulrich Schultheiss, if you care to hear."

She halted. She felt cold, the chill of news she'd have to bear. "What has he done?"

"He was arrested yesterday for the second time in connection with an assault on a colleague who's in intensive care in the Swedish Hospital. The police caught him just as he was about to leave town. He had an air ticket to Berlin in his pocket. His real name is Klaus Ackart."

Everything around Mitra vanished. The ground swayed. Old feelings stabbed her on their way out.

Nobuo clasped her hand, his fingers soft and warm against hers. For a moment they stood in silence.

"It's over with now." Mitra's eyes roamed around. "I must get back to what I love to do."

Nobuo pointed to an empty patch, said in a light voice, "That coleus looks like it could use some company. Do you have anything in mind?"

"Yes, coreopsis, yellow flower with a red center. It'll set off the coleus nicely and they grow well together."

Nobuo smiled. "I'd like to have a sanctuary like this."

"You have a beautiful location. All it needs is sweat, care, and patience." And what she left unsaid: a little help from her.

"Wait, just a minute." He disappeared inside, walking briskly, but with his usual sense of restraint.

For a spell, she looked out over the garden, a tapestry of shrubs and flowers, interspersed with mossy rocks, bounty all around. Plants had always occupied a special place in her heart; it was even more so now. After years of landscaping and the trauma of recent events, she had finally acquired some insight into what her efforts were about: to seek new connections and broader perspective. Some might even call it a quest for love. You worked through cycles of growth, bloom, decline, death, and challenge. Eventually, balance was achieved, beauty awakened, a miracle birthed.

Nobuo handed her a cellophane-wrapped bouquet and said in a soft knowing voice, "Welcome back."

Mitra looked down at the bouquet. What a pretty surprise: at least fifteen long-stemmed creamy yellow tulips, mixed with thick green leaves. Streaked on the outside with red, the bright beauties opened wide to reveal their delicate interiors.

She held them close to her chest, breathed deeply. Smiling through her tears, she looked up at him. He bowed toward her.

Early the next morning, Mitra awoke, nestled with Nobuo on her bed, their limbs tangled. His eyelids heavy with sleep, Nobuo stirred. Disengaging slowly from his embrace, she sat up and smiled at him. His clothes were on the floor, comfortably mixed in with hers. She remembered the long night, full and glowing as the moon. Yawning leisurely, forgetting for now the tough road ahead, Mitra looked out the window to the rosy dawning of a new day. Splashes of flamboyant color had popped up in the pansy patch. A fat lady bug crawled on the underside of a dahlia leaf. The satiny petal of a nicotiana flower quivered, brushed by a wayward puff of the wind.

It was still spring.

THE END

READING GROUP QUESTIONS

By the end of Tulip Season: A Mitra Basu Mystery, how has Mitra changed? What have you learned along with Mitra?

Family, friendship, betrayal, and grief are among the many themes presented here. Choose one or more themes and discuss how they're revealed in the course of the novel.

Did Kareena pay too heavy a price for the course of action she'd chosen? Have you known any one in a similar situation? If you were to meet Kareena face-to-face, what words of wisdom would you pass her along?

How does the setting of a garden contribute to the fuller expression of the story? Comment on Mitra's observations about the cycle of birth, death, and rejuvenation at the end of the book.

Comment on Mitra's various relationships: with her mother, grandmother, Robert, Detective Yoshihama, and Ulrich. Do you have (or have you ever had) a relationship similar to one of these?

How has India become a character for the novel? What aspects of Indian culture, as depicted in the book, interested you the most?

Do you enjoy a mystery series? Does Mitra's attempts at sleuthing open up possibilities for a sequel to this novel?

Have you read other novels by Bharti Kirchner? How does this one compare?

Also by Bharti Kirchner

Fiction

Shiva Dancing

Sharmila's Book

Darjeeling

Pastries: A Novel of Desserts and Discoveries

Nonfiction

The Healthy Cuisine of India: Recipes from the Bengal Region

Indian Inspired

The Bold Vegetarian

Vegetarian Burgers

More Great Reads from Booktrope Editions

Riversong by Tess Hardwick (Contemporary Romance) Sometimes we must face our deepest fears to find hope again. A redemptive story of forgiveness and friendship.

Jailbird by Heather Huffman (Romantic Suspense) A woman running from the law makes a new life. Sometimes love, friendship and family bloom against all odds…especially if you make a tasty dandelion jam.

Don Juan in Hankey, PA by Gale Martin (Contemporary Comic Fantasy) A fabulous mix of seduction, ghosts, humor, music and madness, as a rust-belt opera company stages Mozart's masterpiece. You needn't be an opera lover to enjoy this insightful and hilarious book.

Memoirs Aren't Fairytales by Marni Mann (Contemporary Fiction) a young woman's heartbreaking descent into drug addiction.

Sweet Song, by Terry Persun (Historical Fiction) This tale of a mixed race man passing as white in post-Civil War America speaks from the heart about where we've come from and who we are.

The Printer's Devil, by Chico Kidd (Historical Fantasy) a demon summoned long ago by a heartbroken lover in Cromwellian England, now reawakened by a curious scholarly researcher. Who will pay the price?

Throwaway by Heather Huffman (Romantic Suspense) A prostitute and a police detective fall in love, proving it's never too late to change your destiny and seek happiness. That is, if she can take care of herself when the mob has a different idea.

Moonlight and Oranges by Elise Stephens (Young Adult) Love, fate, a secret dream journal, a psychic's riddle, a downright scary mother of the beau. A timeless tale of youthful romance.

… and many more!

Sample our books at www.booktrope.com

Learn more about our new approach to publishing at
www.booktropepublishing.com

CPSIA information can be obtained at www.ICGtesting.com
Printed in the USA
LVOW12*2300220114

370616LV00003B/15/P